HARRY SIDEBOTTOM

The RETURN

ZAFFRE

First published in Great Britain in 2020 by
ZAFFRE
80–81 Wimpole St, London W1G 9RE

A CIP catalogue record for this book is
available from the British Library.

Hardback ISBN: 978–1–78576–963–4
Trade paperback ISBN: 978–1–78576–964–1

Also available as an ebook

1 3 5 7 9 10 8 6 4 2

Typeset by IDSUK (Data Connection) Ltd
Printed and bound in Great Britain by Clays Ltd, Elcograf S.p.A.

Zaffre is an imprint of Bonnier Books UK
www.bonnierbooks.co.uk

Harry Sidebottom was brought up in racing stables in Newmarket where his father was a trainer. He took his Doctorate in Ancient History at Oxford University and has taught at various universities including Oxford. His career as a novelist began with his *Warrior of Rome* series.

Fiction
The Lost Ten

(The Warrior of Rome series)
Fire in the East
King of Kings
Lion of the Sun
The Caspian Gates
The Wolves of the North
The Amber Road
The Last Hour

(The Throne of the Caesars trilogy)
Iron & Rust
Blood & Steel
Fire & Sword

Non-fiction
Ancient Warfare: A Very Short Introduction
The Encyclopedia of Ancient Battles
(With Michael Witby)

To Jack Ringer and Sandra Haines

GALLIA

Sequani

Narbonensis

Aquitania

HISPANIA

Numantia

Bætica

BALEARES

MAURETANIA

A.

NUMIDIA

N
nw   ne
W   E
sw   se
S

0
0   500km
400mi

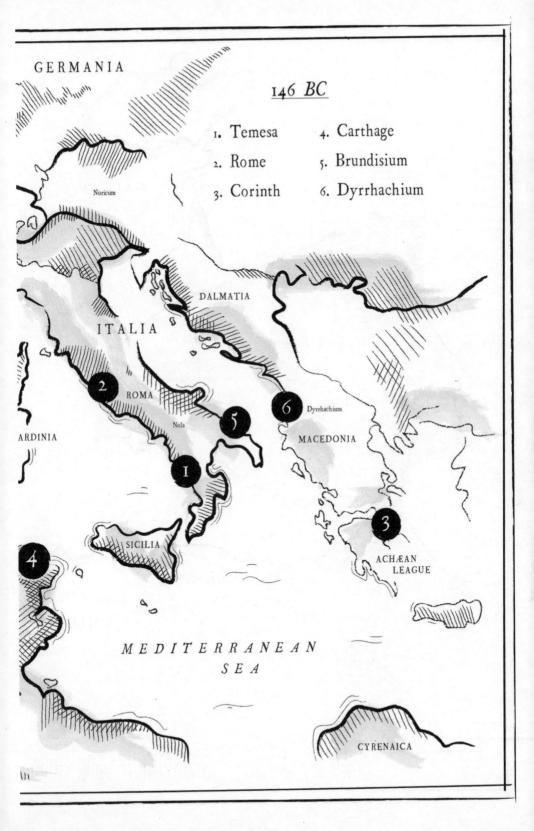

GERMANIA

<u>146 *BC*</u>

1. Temesa   4. Carthage
2. Rome   5. Brundisium
3. Corinth   6. Dyrrhachium

Noricum

DALMATIA

ITALIA

② ROMA

Nola

⑤

⑥ Dyrrhachium

MACEDONIA

SARDINIA

①

④

SICILIA

③

ACHÆAN
LEAGUE

MEDITERRANEAN
SEA

CYRENAICA

Hold out your hands, if they are clean
no fury of ours will stalk you,
you will go through life unscathed.
But show us the guilty – one like this
who hides his reeking hands,
and up from the outraged dead we rise,
witness bound to avenge their blood.
Aeschylus, *The Eumenides* 313–19
(tr. Robert Fagles)

CHAPTER 1

Patria

609 Ab Urbe Condita, From the Foundation
of Rome (145 BC)

ONLY A FOOL OR A MAN TIRED of life travelled alone into the
Forest of Sila.

Paullus brought the mules to a halt. The country here was still flat.
The wheat was almost ready to harvest; just a tinge of green remained
in the gold. The broad fields stretched away into the distance. No
threat could lurk anywhere except ahead.

The two mules were roped together, one behind the other. Paullus dropped the rein of the lead animal onto the road. They were
well trained, and would not bolt unless something disturbed them.
Paullus took a careful look all around. The breeze rippled gently
through the corn. It was the only thing that moved. Not even a bird
crossed the sky. The peaceful landscape dozed under the hot midday Italian sun.

Paullus checked the load of the first mule. Most of the plunder,
discreetly wrapped and bundled, was stowed here. After a time,
when satisfied, he went to the other beast. Apart from a few more
precious things, well hidden, this animal carried his mundane
baggage: food and drink, spare clothes, his shield in its leather
travelling cover strapped to the near-side flank, and his javelins –
one light *pilum*, one heavy – wrapped in canvas to the other. The
pack of this mule had shifted forward.

Having scanned his surroundings again, and taken off his hat, he set to unbinding the many straps that held the load. The pack was ridiculously heavy. Paullus was short, but young and strong. He had the physique of a peasant, one inured to hard labour outdoors in all weathers from an early age. The army had added more muscle. When he got the pack on the ground, he checked the mule's back, then spread and smoothed the blanket. Staggering with the effort, he hefted the pack and slung it back into place. All the while, the mule stood with the resigned, eternal patience of its breed.

Normally rigging a pack mule was a two-man job. They stood on either side, passing the straps back and forth, calling out the immemorial words: *take – cinch – tie*. Although he wanted to get on, Paullus took his time, cutting no corners, and carefully keeping clear of the beast's hooves as he went around its tail.

By the time he'd finished, Paullus was sweating hard. He took a flask from the baggage and drank. Although the container had not been in direct sunlight, the liquid was tepid. Six parts water to one part wine, enough to smother any impurities and to give a little flavour; not enough to intoxicate. After the incidents in the bars at Apollonia and Brundisium on the march home, he had avoided getting drunk. It had taken the intervention of the general himself, Lucius Mummius, to spare Paullus the consequences of the latter. It was unseemly to punish war heroes, especially those who had been awarded the *corona civica* for saving the life of a fellow citizen in battle.

Paullus picked up his hat, knocked off the dust against his leg, and settled it on his head. From under its broad brim, he regarded the way ahead. The foothills were dark green with trees; beyond, the high ridges were misted blue with distance. In the heat of the day no one was about: no peasants in the fields, no travellers on the road. Paullus hitched up his tunic, touched the copper charm in the shape of the Greek letter theta which was attached to his belt, and patted the sword in its scabbard on his hip. Satisfied, he gathered the lead rein, and walked up into the Sila.

At first the slopes were terraced, planted with well-spaced olive trees, vegetables growing between their trunks. There were a few rustic huts and shelters dotted here and there. As the gradient increased the works of man fell away and nature reasserted itself. The timber closed in. Oak and ash, chestnut and maple lined the track. Their boughs met overhead. It was cooler. Only occasional shafts of sunlight penetrated the canopy. Paullus heard the accustomed noises of the forest: birdsong – the twittering of sparrows, the call of doves, the tapping of a woodpecker – the skittering of squirrels and other shy creatures, the soft creak and murmur from above as the wind rubbed branches together. On the forest floor the air smelt musty with centuries of leaf mould. Alert as ever, once he glimpsed a roe deer watching him warily from cover.

Paullus knew the Sila. He had been born on its slopes. Yet only once had he been this far north. That was three years before, marching off to war with Alcimus and the others. Now he was returning alone. He preferred not to think about that.

He had crossed a clearing, a small, natural meadow, and re-entered the dense woodland when he heard the heavy, rasping breathing. It came from off on his right. Although his heart shrank, he stopped. *Be a man.* He squared his shoulders, and turned.

The old woman was some way into the trees, half obscured by a low hanging branch. As always she wore a filthy black dress. Her long straggly hair was unbound and snaked down over her shoulders. This time she was on her own, not accompanied by her two sisters.

Neither spoke. Her eyes were inflamed and rheumy. She regarded Paullus with contempt and hatred.

As he watched, she faded back into the forest.

He remained, rooted where he stood, the blood pounding in his ears, staring at where she had been, blind to everything else.

The harsh cry of a jay brought him back to his senses. Everything was as it had been before her appearance. The sunlight dappled the path. The ordinary sounds of the woods all around seemed to mock him. He half raised his clenched right fist. *It was not my fault. I did not wish it to happen. I should not be cursed.* He marked off each thought by extending a finger. The often repeated ritual calmed him a little. Drawing a deep breath, he looked at his hand. It was not shaking. *Good. Be a man.*

By late afternoon the deciduous trees had given way to pine and fir. Narrow tracks ran off from the road. His nostrils caught the faint tang of tar, and the whiff of wood smoke. In the winter only outcasts and brigands remained in the high Sila. But now in summer there were others hidden in its vastness. Stout shepherds, armed to the teeth, pastured their flocks in the remote glens. In the deep forest were gangs of charcoal burners and timber cutters, and the slaves and landless labourers who tapped the trees for the medicinal pitch to flavour the wine of the rich in distant Rome.

By now, the sun had sunk below the western ridges, and the light was fading. The wind had dropped, and the music of the forest had changed to that of a still evening. Thrushes and other songbirds sang, their notes clear and pure. Furtive nocturnal hunters began to rustle through the fallen leaves and undergrowth. Paullus pulled a light cloak around his shoulders. Going on he spotted a vixen slinking between the trees, already about her murderous quest.

It was getting late. But soon he must come to where the road split in two. One branch ran off east through the wildest of the mountains, eventually to strike the headwaters of the Neaethus and then follow its valley down to the coast of the Ionian Sea above the Roman colony of Croton. The other continued south towards home. He would make camp where the paths diverged, when he was back in territory that was familiar.

He slowed down. Something was moving in the wood, further up the track, and off to the right. Not the soft pad of a wolf or wildcat; this animal made more noise than a badger, but less than a boar. There was only one type of creature that stalked the paths of the Sila.

From under the brim of his hat, Paullus tried to spot the man moving – he was reasonably sure it was only one man – but he did not turn his head or break stride. Then he caught a similar noise from behind.

This was bad. If the bandits had bows, it was very bad. Paullus' armour was stowed on the second mule, and his shield lashed to its flank. If the bandits had bows, it was all over. The old woman and her sisters would get their wish.

Paullus stopped the mules. He went and picked up the left front leg of the foremost. It put the animal between him and the approaching men. He pretended to inspect the beast's hoof.

The subterfuge was unnecessary. The loud crack of fallen twigs and the swish of disturbed branches indicated that the men were not concerned to mask their arrival. Either they had no malicious intent, or they were completely confident.

Paullus pulled the head of the lead mule down and tied its muzzle close to its fetlock. Even the best trained mule would not stand quietly through what was most likely to unfold.

If the man who emerged about thirty paces up the road was innocent, his looks did him a disservice. Long hair and an unkempt beard framed a face stamped with brutality and feral cunning. He had a blade in his hand.

Paullus stepped away from the mules, over to the far side of the road, to give himself room. Facing back to the animals, out of the corner of his eye he saw the other come out of the treeline further away. This one was younger. He had a shock of fair hair, and an air of uncertainty. He too had a sword, but neither carried a bow.

The older brigand walked slowly until he stopped some six paces from Paullus. The younger hesitated a little further off.

'Health 'n' great joy.' The older man spoke in Latin, but his accent betrayed him as a native Bruttian.

'This does not have to end in bloodshed,' Paullus said.

'No, indeed.' The man grinned, revealing snagged and discoloured teeth, the product of a lifetime of neglect and hardship. 'Possessions are a burden, and only what you give to others is yours forever.'

'A kind offer,' Paullus said, 'but I see nothing of yours that I covet.'

The youth sniggered nervously.

'A travelling comedian.' The older man laughed with no trace of humour. 'Take the mules,' he snapped at the boy.

'Do not move.' Paullus pushed back his cloak to reveal the sword.

'A soldier. A Roman soldier.' The man spat. 'Which colony?'

'Temesa.' Paullus took off his cloak and wound it around his left forearm.

'My grandfather had a farm at Temesa. It was confiscated to make way for the likes of you.'

Taking off his hat, Paullus shrugged. 'Following Hannibal was a bad idea.'

'You piece of shit. I was going to let you live.'

'Walk away, and I will do the same.'

With an inarticulate cry, the man leapt forward. In one fluid motion, Paullus unsheathed his sword and lunged. The instant counter-attack disconcerted the brigand. He parried the blow clumsily, staggered across the track towards the mules.

Paullus took two or three steps sideways, turning the fight, putting his assailant between him and the youth.

'Get round behind him!' The brigand shouted over his shoulder.

The boy wavered.

'Do it now!'

Reluctantly the boy started to move around the far side of the animals.

Paullus did not have long. He closed the gap, feinted high, then struck low. The brigand only just got his own weapon in the way of the blow. Paullus pressed his advantage, probing and jabbing, shifting the angle of attack. The brigand was untrained, but he was strong and experienced and fast. He gave only a couple of steps, and remained balanced. Once a sudden riposte nearly got through Paullus' guard.

Both were panting hard. They could hear nothing but the ring and screech of steel on steel, the thud of their boots, their own laboured breathing.

Without looking, Paullus knew that the youth would be at his defenceless back in a moment. This had to be finished fast. If you could not take a wound, you should not stand close to the steel.

Paullus lifted his sword, shaped to take a cut down to the shoulder. The movement opened him up. The brigand saw his opportunity. Quick as a snake, the steel flicked towards the unguarded stomach. Paullus turned the thrust with his left forearm. The blade sliced through the wadded cloak. Pain lanced up Paullus' arm, white hot into his shoulder, stealing the breath from his chest. Closing his mind to the agony, he brought his own weapon down. The heavy edge bit down into muscle and bone.

No time for weakness. No time to inspect the damage. Paullus shoved the brigand away with his injured arm – another sickening surge of pain – and whirled to face his other opponent.

The youth's mouth was open in silent shock.

'Do not run,' Paullus said.

The boy did not move.

'Put down the sword.'

The youth looked at the weapon, as if surprised to find it in his hand.

'Drop it!'

The metal clattered on the road. 'Please, do not kill me!'

'Not unless you force me.' Paullus kicked the sword away.

The boy sank to his knees, stretched out his arms like a suppliant in a sanctuary.

'Stay there.'

Paullus half turned. The older brigand was still alive. Crumpled in the dust, his right hand clamped to the terrible wound to his left shoulder, he was gasping out his life. Bright blood was flowing through his fingers, pooling around him on the track. Paullus went over, gripped the matted hair, yanked back the head, and slit his throat.

Watching the youth, Paullus whipped his blade clean on an unsullied piece of the brigand's tunic. The pain in his arm, which had dulled, now returned and made him clench his teeth. Blood was seeping through the cloak.

'Please, I do not want to die!'

'Do what I say and you will live. I give you my word.'

The boy dropped his hands to his sides and bowed his head like a sacrificial animal.

Keeping an eye on his prisoner, Paullus went and got the flask from the pack. Unpeeling the cloak from his injured arm hurt, washing the wound stung savagely. It was a nasty gash, but he had had worse. He regarded the dead man. Where the brigand's clothes were not soaked in gore, they were filthy. Paullus fished a clean tunic from his baggage. With his dagger, he cut the garment into two unequal parts. The larger he used to dry the cut, the blood blotting on the material. Then he wrapped the other around as a makeshift bandage. Such a wanton waste of a good piece of clothing went against his upbringing. It would take time to get used to being a rich man.

'Just the two of you?' Paullus asked.

'No – I mean, yes.'

'Which?'

Terror seemed to have robbed the youth of his wits.

'Are there other bandits here?'

'Not here, no.'

'Then where?' As he talked, Paullus retrieved the two swords his assailants had dropped. They were worn and rusty. Reverting to the frugality of his peasant origins, he stashed them with his other goods.

'The camp is off the Croton road.' The boy glanced at Paullus, then dropped his gaze. Was he lying or just afraid?

'How far?'

'The pass just beyond the Petra Haimatos.'

It was a likely spot in the most remote part of the Sila. The haunt of robbers since time immemorial, the Blood Rock had not got its name for nothing. But it put the camp half a day's walk from the junction with the Temesa road. If the boy was telling the truth.

Paullus rummaged in his kit and found his entrenching tool. He studied the notch on the blade of the pick, the nicks on the axe. It was easy to kill a man with such an implement. But the youth seemed to have no fight left in him.

'Dig a grave.' Paullus handed over the pickaxe.

The boy did not want to take it. 'You said you would not harm me.'

'A grave big enough for your companion.'

'Why?'

'It is the right thing to do.'

'Where?'

'Here by the track seems as good as anywhere.'

While the boy laboured, Paullus untied and fed the mules, then sat and made a meal of some air-dried beef, cheese, bread, and ate an onion.

'Your accent shows you are a Roman,' Paullus said.

The youth's eyes cut to Paullus, then looked back at his work. He did not answer.

'Why did you end up with a Bruttian outlaw?'

'My father did not return from the wars in Spain.' There was a bitterness beyond his years in the boy's voice. 'My mother got into debt. We lost our land.'

'You could have found honest work.'

'As a day labourer, at the beck and call of another?'

'Sometimes a man has to swallow his pride.'

The youth said nothing.

'You could have enlisted in the army.'

'The unpropertied cannot serve in the legions.'

There was no answer to that.

It was night by the time the grave was dug. But a near full moon had risen. Its light slatted across the road. Somewhere in the distance a wolf howled.

Paullus got up, and together they dragged the corpse to the hole.

'Take anything you want of his possessions,' Paullus said.

As the youth riffled through the brigand's tawdry apparel, Paullus considered the remains of the man he had killed. Gouge out the eyes of your victim and his shade cannot see you, cut off his feet and it cannot follow you, rip out his tongue and it cannot denounce you, sever his hands and the daemon cannot harm you. That was the old way, inherited from the Greeks, enshrined in their literature. No, it was not fitting. This was not murder. It was self-defence. Paullus had given him a chance. The Bruttian had rolled the dice, and he had lost.

Paullus plucked a coin from his own wallet, and placed it between the jaws of the dead man. *Dis manibus*: to the shades below. The outlaw could pay the ferryman.

They tipped the corpse into the grave, and the boy began to shovel the soil back.

'When we get to the Croton road, I will let you go.' Paullus took some high denomination coins from his belt. 'Take these, they will help you take a new course. My advice is go to Rome. There is always building work in the city, or unloading ships at the docks.'

The youth snatched the coins, but offered no thanks.

'Just be sure,' Paullus said, 'if I see you again in the Sila, I will kill you.'

CHAPTER 2

Patria

609 Ab Urbe Condita (145 BC)

PAULLUS CRESTED THE LAST RISE and finally saw the sea. It lay like a silver shield, glinting under the sun. Below him at the bottom of the deep valley the river meandered through wide expanses of pale-grey silt carried down from the mountains. The mudflats were flanked by neat rectangular fields, and beyond these were the hills. The slopes to the south were terraced, set with rows of trees. Those on the far side were steeper, largely untouched by agriculture, with patches of bare, tawny rock. His eyes followed the river down to the sea, and the walls and the jumble of whitewashed buildings of the small colony of Temesa.

The remainder of his journey through the Sila had been uneventful. Last night, when he had reached the turning for the Croton road, he had kept his promise, and let his captive free. The youth had departed in silence, his thoughts unknowable. Paullus had walked on for the best part of another hour, before seeking shelter in a stand of maples well off the path. Only the hooting of an owl had disturbed his brief rest. In the darkness of the last watch, he had tacked up the mules, and continued on his way.

Paullus stopped and studied the vista. There, outside the town, at the foot of the southern side of the valley, was the farmyard of his family; above it the holdings of their neighbours Severus and Junius. From this distance, the countryside looked idyllic and unchanging. But appearances were deceptive. Like one of the Alexandrian poems he had read at school, when you really looked, studied every line and every word, much lurked below the surface. Paullus was almost home. No, now he could see, not everything was the same. The roof of old Severus' place up the slope appeared to have collapsed. The building looked derelict, although his fields were still tended.

After three years, there was no hurry. Paullus let his gaze drift across the river to the spring of Lyka and the Temple of Polites. The sanctuary, gloomy and ancient, shaded by wild olives, was the only thing that the wider world knew about the town of Temesa. Long ago, long before the Romans arrived, Odysseus had come ashore here in his wanderings after the sack of Troy. Polites, one of his sailors, had got drunk and raped a local virgin. The natives had stoned Polites to death. Odysseus had sailed away, leaving his companion unavenged and unburied. Polites had not rested quietly in death. His daemon had stalked the hillsides, murdering old and young alike, mutilating men, women and children. The Oracle at Delphi ordered the locals to build a temple, and every year offer the daemon the most beautiful virgin in Temesa. The girl was locked in the empty temple overnight. Every year in the morning they discovered her dismembered corpse. The grisly ritual continued until Euthymos, three times victor in the boxing at Olympia, happened to pass through the town. His pity for that year's victim turned to love. Hiding himself in the sanctuary, he fought the daemon until it fled and dived down into the sea. Euthymos married the girl, and Polites was gone for the rest of time. Although the superstitious still swore they had seen his shade slipping through the surrounding woods.

Paullus' eyes sought out one particular tree. A huge and ancient wild olive grew close by the temple. One of its upper branches overtopped, and almost reached the roof. As a child he had climbed that tree. It had been Lollius' idea, but he had backed out, leaving Paullus to make the climb with their friend Alcimus. They had made it to the roof, scrambled up to a trapdoor behind the facade. The trapdoor had been locked. Breaking it open had been a step too far. Entering the temple was sacrilege. If caught, they would have been in terrible trouble. But it had been fear of the daemon that had turned them back. Forcing themselves to make the jump back to the branch had been the hardest thing.

The Hero of Temesa, as Polites became known, was the sole claim to notoriety of the town of his birth. It was sanguinary and horrible, but at least, like his childhood adventure, the story of Polites had concluded happily. Paullus was unsure if his own home-coming would end as well. Still, there was nothing to be gained by delay. He gathered up the lead rein, and set off again.

Paullus did not take the direct route, the road down by the river, but instead went along a footpath that clung to the shoulder of the southern hillside. He had no desire to meet any neighbours, answer their banal or intrusive questions.

From up here all the main holding of his family farm was spread out. It was not large, only twenty *iugera*, the standard allocation for a colonist. You could walk its boundaries in well under half an hour. But the soil was good. After the defeat of Hannibal, when the Romans confiscated half the land of his Bruttian allies, they had seized the most fertile. A broad belt of mature oaks and beech trees screened the farm from the road and the river, and provided shelter from the south-westerly wind that in winter whipped up the valley from the sea. The house and barn, the olive and wine presses and storage tanks, the stables and sheds were built up against the timber. They faced inwards, and were connected by a wall to form a small compound. The stone threshing floor was outside, in front of the gate, to catch the breeze. Alongside the homestead stood the cottage garden – vegetables planted between apple and pear trees – and the stock pens. The dung heap was sited downwind to the east. A stream ran from the ridge down to the river. On its west was a meadow where the sheep were pastured when they were driven back from the high Sila in the autumn. There were two fields to the east. That next to the buildings was flat and set with olive trees with wheat growing around them. The enclosure to its south was terraced up the slope. Here vines were propped between the silvery trunks of more olives.

The final piece of Paullus' patrimony, the top field, a five *iugera* plot, the dowry his mother had brought to her marriage, was to the north, on the other side of the river and over the ridge, a couple of hours' walk away. By far the best wheat, as well as the juiciest olives and the sweetest grapes grew there. The top field had a special place in his heart. On the craggy hillside above the cultivated land was a cave. Its entrance was screened by brambles. No one else knew it existed. It was here Paullus had often hidden from his father in his childhood. He had not even told his friends Alcimus and Lollius about this secret place.

Paullus considered the arrangement of his family farm. Such mixed farming of scattered plots – different things growing together in small fields set in widely separated valleys – did not produce the highest yields. The big new estates of the wealthy were buying up blocks of contiguous land and turning each field over to just one crop. They had the money to invest in new planting, and their gangs of slaves and seasonally hired labourers gave them the man-power needed for such extensive harvests. But for a small farmer the old ways were the safest. If a storm swept down one valley, it might spare another. Should disease blight one crop in a field, it might not destroy its neighbour.

Now he was closer, Paullus could see that several tiles had slipped on the roof of the barn, some rails were missing in the fences of the stock pen, and the dung heap was overflowing. This all gave the place a rundown air. It was not unexpected. Counting inclusively, as all Romans did, Paullus had been away three years. Not a day had passed that he had not thought of this place. Now, suddenly unsure of his own emotions, he led the mules along the track that switchbacked down the terraces to his home.

The gate to the farmyard stood ajar. It had sagged on its hinges. As he approached a deep, fierce barking came from within. Paullus stood still. The huge and vicious black dog came hurtling out, hackles up, fangs bared. Paullus hung on to the reins as the mules sidestepped, thoroughly alarmed by the unbridled aggression.

The hound skidded to a stop a few paces short. The hackles still stood in a crest over the bunched shoulder muscles, but the bark changed to a high yelp. The beast shifted from one paw to another. Its lips pulled far back into a foolish, toothy grin. Then it launched itself at Paullus.

'Niger, you lazy old dog.'

The hound forced itself between Paullus' legs. Once through, it turned and repeated the process.

'Were you sleeping? You never bark at someone you know.' Paullus fussed the soft ears, kissed its head. 'Not unless they wake you up.'

Round and round the dog went. Once its hard, bony skull cracked against Paullus' knee.

'You clumsy, great dog.'

Paullus looked up. An old man was standing in the gate. His tunic was ragged, and his hair sparse and unkempt. A scythe was clutched aggressively in his hands. He peered myopically at the newcomer, but did not speak.

'Eutyches.'

Recognition dawned on the aged and unlovely face.

'You are back, then.'

'Yes,' Paullus said. He had forgotten just how ugly his family's elderly slave was. Beetling eyebrows gave Eutyches a look of obstinacy, while his protuberant and loose lower lip hinted at imbecility.

'Your nurse is dead.'

'When?'

'Last winter. The cold got her.'

Rhodope had been nurse to Paullus' father. She had always seemed ancient.

'Has my mother got a new maid?'

Eutyches snorted derisively. 'What with?'

Paullus said nothing. Times would have been hard.

'Don't suppose you have come back weighed down with gold?'

'What happened to Severus up the hill?' Paullus changed the subject.

'Hanged himself.'

'A woman's death,' Paullus said.

'Went off his head. They say he saw the Hero in the forest.'

'People say all sorts of things. Where is my mother?'

'In the house, where else?'

'The fences need fixing in the stock pen.'

Eutyches made a dismissive gesture. 'With the shepherd away up in the Sila, there is too much work for one man.'

'I am back now.'

'Yes,' Eutyches said without discernible enthusiasm. 'You have cut your arm.'

'It is nothing.'

This reunion had gone on long enough. Paullus handed over the lead rein. While the slave held the mules, Paullus unlashed his shield and javelins, retrieved his helmet and armour from his baggage, and also extracted a carefully wrapped parcel. 'Feed and water the mules. I will help get the rigging off them later. Do not touch the packs.'

Niger trotting at his heel, Paullus went to the house. It had two floors, but it was not large. Built of mortared rubble, after seeing Rome and the towns of the east, it now struck him as squat and primitive. The afternoon was hot and the door was wide open, the shutters drawn back from the glassless windows. From inside came the click and shuffle of the loom. He stepped into the gloom.

When his eyes adjusted, he saw his mother, Annia. She stopped spinning wool and stood.

'Health and great joy,' she said.

Paullus repeated the formal greeting.

'Your letter reached Lollius. Your friend came and read it to me.' His mother came and kissed him. Her cheeks were dry and slightly rough, like old papyrus, and smelt of lanolin from the wool.

Paullus held her at arm's length. Her face was strong and mannish, an impression heightened by her scraped-back hair.

'You will make an offering to the household gods.' She stepped back from his grasp. She had not asked after his health, or mentioned the bandage on his arm. If he had hoped for a more effusive welcome, he would have been disappointed.

'In a moment.'

Her silence was eloquent of her disapproval.

Paullus removed the leather covers from his shield and helmet, and unwrapped the oiled cloth from his armour. He checked they were not rusted, and then hung them and his javelins on their accustomed hooks on the wall. He unbuckled the scabbard from his belt and put the sheathed sword on the plinth under the rest of his equipment. Finally he took from the parcel a wreath of oak leaves tied together with a ribbon. The leaves were dry and crackled in his fingers. One dropped to the floor. He stooped and picked it up, before placing it with the wreath next to the sword.

The *corona civica* was awarded to a man who had saved the life of a fellow citizen, and then, for the remainder of the battle, held the place where the exploit had occurred. Such a man was to be honoured for the rest of his life. He was exempted from all public duties. Entitled to a seat of honour at the games, even the senators of Rome should rise when he entered a room.

Paullus regarded the civic crown, trying to sort out his feelings. Yes, there was pride, but also a terrible sadness. He had saved the wrong man.

His mother brought him back from the past. She had lit the fire on the altar, and now handed him a saucer of wine.

A man polluted by blood-guilt should not approach the altars of the gods. It had been unavoidable while he was still in the army. Those under military discipline had to abide by its rituals. But now he was a civilian again, and these were the gods of his own home. The act would be of his own volition, the sacrilege more personal.

Trying not to betray his reluctance, Paullus stood in front of the little shrine. The *genius* of the house was painted as a dignified man in a toga. The divine guardian was flanked by two attendant spirits. The *lares* danced gaily, their short tunics flared; each held a wine jug and a drinking vessel. A snake coiled by their feet. The craftsmanship was local and rough, but that did not lessen the power of the divinities. Paullus bowed his head, placed his right hand flat on his chest, and muttered a few conventional words.

In more affluent houses any scraps of food that were discarded in the dining room were offered to the *lares*. In this home nothing had ever been wasted. Even the saucer contained only a minute portion of wine. Paullus made the libation. The wine hissed in the flames.

'You will want to look over the farm,' his mother said.

'Tomorrow will do.'

'Whenever your father returned he inspected his property.' Her voice was sharp.

'My father never went further than Croton.' Paullus regretted the words as soon as they were spoken.

'Your father was a brave man. It was fate that he was not called to serve. He was a good man, respected the gods, never drank to excess, worked himself into an early grave on our behalf.'

'It has been a long journey, and I am tired.' Paullus attempted to sound conciliatory. 'Today Eutyches will take you into town to see if you can buy a new maid.'

He fished a handful of coins from the wallet on his belt. She took them without speaking.

'You can ride one of the mules.'

'I have walked to Temesa all my life. I am neither infirm nor an invalid.'

Paullus turned and went out of the house.

'I have managed well enough these last three years,' she called after him.

Paullus helped unload the mules. Afterwards he watched Eutyches and his mother walk away.

As soon as they were gone, he set about hiding the plunder. The majority of the coins he buried in the hay barn, along with the swords he had taken from the brigands, all carefully wrapped in oil cloth. Then he raked the hay back to cover the disturbed soil. A few of the highest denomination coins were secreted behind a loose stone in the wall of the olive press. He had hidden things there as a child. Finally he got a ladder and tucked the bag containing the golden drinking set in the rafters of the house, high up under the tiles, well out of sight. He did not unwrap the cups, the mixing bowl, or the wine cooler. Especially not the engraved wine cooler. He had no wish to look at that.

Paullus was carrying the ladder back to the shed when Lollius, his childhood friend, walked into the yard. Paullus had not heard him coming. Niger was winding around Lollius, wagging his tail.

'Busy already,' Lollius said.

'A tile had slipped on the house.'

Lollius pointed. 'There are some missing on the barn too.'

'They can wait.'

Lollius stepped forward for an embrace. Paullus stiffened. Even to touch a man with blood-guilt could bring pollution.

'The winner of the civic crown is too good for his old companions now?'

'Sorry, the army has coarsened my manners.' Paullus hugged his friend.

'Welcome home, neighbour.'

'Neighbour?'

'After Severus hanged himself, my father bought his place.' Lollius tilted his long, almost ascetic face to one side and studied Paullus carefully. 'You look different.'

I am different, Paullus thought. 'I have only just got back.'

'I know, Kaido told me. She saw you cross the bridge at Ad Fluvium.'

'I did not see her.'

'Maybe she transformed herself into a bird.'

'You have not started to believe that shape-shifting nonsense?'

'No, but the natives do.'

Paullus smiled. 'So you have become a familiar of the old Bruttian witch?'

Lollius grinned back. It transformed him from an austere man back to the impulsive boy Paullus remembered. 'I met her on the road. One of our slaves has vanished from the upland pastures.'

'Run?'

'Probably to the brigands. The upper ranges of the Sila are crawling with them. Quite what my father expects me to do, I don't know.'

Paullus held up his bandaged arm. 'I met two on the way down.'

'What happened to them?'

'One dead, the other got away.'

Lollius laughed. 'Kaido was right. She was muttering that you had blood on your hands, something about a harbinger of death.'

'You don't need to commune with the gods to make that assumption about a veteran.' Paullus spoke calmly, not giving away the sudden lurch of his heart. 'The barracks have robbed me of all civility. Come inside and have a drink.'

'Thank you, but no, I had better get on and carry out my father's bidding. Speaking of my father, you must come to dinner. He is holding a feast the day after tomorrow, the kalends of August.'

'I do not know.'

'He will want to see you.'

'Then, thank you.'

Lollius paused, weighing his words. 'Fidubius will be there.'

Paullus flinched, as if he had been slapped.

'You have to see him sometime,' Lollius said with genuine concern. 'Best get it over with. We all read the consul's letter. What happened to his son was not your fault. No one will grieve for Alcimus more than you. Everyone knows you were not to blame for his death.'

CHAPTER 3

Patria

609 Ab Urbe Condita (145 BC)

THE SUN WAS DIPPING into the sea, and waders and other sea-birds were lifting off the estuary as Paullus walked to Temesa. The air was full of the clamour of the birds. Paullus was tired. It had been the first day of harvesting the wheat. Although you could not start until the sun had burnt off the dew, each of the twelve hours of daylight was long in the summer. But it was not the hard physical labour or the relentless swing of the scythe that accounted for his weariness.

Paullus had woken in the dead of night and known they were there before he had seen them. They were asleep on the floor of his room: three dark, humped shapes. The breathing of the three old women was regular, their slumber undisturbed. Through the watches of the night he had lain rigid, afraid of waking them, unwilling to hear their recriminations. In the end he must have slept. When Eutyches roused him, they were gone.

The town house of Vibius, the father of Lollius, occupied an entire block of the main street of Temesa. It presented a blank face to the world, a tall wall of dressed stone. At the gate a porter took his cloak and conducted him inside. The atrium was wide and porticoed, the columns of fine marble. Paullus recognised several of the torchbearers and attendants of the other guests. They got to their feet and respectfully touched their fingers to their lips and bowed their heads. One whom he did not know was slow to rise, and made an offhand obeisance. The slave was very broad shouldered, with a jutting chin and a palpable air of menace. As Paullus passed he got a waft of perfume of spikenard and cinnamon. Obviously the pampered and thuggish favourite of a local dignitary.

The dining room opened onto a garden with a fountain and artfully lit Greek statues. The guests were still standing, sipping drinks and talking quietly. Fidubius was the very first man Paullus encountered. At least Alcimus' father would not have to rise as he entered. That would have been too awkward.

'Health and great joy, Gaius Furius Paullus.'

Paullus returned the greeting. 'Alcimus was a good citizen, a brave soldier and a loyal friend. May the earth lie lightly on him.'

Fidubius' broad face was pale, as immobile as a waxen death mask. 'I always knew my son was mortal. As you say, may the foreign soil rest softly on his bones.'

As a good host, Vibius had waited until the painful exchange was completed. Now he came forward and embraced Paullus.

'Welcome home, Paullus. Thank the gods that you were spared.'

Without waiting for a response, Vibius took Paullus' arm and led him away.

'Let me introduce you to our fellow diners.'

There were three couches set for nine men. Apart from his friend Lollius, Paullus already knew Ursus, the priest of the Temple of Polites, and two of the three other local landowners. The last guest was a Greek philosopher, whose name he did not catch.

Vibius poured a generous libation and guided them to their places.

Before they reclined, house slaves took their shoes, washed their hands and feet, anointed them with balsam and wreathed their heads with roses. The slaves themselves wore wreaths of myrtle. Paullus was glad that he had left the *corona civica* on its plinth. The oak leaves would have drawn unwelcome attention and been a hurtful reminder both to Fidubius and himself.

Paullus was placed on the right-hand couch between his friend Lollius and Ursus. Paullus was relieved that one of the land-owners had been given the place of honour on the middle couch. In this household, age and *dignitas* must outweigh military service, or, given the presence of Alcimus' father, perhaps it was another example of the tact of the host.

The servants set the first course on little tables in front of each couch. Hard-boiled eggs and small fried fish, a salad of lettuce and rocket – nothing extravagant, but it was good, and the bread was warm from the oven. After his day in the field, Paullus was hungry, yet he was careful not to snatch more than his share or eat greedily. His father had not stinted in beating good manners into his son.

'Who owns that large slave in the atrium?' Paullus spoke quietly to Lollius, so that the priest did not hear. 'The one with the big chin and the insolent manner?'

'Croton belongs to Fidubius.'

'Croton?'

'Fidubius bought him in Croton.' A look of distaste crossed Lollius' features. 'Nasty brute, town bred, but now bailiff on Fidubius' main estate. Croton has got above himself since we heard the news that Alcimus was dead. It could be that even stern old Fidubius needs to lavish affection on someone. If so, Croton is a poor choice.'

Conversation became general throughout the room. The topic was land: its properties and price, the shortcomings of slaves and hired labour. The philosopher aside, the guests knew of what they spoke. Between them the host and the other five elderly farmers owned a great deal of land around Temesa and in the Sila. In the time of Paullus' grandfather, Rome had confiscated half the land of the Bruttians, punishment for the locals' loyalty to

Hannibal. Most had been declared public land, available for citizens to rent as pasturage, but the best farming land had been
reserved for the new colonists. Three hundred veterans and their
families had been sent. Each had been given twenty *iugera*, except
for thirty cavalrymen who had been granted twice as much. Of
course such equality had not lasted into even the second generation. It was not so much the diligence of the farmers, or even the
fertility of the soil, as the vagaries of marriage and inheritance.
Roman custom demanded that an estate be divided between the
children. Having just the one son ensured the holding of a family
remained intact, and a well-placed marriage would see it increase.
Paullus himself was an only child, as had been his father, although
his mother had been one of four, and had not added much land.
Other families had done much better, including all those repre-
sented at this meal.

And other ways to make money were available to those who
had the capital to invest. Those not averse to risk could buy a
share in a vessel trading out of the port. But only the foolhardy
took this course. One shipwreck and a family might be ruined.
Property was much safer. Acquire a town house or shop, an olive
grove or meadow, and you could always find a tenant to bring
you a steady return. Greater profits could be generated by band-
ing together and forming a company to bid for the contracts to
fell timber or tap pitch in the high Sila. The produce was floated
down the Sabutus to be exported from Temesa. Paullus' father
had often talked of such projects, but had always lacked the
wherewithal.

The main course arrived. There was chicken with chickpeas
and lentils, but also a suckling pig to each couch. The latter were
an expensive indulgence, and utterly delicious. Again Paullus had
to exercise self-control. Not wanting to drink too fast, he took in

his surroundings. There were pictures that he had not seen before on the walls: the labours of Hercules, obviously by a Greek artist. For a moment he was transported somewhere else. The stench of burning was in his nostrils. He saw the soldiers, blind drunk and laughing, playing dice on the picture they had ripped from its frame. Hercules writhing in agony as the poison in the shirt ate into his skin. Surreptitiously Paullus extended three fingers, one after another – *It was not my fault, I did not wish it to happen, I should not be cursed* – ticking off his defence.

Dragging his gaze away from the pictures, Paullus reached for his cup. His hand was steady. He took a sip and looked at the familiar display of Carthaginian weapons. The two broken spears, the hacked shield and dented helmet, and the broad slashing sword had been there when he was a child. They had been stripped from the dead on the battlefield of Zama by Lollius' grandfather. Again the past threatened to overwhelm Paullus. Once more he smelt the stench of burning. This time he heard the piteous cries of the women and children. He closed his ears to their terror, took a deep pull on his wine and forced himself to listen to what the Greek philosopher was saying.

'Hunting is undoubtedly the finest training for war. In the heat of the summer or the icy blasts of winter, ranging across the wild country, it toughens the body. Yet its greatest benefits are those of the spirit. The hunter glimpses his prey, then loses its track. It trains the soul to deal with all the vicissitudes of fortune.'

Ursus touched Paullus' hand. 'Typical Greek impertinence.'

The priest was very old, his cheeks sunken, his face seamed with deep lines. Beneath his long nose, his thin lips were taut with disapprobation. 'How dare that hirsute Greekling presume to lecture this company? Let alone you, a Roman who has won the civic crown.'

'You do not care for the Greeks?' Paullus had no wish to talk about the *corona civica*.

Ursus looked into Paullus' eyes. 'I advised your father not to waste his money when he sent you to that Greek schoolteacher. Everything Greek – hot baths, sitting in theatres, futile contemplation of the soul, questioning the existence of the traditional gods – it all undermines the very manliness of a Roman. It digs up the roots of the *mos maiorum*, and without the ways of our ancestors we are nothing.'

The priest paused, then spoke so that all could hear. 'The only good Greek is a slave or dead.'

The ensuing silence was uncomfortable.

The philosopher rallied. 'For the wise man death holds no fear.'

Ursus fixed him with a fierce gaze. 'The pious man always fears the punishment of the gods.'

Vibius gestured for the slaves to bring in the nuts and fruit and more drink.

'Paullus, tell us about the campaign in the east,' Ursus said. Doubtless the killing of Greeks was a congenial subject.

'It would be too painful to Fidubius.' Again Paullus caught the smell of burning.

'It is a fine thing to die for your *patria*,' the priest said. 'We all grew up hearing the tales of our fathers' battles against Hannibal.'

Paullus glanced at Fidubius. The mask had slipped. Alcimus' father looked back at Paullus with utter hatred.

'We marched a long way, fought two battles, and burnt the city of Corinth.' Paullus' head was pounding, the screams of the women and children ringing in his ears.

'Corinth,' one of the landowners said, 'the richest city in the east.'

'Not any more,' Paullus said.

'But the plunder.' Naked avarice shone in the eyes of the small-town worthy. 'There must have been wagonloads.'

'Most of the precious things were destroyed or burnt. As military discipline ordains, the rest was collected together, then distributed to the soldiers.'

'Then you must have returned as rich as Vibius here.' The land-owner laughed, intoxicated by his own wit.

Paullus felt as if a band of iron was tightening around his temples. It was hard to draw breath. 'The centurions and higher officers did well. Not so much reached ordinary legionaries.'

'Come now,' the man said, winking.

Vibius intervened. 'Let the boy keep his becoming modesty. I have hired a flute player for our entertainment.'

Paullus had to leave. Unsteadily he pushed himself to his feet. 'Vibius, my thanks. Gentlemen, you must forgive me, but I have a long day ahead tomorrow. The harvest does not gather itself.'

There was a fleeting look of annoyance on the host's features before they relapsed into their usual suavity. 'Of course, Paullus. Those of us who are old and no longer toil ourselves forget. May the gods hold their hands over you.'

The slaves were still waiting outside in the atrium. Paullus glowered at Croton. The bailiff stared coolly back, with just a dip of the head, perhaps even a slight smirk. Paullus felt his anger rise. He would wipe the smile off his face. Before he could act on the urge, the porter brought him his cloak and escorted him to the gate.

Unable to face going home yet, Paullus walked down through the town towards the sea. He considered going to the tavern of Roscius. The innkeeper was empty headed, and much given to the most ludicrous superstitions. In his cups Roscius was bitter, fulminating against the fate that had robbed him of his family farm and reduced him to running a bar. Was he not a Roman citizen, descended from good, colonist stock? But, when sober, he was amiable, kept a good cellar, and the girls in his establishment were clean and willing. Paullus remembered Apollonia and Brundisium, and dismissed the idea. It would mean more wine, and most likely in his present mood lead to a fight with another customer.

The streets down to the port were dark and empty. Paullus took little notice of his surroundings, lost in his thoughts. It was not the fault of those at the dinner. Of course Fidubius hated him. It could not be otherwise. Paullus had returned, and Alcimus had not. There was no tragedy worse than a parent mourning a child. As for the rest, they could not understand. The original colonists might have known. They had fought in Italy and Africa. Temesa had been their reward. The colony had been founded to watch the Bruttians, and suppress brigandage in the Sila and piracy along the shore. The settlers and their descendants were exempt from other military service. The next generation, the landowners at the dinner, had never followed the standards, never had to stand close to the steel.

When the recruiting party came, Paullus and Alcimus had volunteered. The Bruttians had not had a choice. Debarred from serving in the Italian allied legions, they were conscripted as camp servants. They endured the discipline and privations of the army, shared its dangers, but enjoyed few of its rewards. Thirty of them had marched out of Temesa. Just six had returned. Neither those Bruttians who had survived nor those who had died had been mentioned at the dinner. They were beneath notice. But, now and then, when the dead crossed Paullus' mind, he thought about their parents and wives and children.

The docks were almost empty. A couple of warehousemen regarded the wreath of roses on Paullus' head and his fine clothes with suspicion. Young men returning from a drinking party were often trouble. When they saw he was alone, they bade him a civil good evening.

Paullus walked to the end of the jetty. Out beyond the moored merchantmen, the shadows of the clouds played on the sea. The night air was cool, and smelt of salt and fish, of tar and sun-bleached wood. Alcimus and he had enlisted for the eternal reasons that drew young men to the army. They had wanted to prove themselves, to see the world and to make their fortune. The former aims both had achieved; the latter only Paullus. They had been inseparable. Then Tatius, the smart youth from the backstreets of Rome, had joined their brotherhood. The Three Graces, the centurion had mockingly dubbed them. United until death, Alcimus had said. Alcimus' words had been prescient.

Between the scudding clouds, the stars shone bright: the Pleiades, the Belt of Orion. The same constellations that shone over Corinth. And suddenly Paullus was back there outside the last house.

The street was full of smoke. Soot, like black snow, eddied in the backdraught of the fires.

'One more house,' Tatius said.

'We have enough.' Alcimus coughed. It was getting hard to breathe.

'Alcimus is right,' Paullus said. 'The flames will cut us off.'

'No, one last house,' Tatius said. And there was a strange, mad light in his eyes.

CHAPTER 4

Militia

One Year Earlier

608 Ab Urbe Condita (146 BC)

THE CONSUL ASCENDED THE TRIBUNAL backed by his senior officers. Calm and dignified, Lucius Mummius prepared to address the troops. Beyond the tribunal were the walls of Corinth, and beyond them, towering above the city, was its two-peaked citadel, the impregnable Acrocorinth, one of the fortresses called the fetters of Greece. For two whole days the army had been camped on the plain. For all that time the gates of Corinth had stood wide open. But no one had emerged. No armed men had issued forth offering battle or intent on raiding the Roman camp. No heralds or deputations of citizens had come out hoping to negotiate a surrender. Not even refugees, fleeing the impending danger, had slunk through the portals. Yet the city was not totally abandoned. The army had seen the smoke of cooking fires in the evening, and now and then in the day had glimpsed furtive movements along the battlements. Mummius had bided his time, suspecting an ambush. Now the waiting was over.

'Soldiers of Rome, our cause is just.' Mummius measured out the weighty and sonorous phrases as a general should. 'The gods are on our side.'

Paullus, standing with Alcimus and Tatius at the front of the throng, had a fine view and could hear every word. The position was fitting as their maniple had cut and stacked the turf to build the tribunal.

'We did not seek this war. Our empire is built on good faith and guarding the safety of Rome. We always honour our word, and protect ourselves and our allies.' Mummius gestured to the city. 'The Achaeans who hold Corinth took a different course. They rejected the reasonable terms we offered.'

Mummius flourished a toga, its snowy whiteness fouled with brown stains. 'The Achaeans insulted Lucius Orestes, even tried to lay violent hands on him, impiously sought the death of our envoy. In their madness the Achaeans declared war. These little Greeks had the temerity to face Romans on the field of battle. They lost, and now they must suffer the consequences.'

Tatius smirked. 'And we will all get rich.' The centurion snapped for silence in the ranks.

'The senate has decreed the total destruction of Corinth.' Mummius paused to let the soldiers appreciate the enormity of the statement. 'Long ago the Achaeans sacked Troy. We Romans are of Trojan stock. Today we take revenge.'

Warming to his task, Mummius began to pace the tribunal.

'Justice and necessity combine to demand this terrible devastation. Wealthy Corinth must never rise again.'

Tatius nudged Paullus. The centurion stilled the movement with a glance.

'The soil here is too fertile, the isthmus a conduit for trade. Men who inhabit this city become too rich. Wealth leads inexorably to luxury, and luxury to vice. Men of vicious habits are the enemies of Rome. To prevent another war, to preserve our virtue, to guard our safety, Corinth must be destroyed!'

'And as a warning to the rest of the Greeks,' Tatius said quietly.

'One more word, and you are on a charge,' the centurion hissed.

'A picked body of men has been ordered to go ahead and seize the Acrocorinth.' Mummius had stopped moving, his tone become brisk. 'Soldiers of the Second Legion, you will enter the city by the Isthmian Gate, proceed under arms to the Temple of Apollo. There you will wait in good order. No legionary will fall out, and there will be no plundering, until the signal that the citadel has fallen.'

A soft murmur of excitement, an exhalation of compounded greed and lust and ferocity, ran through the ranks.

'March in silence. Listen for the words of command. Keep your discipline. Do your duty. When the trumpet sounds, kill all the males of military age, spare only those civilians who will fetch a good price. The property of Corinth is ours by the laws of war. Do not burn the city until you are ordered.'

Mummius turned to leave the tribunal.

'Achaicus! Achaicus!' Tatius started the chant. Others soon joined in.

Mummius stopped, and raised his arms for silence.

The acclamation faltered and died.

'This campaign was not fought for my personal glory. I am satisfied with the names my father gave me.' Mummius descended the steps and walked away.

'Well that piece of flattery did not work,' Alcimus said.

'You always have to try.' Tatius was unabashed. 'You get nothing unless you try.'

Two long walls linked the city to its western port of Lechaion on the Corinthian Gulf. They were obviously very old, overgrown with weeds, and in places bulging or partly fallen. Here and there were piles of fresh stones and builders' materials, recent attempts at repairs that had been abandoned. The Achaean leaders must have thought to ready Corinth to withstand a siege, then given up the idea.

The Isthmian Gate was open. The legion was drawn up in a cypress grove. They had been here before: the centurion Naevius, along with Paullus and Alcimus and Tatius. Their century was posted at the front of the *hastati*. They knew the way. The rest of the legion, the *principes*, the older men, and the veteran *triarii*, would follow. With luck, Paullus thought, this visit to Corinth would go better than the last.

They watched the light infantry jog forward. The *velites* were the youngest and poorest recruits. Unlike those older and richer, they wore no armour; some lacked even a helmet, and carried small shields and light javelins.

Their approach triggered no response. Nothing moved along the wall.

Some fifty paces out – beyond the range of a hand-hurled weapon – the *velites* paused. The wolfskins many wore over their heads turned this way and that, as if they were still predatory animals scenting danger.

A trumpet sounded the advance. The *velites* gathered themselves and went forward.

After they had vanished under the arch of the gate, there was no sound except the wind sighing through the branches of the trees. Everyone was listening for the clamour of an ambush.

The ears and muzzle of a wolf appeared on the battlement above the gate. The youth gestured that all was clear.

'Our turn, boys,' the centurion said. 'Take it slow, keep together. Still no telling what we will find further in.'

Through the gate there was a range of workshops. They were in good repair, and a wagon was parked outside by a stack of hundreds of tiles. The workmen might have downed tools but moments earlier.

The column turned left and halted facing the next obstacle, the actual defences of the city. This wall was higher, made of smooth, dressed stone, impossible to climb unaided. But again no defenders were in sight, and the gate gaped wide.

'Close order,' the centurion said. 'Dress the ranks.'

There was a primitive comfort in the proximity of tent-mates and fellow soldiers. The veterans said there was nothing worse for regular troops than fighting in a city. Disorientated and lost in unfamiliar streets, unable to keep formation, deafened by the noise, the enemy appearing from anywhere – a tile thrown from a roof by a woman or child could kill more easily than any sword thrust. All the advantages lay with the defenders.

'This could be worse than last time,' Tatius said. 'It could be another Carthage.'

Everyone had heard the stories of the terrible house-to-house fighting when the North African city was taken earlier in the year. The days of unrelenting horror had driven some of the attackers out of their minds.

'Silence, you fool.' The centurion spoke harshly. The muscles in his jaws worked as he forced himself to relax. 'If there are any Greeks who have not run, they are hiding.' He forced himself to smile at Paullus and his companions. 'They have heard the Three Graces here are coming back. Who would not piss himself with fear?'

The *hastati* laughed. The sound was thin as it floated up to the brazen sky, but a little of the tension had been released.

Centurion Naevius might be a bastard, but he was a good man to follow into a bad place.

Again the *velites* went first. Again they met no opposition.

'Here we go, boys,' Naevius said. 'Shields up. Stay alert. Keep quiet. Listen for my orders.'

They emerged into a long colonnaded street. True to their lupine costume, the *velites* slunk ahead. Nothing else stirred in the bright sunlight. The column moved slowly. The tread of the legionaries' hobnailed boots and the metal jangle of their equipment echoed back from the buildings. Nothing else could be heard.

Paullus studied the rooftops. An unexpected movement ahead brought his attention back down to the street.

A solitary Greek – a young man, unarmed – walked out from behind a pillar.

For a moment no one reacted.

In the middle of the road, the youth dropped to his knees, held out his hands.

One of the *velites* took a couple of rapid steps, and threw. The javelin missed by a hand's breadth. The Greek scrambled to his feet and turned to run. The next missile struck him between the shoulder blades. As he sprawled in the dirt, two more javelins thumped into his body.

'Recover your weapons,' the officer with the *velites* shouted. 'Leave him. Keep moving.'

The blood was running along the cracks in the pavement when the *hastati* reached the corpse. Tatius darted forward to search the body.

'Back in line!' Naevius roared.

Reluctantly Tatius did as he was told.

The centurion rounded on him. 'Don't even think about doing something like that again. You leaving the ranks endangers all of us. Don't imagine your friendship with Paullus here will stop me putting you on a capital charge.'

'Sorry, sir,' Tatius said. This time even the sharp boy from the city seemed somewhat chastened. It would not last long. It never did.

In the heart of the city the column turned right and ascended a steep, short road shaded by tall buildings. Paullus remembered it all too well. It was best not to dwell on bad memories. Such introspection robbed a man of his courage. When they emerged onto a sunlit eminence crowned with a temple, he did not look to his right at the arsenal or the house.

The temple would be easy to defend. An outer wall enclosed the sanctuary. Inside, the temple itself was squat and massive, its columns solid and obviously ancient. The heavy infantry halted and the *velites* swarmed through the gate.

'It still does not seem right,' Alcimus said. 'Armed men setting foot in holy places is tempting fate.'

'You need to listen to the officers, my innocent country lad,' Tatius said. 'Remember what the Corinthians did to us. The gods have deserted the bastards. They have come over to our side. Apollo has moved out. The god wants us to have his possessions.'

Alcimus was not reassured. 'What do you think, Paullus?'

'Paullus thinks what the officers tell him to think,' Tatius said. 'He is the very model of discipline.'

'I don't know.' Paullus was not going to rise to the teasing. Unlike Tatius, the traditional morality of his upbringing had not deserted him. The gods were jealous, their power not to be mocked.

The *velites* came out and declared the building safe. Despite the strict injunction against looting, the tunics of some of them bulged with hidden items and there was an audible clank of metal when one or two of them moved.

'Lucky swine,' Tatius muttered.

The order came to form up in a square around the sanctuary.

'It would be safer inside the wall,' Tatius said.

'Really?' the centurion snapped. 'Really? Why don't I go and tell the legate? Please, Lucius Aurelius Orestes, sir, one of my soldiers thinks he knows better than an ex-consul like you.' Naevius brought his face very close to that of Tatius. The centurion was a short man, shorter than Tatius, but his presence was intimidating. 'We are here to sack this city, you snivelling little shit, not cower from a bunch of effeminate Greeks.'

'What happens next?' Paullus wanted to deflect Naevius before the centurion worked himself into a rage. No legionary was immune when he lashed out with the vine stick that was his badge of office.

'Now we wait.' Naevius looked up and down the line. 'Ground shields, but stay in your ranks. And Tatius – shut the fuck up.'

Gratefully Paullus leant the bulky oval shield against his thighs and propped his two long javelins against its face. He stretched and rolled the ache out of his shoulders and neck.

It was a beautiful early autumn day. A gentle breeze shifted high white rafts of cloud across a pale azure sky. Gulls soared on the updraughts. There was a faint hint of incense on the air. A glorious and peaceful day.

At the foot of the incline was a road with a running track on the far side. According to Tatius the locals loved athletics because the competitors were naked and every Greek was a dedicated pederast. Either that or in the bedroom they liked to play the part of a woman. Beyond the stadium stood a long and elegant covered walkway. Beyond the stoa the land started to lift again and was covered in houses. The jumble of red tiled roofs ended at the base of the Acrocorinth. Its lower slopes were green, but steep. The upper were vertical bare grey rock. Paullus could see the fortifications on the higher of the two peaks, but from where he stood any tracks running up were invisible.

What could have induced the leaders of the Achaeans to abandon this superb natural fortress? The approaches would be too precipitous to bring up battering rams or siege towers. They must all be overlooked, and exposed to a murderous hail of missiles. The Acrocorinth reared far too high for even the most powerful torsion artillery to reach. Well provisioned, the citadel could withstand a siege for months, if not years. Perhaps they had struck a deal with Mummius. At Carthage the general Hasdrubal had deserted his garrison in return for his own life. It was rumoured his wife had cursed him for his cowardice, killed their children with her own hands, then thrown herself into the flames of the burning citadel.

One of the surviving Bruttian camp servants appeared carrying a flask of wine and some bread and cheese. He was a small thin youth called Onirus, and he looked after Paullus and his tent-mates. His task was easier now there were only three left from the original eight legionaries. The casualties of this campaign gave the lie to the often expressed Roman belief that the Greeks were cowards who could not fight.

The wine was good. Onirus must have lifted it from a wealthy suburban house. It was not mixed with water. Paullus drank his share. It would put some fire in his heart for what was to come.

'There!' Tatius had keen eyes.

High up on the summit of the Acrocorinth could be seen a repeated flash of light. The sign they had been told to expect: sunlight reflected off a gilded shield. A stir of excitement ran through the assembled troops.

'Wait for the order, boys,' Naevius said. 'Wait for the order.'

Everyone knew what should happen next. It was in the regulations. When the trumpet sounded half the men were to remain under arms, guarding the camp and key places in the town. The rest, maniple by maniple, were to disperse and gather the plunder. All was to be done by units, soberly and in good order. No one was to pilfer anything for himself. When darkness fell the tribunes would summon them back to the marketplace. There all would sleep, watching over the loot. The next day the officers would auction the goods to the merchants that followed every army. The money raised was then to be distributed among the troops according to their rank. Everyone, including those who had stood watch as the sack progressed, received his rightful share.

The trumpet rang out. In a heartbeat all was chaos. The lines of soldiers dissolved into a mob. Men discarded their shields and anything else that might encumber them. Men pushed and shoved to get a head start. The centurions, Naevius among them, made no attempt to intervene. The prospects of loot, drink and rape were not to be controlled. The legionaries had marched hard, had fought and suffered, had seen friends die. The impending agonies of the city were their reward.

The majority clattered off to the temple. It was at hand, and an obvious choice. Temples were repositories of all sorts of costly offerings. There might be precious metal to hack from the cult statues themselves.

'Onirus, stay here. Look after our shields.' Tatius had taken charge.

'Which way?' Alcimus looked around, as if almost overwhelmed by the expanse of the city.

'To the west are just potteries. There are rich houses in the east.'

'How do you know?' Alcimus asked.

A sly grin cracked Tatius' face. 'Last time we were here, unlike you, I actually talked to one of those whores. It is fortunate that at least one of us thinks ahead.'

Onirus was looking mutinous.

Tatius rounded on the Bruttian servant. 'If I find you have wandered off, I will have your balls.'

Onirus nodded.

'Don't worry,' Paullus said to Onirus. 'You will get your share.'

'Enough,' Tatius said. 'Time and tide wait for no man. Come, brothers, let us go and make ourselves richer than Croesus.'

They skidded and slipped down to the road. It was hard work running in armour, but soon they had outdistanced all the other legionaries. Tatius turned into a broad street of affluent-looking houses.

'Let the play begin.'

The gate was shut, but not bolted. In the atrium they found others had got there before them. Not other Romans, but Greek allies from Pergamum. They were already very drunk. A painting had been ripped from the wall. Two soldiers were gambling for its ownership. The dice rattled across the depiction of Hercules writhing in his death agony. The corpses of three men lay in the open. Two were already mutilated: hands and feet severed, eyes and tongue gouged out. A Pergamene was hacking at the feet of the third.

'The shade of this fucker is not following us,' the soldier said.

Paullus stared at the injuries that had killed them. The Greek slashing sword left longer and wider wounds than the Roman *gladius*: great open trenches, as if the flesh had been peeled back by a plough.

A scream from above. Clutching her ripped clothes, a girl fled down the balcony. A soldier caught her by the hair. Bending her over the balustrade, he hauled up her skirts, fumbled with his own tunic, then mounted her like an animal.

'We are too late,' Tatius said. 'Come on, we need a house to ourselves.'

Alcimus was staring up at the girl.

Tatius cuffed him. 'Come on, you lascivious rustic. No time for that. When we are rich, we can have any women we want.'

Outside in the street, Paullus thought he could smell burning.

The door of the next house was locked. It took all three of them to kick it open. It robbed them of any element of surprise, but that was not something they needed.

There was a fountain in the courtyard. Columns lined all four sides. Nothing had been disturbed.

'Very nice,' Tatius said.

The men must have been hiding behind the pillars. There were two of them. One had a hunting spear, the other a sword. Tatius was not wearing mail, just a chest plate. Although he tried to twist out of the way, the spearhead caught him in the left shoulder. Instinctively Tatius doubled up and clutched the wound. For a moment he was at the mercy of his assailant. As a civilian might, the Greek hesitated. Just long enough for Paullus to get between them.

Off to his right Paullus heard the rasp of steel as Alcimus fought the other man. Paullus did not take his eyes off the fiendish point of the spear. The Greek feinted at Paullus' face, then jabbed down at his stomach. Gripping his sword two handed, Paullus deflected the blow. The momentum of the attack drove them together. Paullus brought his hobnailed boot down on the man's sandaled foot. The Greek grunted with pain. Paullus smashed the palm of his left hand into the man's nose. He felt the crunch of delicate bones breaking. The Greek staggered back a couple of paces. In one motion Paullus recovered his blade and lunged. The steel snagged on the man's ribs, then was hilt deep in his chest. For a moment they gazed into each other's eyes in a horrible intimacy. Then Paullus pushed him away and he fell to the floor.

The quiet in the atrium was unnatural. Apart from his own breathing, all Paullus could hear was the water playing in the fountain. Alcimus had killed the other man.

'Fuck!' Tatius started swearing monotonously. 'Fuck!'

Alcimus moved to tend to his injured companion. The injury was painful, but superficial.

Paullus walked to the fountain, put his sword on its lip and started to wash the blood off himself. He felt tired, and strangely drained.

The old woman appeared like an apparition. Bent over the seated Tatius, Alcimus had his back to her. She flew at him, a long kitchen knife in her hand.

As if trapped in a dream, all Paullus' movements seemed sluggish. His fist grabbing the hilt, his legs propelling him forward, his mouth opening to yell a warning.

Alcimus straightened and started to turn.

Somehow Paullus was there. He knocked the knife aside with the edge of his blade, drew the sword back and stabbed her in the throat. The hot blood blinded him. Automatically he crouched, got his weapon out in a guard, wiped at his eyes with the back of his left hand.

When his vision cleared, she was down. Her body convulsed as she choked out her life. Her long hair was bright with blood.

They all stood, as if turned to stone.

'Fuck!' Tatius broke the spell.

Somewhere in the house a child was crying.

Paullus scanned every corner of the yard. No other threat was concealed there. He bent and cleaned his sword on the old woman's dress. When it was spotless, he sheathed the weapon, then went back to the fountain to carry on washing.

Tatius walked out of sight.

Alcimus joined Paullus at the fountain. Neither spoke.

The child stopped crying.

The water in the pool at the base of the fountain was discoloured.

Tatius came back out. He was carrying an amphora. They all drank as Tatius dressed his wound.

'Now to work,' Tatius said.

They only took items that were valuable and easily carried: coins, jewellery, small statuettes of precious metal from the household shrine. Even so, back in the street, each had a sack or pillowcase of plunder. Now there was a strong smell of burning. By accident or design someone had fired the city. The drunken shouts of others looting were much closer.

'We need to move fast,' Tatius said.

They ransacked two more households. Their inhabitants had fled. No soldiers challenged them. When they emerged from the second they were heavily encumbered. The street was full of smoke. Soot, like black snow, eddied in the backdraught of the fires.

'One more house,' Tatius said.

'We have enough,' Alcimus coughed. It was getting hard to breathe.

'Alcimus is right,' Paullus said. 'The flames will cut us off.'

'No, one last house,' Tatius said. There was a strange, mad light in his eyes.

CHAPTER 5

Patria

609 Ab Urbe Condita (145 BC)

ACROSS THE CLOUDLESS SUMMER sky great flocks of gulls flew inland in serried ranks. The crow flapping its wings on the roof of the barn had emitted two deep croaks, then a long, strident cry. They were both sure signs of rain. The wheat was harvested, but not threshed or winnowed. Although there was not a breath of wind and the day was stifling, the tasks could not be postponed. Eutyches claimed that last night the fleas had bitten more vigorously, had thirsted more greedily for his blood. The old slave was adamant that it meant a coming storm.

The threshing floor was of well-rammed clay. It was circular, a little raised in the centre so that the rain would run off and the water not stand. While Paullus had been away, Eutyches had maintained it well. He had drenched it with the dregs of the oil harvest, and there were no fissures to make openings for mice or ants, nowhere for the grains to get lost.

At first light Paullus had gone up to the farm of Junius to borrow his ox. Each family owned one half of the team. It was an arrangement going back to the time of Paullus' grandfather. Neither holding was large enough to justify keeping a pair of oxen. It had been odd driving it down past the ruin of the house of his neighbour Severus. Paullus had not cared for Severus. But it was strange that the stern old farmer was gone. He was an unlikely man to have killed himself, especially by the woman's method of the noose.

They had harnessed the oxen to the threshing sled. Paullus had stood on the sled, guiding the beasts with the crack of the whip. Round and round they had gone, the sharp hooves and the stones embedded underneath the heavy beams of the sled rubbing the grain out of the ears of the wheat. Eutyches had pitched in more sheaves. It was usually a task Paullus enjoyed. There was something soothing about the tread of the oxen and the weighty drag of the sled. But today he had been distracted. His mother had returned to her favourite theme over the last few days. It was time he married. Each evening she had discussed at length the suitability of various families with unwed daughters. This one was wealthy, and the dowry would be worth having, but their women were prone to miscarriages, their natures shrewish. That one had less land, and their girl was ill-favoured, but she was hard working and docile, and their females had a record of fertility.

Paullus had been taciturn and noncommittal. As his mother talked, the words spoken by Tatius in Corinth had run through his mind. When we are rich, we can have any women we want. For now the serving girl in Roscius' inn, the lascivious one from Gades, was more than enough to take care of any physical needs. There was plenty of time. Paullus was still young, just twenty-five, and now he was rich. It was not just the items hidden on the farm. Most of the coins and jewels he had left in Rome, deposited for safekeeping with Lucius Aurelius Orestes. The legate of his old legion might carry an unlucky last name, but he was a man of honour. The wealth of Paullus would be safe.

There was no hurry for matrimony. With the new maid, his mother ran the household well enough. That thought brought another irritation. His mother was full of complaints about the new servant girl. She was lazy and slovenly and greedy. Things had gone missing and there had been accusations of petty theft. The other day his mother had beaten the girl when she could not find a pair of earrings. Paullus suspected they were merely misplaced – most likely by his mother herself – but it was not the place of a man to intervene in such domestic affairs.

By mid-morning the threshing was done. As there was no wind, Paullus and Eutyches fetched the winnowing baskets. Paullus was annoyed. Yesterday the day labourer he had hired in the market-place had announced he would be working for Ursus instead. The bigger farms were paying more. Of course Paullus could have matched the offer. But he had no wish to fan any rumours of the plunder with which he might have returned. Instead he had punched the impudent bastard in the face, knocked him down and kicked him. The bruises would win no sympathy from Ursus. Should the beating hamper his work, the labourer might find himself laid off without remuneration. An old priest like Ursus was a man of traditional ways, stern and unbending. It would serve the labourer right. A man should stand by his word.

When there was a breeze winnowing was not too bad. You took a shovel or a fan shaped like an oar, and tossed the threshed crop high in the air. The lighter chaff blew away on the wind, and the heavier grain fell to the ground. On a still day the task was more unpleasant. Paullus and Eutyches loaded their baskets, rotated them like a sieve, occasionally flipping the contents, then they had to pick out the chaff from the top. It was a slow process, basket after basket. Almost at once they were working in a choking cloud of dust. Despite the sweat, their hands soon became dry, the skin on their knuckles began to crack. They were breathing chaff. It clogged their nostrils, irritated their eyes, worked its way under their tunics. It was everywhere, itching and scratching.

Paullus was not sure how long they had been working when he saw Kaido. The old wise woman was by the tree stump in the lower field. She was burying something at its base. Paullus felt his anger rise. He threw down his basket and rounded on Eutyches.

'You know my orders. There is to be no meddling in forbidden things.'

The slave looked sly but unrepentant.

'No consulting fortune tellers, astrologers, magicians, certainly not that old witch.'

'It was good enough for your father,' Eutyches said. 'Kaido has powers.'

'Superstitious nonsense.'

'It can do no harm.'

'It is against the law.' Despite the firmness of his words, the anger of Paullus was ebbing away.

'Who will tell the magistrates?' Eutyches said.

The question was rhetorical. Paullus' resolve faltered. It was not that he doubted the powers of the old woman, more that he feared them.

'What did you promise her?'

'Some food, a few coins if her spell succeeds.'

Paullus did not reply, but bent to retrieve his basket and resumed work.

Her arcane ritual complete, Kaido sat by the tree stump and watched them.

After a time, Eutyches nudged Paullus.

The leaves at the very top of the chestnut and beech trees by the road were stirring. As Paullus watched, the thin very uppermost branches were beginning to sway slightly. There could be no doubt that a west wind was getting up, moving in off the sea and up the valley.

There was a look of self-satisfaction on the ugly face of the slave.

'Nothing but coincidence,' Paullus said, but his voice lacked conviction. The sun was directly overhead. It was very hot, and Paullus' throat was parched and raw. 'We will take a break.'

Paullus went to the well and drew up a bucket. He stripped to his loincloth and sluiced the water over his head and body. The wound on his left forearm that he had taken in the Sila was still pink. The old scar was white against his tanned thigh.

Eutyches was stretched out in the shade of the barn, eating, as passive as the oxen stalled behind him. After he had swilled out his mouth with watered wine, Paullus drank deeply. He picked up a loaf and a hunk of cheese, and carried them with the flask over to Kaido.

As he approached, he saw the old woman put her thumb between her first two fingers.

Paullus put the food and drink down by her.

Before she reached for the meal, quite deliberately she spat on her own chest.

'You think I carry bad luck?' Paullus said.

She started to eat, not looking at him. 'Your hands reek of blood.'

'I was a soldier.'

'You bring death to the valley.'

Paullus said nothing.

'It will take more than blood and water, more than a shaven head, to purify your pollution.'

Still Paullus did not speak.

'I have seen the ones that hunt you like hounds after a wounded fawn: Tisiphone, Allecto and Megaera.'

As she uttered the ill-omened names, Paullus could not stop himself looking around. The farm slumbered in the haze of the midday heat. There was no sign of the three dark sisters.

'What should I do?' Paullus asked.

'Only the Hero of Temesa can turn them from your steps.'

Paullus turned away.

'Your man promised me money.'

Paullus walked to the well, where he had left his belt. The theta-shaped ornament shone in the sunlight. He took some coins from his wallet, then went back and crossed Kaido's palm with silver.

She did not thank him, but her face creased into a senile smile.

'Intercede for me,' Paullus said.

'Only you can save yourself.' The coins vanished into her grubby dress. She drained the last of the wine and, with no further valediction, clambered to her feet and limped away.

Paullus roused Eutyches. They collected the winnowing fans from the barn and returned to work. As the afternoon wore on the gusting wind cooled their labours, pulling the plumes of chaff off the threshing floor and high out over the fields.

They did not talk. The thoughts of Paullus took their own unhappy course.

Kaido had named the Furies. Safer to call them the Kindly Ones. To utter their names ran the risk of summoning them. But, mercifully, they had not appeared.

The poets and artists were wrong. The Furies did not have the heads of dogs, nor did they possess the wings of bats. They had no scourges in their hands, and their hair was not full of snakes. They looked like old women with dark faces and ragged clothes. But that made them no less terrifying.

Kaido was right at least in part. On the long journey home from Corinth, Paullus several times had sacrificed a pig, had dug a trench, and let the blood flow into the black earth for the ghosts. Afterwards he had washed his hands in running water. In Brundisium he had shaved his head. None of it had bought more than a few days respite, sometimes no more than a few hours.

In the old stories the Furies had pursued Orestes for years. Orestes had killed his mother. The Furies had driven him insane. Paullus envied Orestes. The matricide had a loyal companion, and the goddess Athena had annulled the curse. There were neither gods nor man to help Paullus.

To seek absolution at the shrine of the Hero of Temesa, the priest would have to know what happened in that last house in Corinth, both the crime and the curse. Paullus had not told anyone, and he could not tell Ursus. The aged priest could not be trusted with such awful secrets. The curse echoed in his memory, like a stone in a dry well.

Hades, hear me – Furies hunt him across the face of the world.

CHAPTER 6

Patria

609 Ab Urbe Condita (145 BC)

*T*HE MONTH OF AUGUST. *Thirty-one days. The nones fall on the fifth day. The day has thirteen hours. The night has eleven hours.*

Junius was illiterate. It did not matter. Years before someone had read to him the calendar inscribed on the wall of the forum in Temesa. Junius had a good memory.

The sun is in the sign of Leo. The month is under the protection of Ceres. The stakes for the vines are prepared. Cereals are harvested, likewise the wheat. The stubble is burnt. Sacrifice to Hope, Safety and Diana. Celebrate the Volcanalia.

The festival to Vulcan had been the previous day. Junius knew more than the words on the stone. In August the ides were sacred to Jupiter, and there were also festivals to Portunus, Venus, Consus, Ops Consiva and Volturnus. A man of traditional devotion, on the correct day Junius offered a small libation to each divinity. If he was not too busy, and if he had the energy, he walked into town to watch the processions. A lifetime of piety had brought him few rewards.

At the start of the day Junius would have liked porridge to eat. But it was summer, and not worth lighting a fire. He rummaged in the meagre store cupboard of his hut. Yesterday's flatbread and a piece of cheese would suffice. The dog sat at his feet as he washed down the food with a cup of his own wine. As a tiny indulgence, he let the dog have the last of the bread. Its teeth took the morsel delicately from his fingers. The once black muzzle of the hound was silver. It appeared nearly as ancient as its owner.

Life had not been kind to Junius, or to his family. One of four children, he had inherited just the five *iugera* of land where his hut stood overlooking the valley of the Sabutus. His wife, from a similarly large family, had brought the same amount. The dowry land was over the crest of Mount Ixias, two hours walk to the south. The path was steep, flanked with holm oaks, and invaded by brambles.

They had had a son. Mindful of the previous generation, Junius had employed the method peasants had always used to ensure the boy was an only child. The birth had been difficult. For all her herbs and lore, old Kaido had nearly lost both mother and baby. Junius' wife had wanted no more children. The boy had gone east into the Sila to work in a logging camp. He had not returned. Junius had never discovered the fate of his son. Most likely he had been killed by brigands. It had been too late to think of starting another family. Five winters ago Junius' wife had caught a fever. Junius had given the few coins he had hoarded to the Bruttian wise woman, but her ministrations had done no good.

After his wife died, Junius had not felt too lonely. There had been his neighbours. Some evenings he had walked down to see Severus or Furius, or they had come to him. The three old men would sit and drink their wine, talk of the weather and the crops, complain of the lack of respect and the indolence of the younger generation. Then Furius had died. Junius had little time for Furius' son. Even before he went with the legions, Paullus had been too full of himself. Junius blamed the Greek schoolmaster in town. His friend Furius had paid good money to give the youth ideas above his station. Since he had returned, Paullus barely deigned to talk. Having won the *corona civica*, Paullus was yet more stiff and proud. There were stories that he had returned with his saddlebags bulging with gold.

Then Severus had been found, the noose around his neck, his feet dangling. Junius still could not believe that his neighbour had hanged himself. If, as people said, he had encountered the Hero somewhere on the hillside, if Polites had driven him out of his mind, Severus would not have taken that way out. No, Severus would have ended his life like a man. He would have opened his veins, or fallen on his father's sword. Junius had voiced his doubts to the magistrates. They had pointed out that the sword was not in its accustomed place, hanging by the fireplace. Severus had lost his wits. There was no telling what a man might do in such a condition. Junius had not been convinced.

Now Junius was alone. He tended the land. What else was there to be done? One day soon he would go into Temesa, have a will drawn up and make his mark on the document. The land he would divide between his brothers, his few possessions could go to the husband of his sister. He was not close to any of them, but it was the dutiful thing to do. Land should stay in the family.

The thought brought an annoying memory. Fidubius had made an offer to buy him out. That was fair enough. A rich man always looked to increase his estate. It was the way of the world. Vibius had snapped up the farm of poor, dead Severus. What galled Junius was that Fidubius had not had the courtesy to come himself. Instead the equestrian had sent his upstart bailiff, that insolent slave Croton. Of course the answer would have been the same had Fidubius had the civility to speak to him as one citizen to another.

Still it was no use dwelling on the past. Junius got to his feet and stretched his aching back. He put some more bread and cheese, an onion and a flask of wine in a knapsack, then collected a pitchfork and his tinderbox, whistled the dog to heel and went out, securing the door behind him. A long, tough walk, but the stubble needed burning. As he set out up the slope, his mood lifted.

The dowry land was not large, but it was a gift from the gods. The flat field was tucked high up on the shoulder of the range. Although surrounded by scrub oak and thorns, it was free of weeds. It was high, open ground, south facing and catching the sun, ideal for wheat. Junius regarded it with quiet satisfaction. The dog quartered the field, tail up, every sense alert.

Stiff joints complaining, Junius bent and tested whether the dew had gone. The storm had passed some days before and the surface was bone dry. Straightening, he threw a few stalks into the air. They fluttered away on the steady breeze that blew from the south-west.

Getting on a scent, the hound went away at a half-run, nose close to the ground. Junius let it hunt. It would come to no harm up here.

Walking to the north-east corner of the field, Junius forked some straw onto the tines of his pitchfork. He fished out his tinder box and struck the iron over the flint until the sparks caught. Wielding the bundle of burning straw, he moved methodically, setting the stubble alight.

Stubble burning took him back to his youth. He and his brothers had always helped his father. Even his sister and mother had joined them in the fields. He could not remember a time when his mother had been happier. The world had seemed young then, safe and full of promise. His whole life had stretched ahead.

Above the crackle of the fires, Junius thought he heard the dog yelp. He stopped and looked around. It was out of sight, and he heard nothing else. Most likely it was on the trail of a deer or fox. There were wolves in the high Sila, but only in winter did they venture this close to the coast.

Junius worked steadily, his back to the breeze. It was important to take care. When the stubble was tinder dry like this, if the wind shifted, a man could get cut off by the fires. Not many years ago a farmer over by the village of Ninaia had been overcome by the smoke. When his corpse was found, it had been blackened and twisted, somehow smaller, completely unrecognisable.

Three-quarters of the way across, Junius stood and eased his back. Smuts of soot circled in the air. Still no sign of the dog. This time he called. His voice echoed down the hillside, through the timber. A slight stab of unease struck him. He called again. The dog did not bound out of the undergrowth. Junius thought he glimpsed a movement in the trees. He whistled. The dog did not appear. Perhaps it was no more than a gust of wind. The dog had roamed these slopes all its life. It would be fine. Meanwhile there was work to finish.

Yet Junius could not shift an ill-defined sense of foreboding. He stepped away from the fires and gazed at the woods. The wind was stirring the tops of the trees. Nothing moved at ground level. Suddenly in the shade he saw the ears and mask of a wolf. His heart lurched. It was the wrong season. The wolf rose on its rear legs. It had the body of a man. Deliberately it walked out into the field. There was a sword in its hand. Bright blood dripped from the blade. Dark skinned and muscular, clothed in the pelt of a wolf, its face partly obscured by the head of the beast, it was identical to the painting in the Temple of Polites. The tales were true. The Hero of Temesa had returned.

Junius felt his legs tremble. The flames were at his back. There was nowhere to run. But Junius was no coward. He hefted the pitchfork, faced his assailant. Daemon or whatever, it would not take him easily.

The impact was completely unexpected. Junius staggered. The pain came a moment later. He dropped the shaft of the pitchfork, clutched at the wound. With incomprehension, he saw the bright fletchings of the arrow embedded in the back of his thigh.

The steady crunch of boots coming closer through the stubble.

Defenceless now, doubled over with agony, Junius looked up into the face under the wolf's head. And then, at the last, he recognised his killer.

CHAPTER 7

Militia

Two Years Earlier

607 Ab Urbe Condita (147 BC)

'Y OU READ THE edict?'

They were in Roscius' inn: Alcimus and Lollius, and now Paullus.

'I didn't come through the forum.' Paullus had been down at the docks watching a merchantman putting out for Sicily, bound for Tauromenium, Catania and Syracuse. It was loaded with pitch and timber. Paullus had never been to the island. He had never been anywhere but Temesa and the Sila.

'So you did not see the red flag?' Alcimus had his attention now. Alcimus looked apprehensive – excited but very apprehensive.

The broad, bulky figure of Roscius came over with another cup. As ever, the barkeeper reeked of strong perfume. 'That will put the fear of the gods into the Bruttians, eh boys? It is a hard life as a servant in an army camp.'

They murmured agreement, but did not speak until the barkeeper had left.

'When is the Choosing?' Paullus noticed that his hand was shaking slightly as he took a drink.

'The Prefect Lucius Aurelius Orestes will come and hold the *Dilectus* thirty days from now,' Alcimus said.

'As Roscius said, bad news from the Bruttians.' Lollius was not looking at his friends. 'If any who are summoned own an estate and do not appear the land is laid waste and their houses demolished. Farmers who till the fields of others lose their yokes of oxen, cattle and all other beasts of burden. Those who have nothing are stripped, beaten and sold into slavery. Rome has no use for allies who do not obey orders.'

Lollius still did not meet their eyes. 'Anyway, the families of the colonists of Temesa are exempt from the legions. It has nothing to do with us.'

'At the Choosing a Roman citizen can volunteer for the legions,' Paullus said.

The other two did not speak.

'It is what we have been waiting for. Our chance to get away, see the world, make our fortune.'

'Get away where?' Lollius said. 'You want to be sent to Spain – endless barren mountains, hordes of savage tribesmen, end up dead before the walls of Numantia? Or maybe you fancy the forests of Gaul and some hairy Celtic warrior chopping off your balls?'

'There are four legions in Africa,' Paullus said. 'Think of the wealth of Carthage.'

'And think how long they have been there, and how many will not be coming back. Carthage must be destroyed, so Cato said. Easy for the senator, he does not have to stand in the front line. This is the third year of the war, and still Carthage has not fallen.'

Alcimus joined in. 'There are two legions in Macedonia. The war there is almost over. The east is full of rich cities.'

'There is another pretender to the throne. The Macedonians are not beaten yet.' Lollius took a pull at his wine. 'Still plenty of time to get a pike in your guts.'

'Down at the docks the sailors from Rome say there is trouble coming in Greece with the Achaean League,' Paullus said. 'Everyone knows that little Greeks are too cowardly to stand close to the steel.'

'You don't get to choose where you go,' Lollius said. His thin face was etched with concern.

'But you said we would go together. It was your idea.'

After Paullus had named the thing that had been at the edge of their conversation, had been lurking in the shadows of the bar, there was an awkward silence.

'We swore an oath,' Paullus eventually said.

'We were young, little more than children.' Lollius looked shamefaced.

'It was only a couple of years ago,' Paullus said.

Lollius sighed. 'Our families need us here. Alcimus, you are an only child. Paullus, what would your mother do without you?'

'A man must keep his word.' Alcimus smiled diffidently, as if that might take the reproof from his words.

Lollius looked crestfallen. When he spoke it was very quietly. 'My father would not let me enlist.'

Paullus looked away, ashamed for his friend. It was hard to believe. Lollius had always been the wildest of them, wild beyond the point of irresponsibility. Paullus remembered with a certain guilt when Lollius had convinced them to beat up and rob that merchant on the other side of Mount Ixias. And then there was the time he had led them to sneak onto a moored vessel and steal two amphorae of wine. They had drunk themselves insensible. The beatings they had received from their fathers the next day had been mild compared with their hangovers. And now Lollius lacked the nerve to keep his word.

'Alcimus?' Paullus said.

'I don't want to live my whole life in this backwater.' Alcimus' broad peasant face was set in stubborn resolve.

'You have made up your minds.' Lollius started to rise. 'I had better leave.'

Paullus gripped his arm. 'You will do no such thing. Stay and let's get drunk. After all, when Alcimus and I return we will both be so rich and famous we will not even cross the street to talk to you.'

There was much to do in the spring. The grain fields had to be cleared of weeds. The sheep needed to be shorn, their wool washed. Trenches and furrows had to be dug, ground turned for olive and vine nurseries. The vines had to be set out. Figs, olives, apples and pears needed to be grafted. Tradition held that the grafting be done after noontime, when the moon was waning, and the south wind not blowing. All this and more before the ploughing. And the gods must be given their due. Sacrifices made to Mercury and Flora. A lustration performed to purify every field of grain. May was a busy month.

Paullus was cutting vetch for fodder. The shepherd was out of sight in the meadow shearing the sheep. Unimaginatively, he was named Pastor. Eutyches was helping. Paullus wondered how they would manage the farm when he was gone. Neither slave was young. But they knew the land. They had worked it almost all their lives.

Paullus looked over at the farmhouse. Since his father died, he was the head of the household. He could have told his mother to go to a neighbour's on some errand. But Rhodope could not be sent away. His old nurse was infirm. Unable to hobble any distance, she sat and worked the loom, permanently ensconced by the fire. There was no way Paullus could remove his grandfather's war panoply from where it hung on the wall without it being noted. He would have to hope that the prefect believed him when he stated that he possessed mail coat and helmet, two javelins and a sword, and one greave to protect his left shin. The value of his estate was a matter of public record. Paullus had made no mention of his intention. He had told himself it was for the sake of domestic harmony. In fact he had not dared tell his mother.

Gathering two sacks of vetch, Paullus walked towards the farm-yard. Niger padded out silently, wagging his tail, baring his teeth in a welcome. Paullus stopped and fussed the dog's ears. It was sad, he realised, that he would miss the hound more than his mother, or any other person in Temesa.

Paullus placed the sacks in the barn, then let himself out of the back gate. Unseen, he slipped into the belt of beech trees and oaks by the road. A thudding of paws, and Niger trotted around the side of the compound. It was ridiculous that a dog could almost weaken his resolve. Again, but more briefly, Paullus played with Niger. Then ordered him to stay.

Paullus went through the trees and out onto the road, without looking back.

Alcimus was waiting where he had said by the first of the tombs outside the town.

'We are set on this?' Alcimus said.

'As far as a man can be sure about anything.' In truth Paullus had his doubts. But he would lose too much face to say so.

'Then we had better get moving.'

'Gods below, you stink,' Paullus said.

Alcimus grinned. 'Manure the meadows at the opening of spring, in the dark of the moon. My father holds to the old ways.'

'I hope the prefect is upwind of you.'

'Some general said he preferred his soldiers to smell of garlic, not perfume.'

'They all say that. It shows what tough, earthy stock our soldiers are drawn from, explains why we have conquered most of the world.'

Alcimus looked puzzled. He was not always sure when Paullus was being serious.

'And it was garlic, not manure.'

The forum at Temesa was unimpressive. Paullus realised that and he had travelled no further than the nearest colonies of Croton and Vibo Valentio. The temple of the triad of Capitoline gods at one end was linked to the basilica at the other by two colonnades. But the buildings were undistinguished, and the space enclosed appeared cramped and mean. Never more so than today, when the open area was filled with locals for the Choosing.

The edict had announced that thirty Bruttians would be conscripted from Temesa. At least four times that number had been summoned. They stood muttering in groups, sullen and unhappy. It was odd, Paullus thought. They looked just like Romans, but you could always tell them apart. Of course if they spoke it was easy. Either they talked in their native language or, if they spoke Latin, their accent betrayed them. A native pronounced 'qu' as 'p', and swallowed both 'a' and 'ae'. But, even when they were silent, they were marked out. It was an attitude of passive hostility. Three generations and they still bore a resentment to the colonists, and were not yet totally reconciled to Roman rule.

The murmur of the crowd died away as Lucius Aurelius Orestes walked out and took his stance in front of the basilica. The prefect of the Bruttians was flanked by the *duoviri*, the two annually appointed chief magistrates of Temesa. The latter would draw the tokens.

The names of the first four Bruttians out of the lot were announced. Unwillingly they came forward. The prefect studied them. Lucius Aurelius Orestes was in the prime of life. But he was totally bald, and his face deeply lined, as if aged by the cares of public duty. Such an appearance was fitting for a man who had spent his life in the service of Rome, had held the exalted office of consul. It added the very Roman quality of *dignitas*.

Orestes ordered the Bruttians to run on the spot, then to jump in the air. One of them appeared lame. Orestes inspected him closely, prodding his unsound leg to make sure that he was not feigning. When satisfied, Orestes dismissed him, and indicated that the other three were chosen.

Only three of the next four appeared. The *duoviri* noted the name of the absentee. Unless he had a watertight excuse, things would go badly for him. Of the three who had presented themselves, one claimed to have an exemption. He produced a document. Orestes scrutinised both the seal and the writing before announcing it genuine and letting the man go. Previous good service in the camp had avoided its repetition.

Four at a time the Choosing proceeded. In the shade of a colonnade Paullus and Alcimus watched and waited. Eventually thirty Bruttians had been chosen and the ceremony drew to a close.

'No turning back,' Alcimus said.

Paullus agreed, although part of him wished that there were an honourable way out.

'Time to go,' Alcimus said.

Together they walked out towards the basilica. The throng of relieved locals parted. The two youths stood before the prefect and the *duoviri*.

'My name is Gnaeus Fidubius Alcimus, son of Gnaeus, a Roman citizen in the voting tribe Quirina, and I want to join the legions.'

Paullus gave his name, that of his father and tribe, and repeated the request.

Orestes regarded them not unkindly.

Behind the prefect's back, the two town magistrates glanced at each other with some consternation. One gestured over a servant and spoke urgently in his ear. The slave scurried away.

'The families of the colonists of Temesa are exempt from military service,' Orestes said.

'We wish to volunteer,' Alcimus said.

'You have the necessary property qualification?'

Paullus spoke first. 'I meet the requirement, and have the panoply, to serve in the *hastati*.'

'My family hold equestrian rank,' Alcimus said, 'and I own the war gear to serve in the *hastati*.'

'How old are you?'

They both said that they were twenty-two.

Orestes smiled. When he did so his face was transformed. There were deep laughter lines around his eyes. Despite his dignified manner, Orestes obviously was a man who often smiled.

'You are both aware that if you swear the military oath you may be required to serve on campaign continuously for six years?'

Paullus' heart sank. Six years was an eternity to a young man. It was impossible to imagine that far into the future.

'And after you have been released you will be registered as an *evocatus*. As a veteran, you will be liable to be recalled to the standards for up to sixteen years.'

Before they could answer there was a commotion behind them. Fidubius was bustling towards the basilica. His slave Croton preceded him, wielding a stick to encourage loitering Bruttians to get out of the way.

'Stop the ceremony!' Fidubius commanded. 'It is illegal to con-script colonists of Temesa.'

The laughter lines disappeared from Orestes' face. No matter how amiable, an ex-consul of Rome would not tolerate being spoken to in such manner by a mere equestrian.

'There is no question of conscription,' Orestes said coldly. 'These men have volunteered.'

'That one is my son.' In his agitation Fidubius had not heeded the warning signs. 'I have the legal rights over him of the head of a household. A son may not go against the decisions of a *pater familias*.'

'Military law takes precedence,' Orestes said.

Belatedly realising his error, Fidubius checked himself, rearranged his features into a more unctuous expression. When he spoke again his tone was conciliatory, even wheedling.

'They are very young and immature, Prefect. Alcimus is my only son. The father of Paullus is dead. They have duties to their families.'

Orestes nodded gravely. 'Long ago the general Aulus Postumius had a son. He wanted him to carry on his line and the rites of his household gods. When the lad was young he taught him to read and write, when a youth to fight. The youth was upright and brave. But in battle he left the line on his own initiative to attack the enemy. He was victorious, but Aulus Postumius ordered his execution for disobeying orders.'

Fidubius spread his hands, as if unable to comprehend the rel-evance of the story.

'The duty of a citizen to Rome comes before his duty to his family,' Orestes said.

Fidubius stood silently, unable to muster any response.

The prefect turned to Paullus and Alcimus. 'You will present yourselves here in four days' time with your equipment. You will march to Rome with the Bruttian camp servants under the command of a military tribune. Your patriotism is an example to us all.'

Fidubius rounded on Paullus. There was loathing in his eyes. 'This is all your fault!'

CHAPTER 8

Militia

607 Ab Urbe Condita (147 BC)

THE CAMPUS MARTIUS WAS a low meadow between the city and the Tiber. In the south were the voting pens, where the people elected the higher magistrates of Rome, and various temples, each erected in fulfilment of a vow made on some distant battlefield by a subsequently victorious general. The north, where the troops were camped, was mainly open parkland. The recruits were quartered in tents. The new legions and the reinforcements for those already serving overseas had been raised the month before, and Paullus and Alcimus were with those levies from the more distant parts of Italy that had not yet taken the military oath or been assigned to their units.

The atmosphere varied in the different camps. Those bound for the endless hard campaigning in Spain were evidently unhappy. There were desertions, and sometimes fights broke out, although the overriding mood appeared to be one of miserable resignation tinged with dumb insubordination. Some of the men heading for North Africa gloated avariciously over the riches waiting for them in Carthage, while others were openly fearful of the dangers of a long siege. It was not just the cruel desperation of the Carthaginians, the veterans among them said, disease had run through every besieging army since the Achaeans spent ten years before Troy: always had, always would. The soldiers in the new legions which would be commanded by the consuls who took office the following January tended to be more content. After all it was many months before they might see action. Those with the two legions that would follow the consul-elect Lucius Mummius were convinced that they would be sent to Achaea. Corinth, the capital of that insubordinate league, was as wealthy as Carthage, and it was an accepted fact that all Greeks were cowards. The Macedonians had defeated the Greeks, and now the Romans were stamping out the last embers of Macedonian resistance. In fact the chief concerns were either that there would not be an Achaean war at all, or that the Roman army in Macedonia under the praetor Metellus would end it before Mummius could reach Greece.

Paullus and Alcimus were not long arrived. Army life so far had not treated them badly. They had plenty to eat, and both drink and girls were readily available. Indeed there was a surprising number of brothels around the Campus Martius. These varied from rough lean-tos to affluent houses a little further off. Released from the influence of his father, and freed from the close scrutiny of a small town, Alcimus had developed a strong taste for their varied pleasures.

All in all it was a great deal better than the days between the Choosing and leaving Temesa. Paullus' mother emphatically did not share the opinion of the Prefect Orestes that duty to Rome outweighed that to one's family. Her cold silences were almost worse than her bitter recriminations. *Your father would not have done such a thing. Small farms foundered when the head of the household was away. Your father would not have deserted us.* Of the three slaves Rhodope seemed unmoved. Perhaps in extreme age the full significance of Paullus' imminent departure had been unclear to the nurse. Pastor said nothing, but the shepherd was a man of very few words. Eutyches, on the other hand, had had much to say. How was he to cope when Pastor drove the flock up into the Sila and Paullus was away? He was an old man, broken with a lifetime of hard labour. Many owners would have given him a beating. Paullus suspected that guilt stayed his hand. The complaints had justification. Paullus had consoled himself that no matter how bad things were in his household, they would have been far worse in that of Alcimus.

Any apprehension on leaving Temesa had been overcome by relief. Neither Fidubius nor Paullus' mother came to see them off.

Under the command of a military tribune, Paullus and Alcimus and the conscripted Bruttians had marched north through the Sila. The young equestrian tribune travelled in a mule-drawn carriage. The rest walked, the two Romans carrying their own equipment. But they went in easy stages. By the time they were clear of the forest and descended into the valley of the Crathis river even the Bruttians seemed reconciled to their fate, and the expedition had something of the feeling of a festival procession or a hunting party.

At the town of Interamnium they entered the hill country of the Oenotri. Beyond the lake by Forum Popili, they turned west and followed the Silarus river to the coast. From there the sea was on their left until the road skirted inland of the green mound of Vesusius. When they reached Capua, they picked up the Via Appia to Rome.

They could hear and smell Rome before they saw the city. A distant murmur, like the sea on shingle. The mingled odour of wood smoke and dung, human and animal. It was a windless day and a thick pall from thousands of cooking fires hung in the sky. The road was flanked with tombs, and then they were in the city.

The size of Rome defied comprehension. Paullus thought Temesa and every town through which they had passed, even the city of

Capua, put together would occupy only one of its innumerable districts. Perhaps every town in the world could be dropped around the seven hills and still not match the extent of the metropolis.

'Think of all the women,' Alcimus had said.

But Paullus had been thinking he was already lost. How could anyone hope to navigate the myriad streets and alleys?

There were paved roads and tall, fine buildings. The Temple of Jupiter Optimus Maximus shone up on the Capitoline. But there was noise and mud and filth and unimaginable squalor. And everywhere there were people, as if every inhabitant of Italy and beyond had migrated here.

Paullus and Alcimus had been left on the Campus Martius with the other citizens who had yet to take the oath, and the Bruttians were taken off somewhere else. Another military tribune had registered the newcomers and shown them where to mess and which tent they were to share.

There had been nothing to do but wait. Apart from accompanying Alcimus to brothels, Paullus had hung about the tent. In truth the size of the city daunted him. But today the waiting was at an end.

A trumpet sounded, and the recruits formed up in a rough column in front of the tents. The tribune walked the line, shaking his head as if finding them a sorry lot. The officer was young, but he had the air of a veteran. Or perhaps, Paullus thought, it was just the confidence that came from his equestrian background. If the latter, Alcimus did not share his assurance. Alcimus' face, usually so stolid, was anxious.

'Gods below,' Alcimus breathed, 'please let it not be Spain.'

The trumpet rang out again, and, in a poor approximation of military order, they shuffled off to the Capitoline.

Several hundred men were assembled in the open space in front of the Temple of Jupiter. The sun beat down, and they were on edge as they watched the sacrifice. When the water splashed its head, the animal seemed to bow its head in acquiescence. The executioner knew his trade, and the beast fell cleanly. The priest, his hands and arms red with blood, pronounced its intestines propitious.

The rites of religion satisfied, a tribune read the register. As their names were called the recruits were directed to one of three groups. The tribune announced that those who took the oath today would fill the ranks of the legions in Africa and Spain and those under Lucius Mummius.

Paullus and Alcimus were in the central group. Thank the gods, they were together.

When everyone was in his allotted place, the officiating tribune approached the men on the right. He called an individual forward.

'You will take the *sacramentum* on behalf of your fellow soldiers.'

The man said he would.

'You are bound for Africa.'

The man remained impassive.

'You will repeat the oath after me.'

The man nodded.

'I will obey my officers, follow them wherever they might lead, and execute all their orders. I will defend the Republic of Rome. In battle I will not abandon the ranks in flight or fear, but only to take up or seek a weapon, or to save the life of a fellow citizen. If I see another fleeing, I will cut him down. I will not with malice aforethought commit any theft. Except for one spear, a spear shaft, wood, fruit, fodder, a water skin, a purse and a torch, if I carry off anything worth more than a silver sesterce from the enemy, I will bring it to my officers. Should I break my oath, let the gods curse my household, my family and my own head.'

After the recruit had recited the lengthy formula, one by one the others were summoned forward. They merely said: *Idem in me*.

The same for me. None of them had a choice. Paullus and Alcimus had no choice. For them it was either Spain or Achaea.

The tribune walked to the front of the central group, called a man to come forward.

Dear gods, not Spain! Paullus was unsure if he had said the words aloud.

'You will take the *sacramentum* on behalf of your fellow soldiers.'

Paullus was sweating. He could feel his heart thudding, as if it were too big for his chest.

'You will serve in the army of Lucius Mummius.'

Relief flooded through Paullus. Beside him Alcimus exhaled noisily. Paullus felt weak. He could hardly wait to say *Idem in me*, and leave. When he got back to the Campus Martius, he would buy a really good amphora of wine – hang the expense – make a generous libation to the gods, and drink the rest with Alcimus.

'My name is Naevius, but you will call me sir.' The centurion was short and thickset. Everything about him – the jut of his jaw, the thin line of his lips, even his cropped hair – somehow exuded barely controlled anger.

Paullus stood in the front rank of the *hastati*, hoping not to be noticed. Alcimus was on one side, a legionary called Tatius on the other. After the oath, when they had returned to the Campus Martius, they had been assigned to a squad of eight sharing a tent. Paullus had bought the good wine he had promised himself, but there had been no time to drink it before they were summoned to parade in full armour.

Naevius paced up and down in front of the hundred and twenty men of the maniple.

'You will come to think of me as a stepmother: cruel and hard, with no natural affection. It is my task to turn you into soldiers. You will not enjoy the transformation. You will feel my stick across your back.'

The centurion swished the vine stick of his office in the faces of Paullus and Alcimus.

'My task is made harder by these two peasants just assigned to us.'

Paullus stared straight ahead over Naevius' shoulders.

'Now you rustics are under military law. For those who steal in the camp the penalty is death. Those who give false evidence, the penalty is death. Those who fuck their tent-mates, death. Those who commit any less serious offence three times, death. For these crimes you will be executed. Do I make myself clear?'

'Yes, sir,' Paullus and Alcimus both said.

'The following actions are unmanly and dishonourable: leaving your post, throwing away your weapons, feigning sickness to avoid battle, making a false report of your actions in the hope of commendation. The punishment for these is also death.'

'Yes, sir.'

'When found guilty by court martial, after the touch of this vine stick, it is the duty of your fellow soldiers to fall on you with clubs and stones. Here in the camp they will beat you to death.'

'Yes, sir.'

'Should you contrive to escape, you are no better off. You are not allowed to return to your home. None of your family would dare to receive you in their house. You are completely and finally ruined – worse than an outlaw, denied fire and water.'

Tell that to the brigands in the Sila, Paullus thought. He tried very hard to keep the defiance from his face.

'On campaign should any soldier attempt to desert to the enemy, or betray any information, he will be killed in the ancient fashion: tortured at length, then bound to the 'fork' and beaten to death.'

It was the ultimate degradation. Only a slave should be tortured, not a citizen.

'Should you mutilate your sword hand, cut off your thumb, the punishment is death. Should you attempt suicide and fail, the punishment is death.' Naevius laughed, quite happily. 'In this the army is too generous.'

In a moment the mirth was gone. 'All other misdemeanours will be punished according to their severity: dishonourable discharge, flogging, short rations or stoppage of pay.'

Naevius stepped back, ran his gaze over the whole unit.

'As we have two new recruits, they must be introduced to discipline. Five hours of daylight remain. In five hours at the military step a unit should cover twenty miles in summertime. Ten miles out, ten back. Take up shields. Form column of fours. Prepare to march.'

Naevius went to the head of the column.

'This is the fault of you fucking peasants,' Tatius hissed.

'Go fuck yourself,' Paullus muttered. Although Tatius had delicate features, almost like a girl, he was a re-enlisted soldier. Paullus had not liked the look of his new tent-mate from the start.

'Forward!' Naevius shouted.

They took the Via Flaminia north. On the water meadows to the west were the camps. To the east, garden-covered slopes, dotted with villas. Where the hill came down close to the road, the soldiers were held up by a throng of travellers and carts waiting to pay their tolls at a customs station. Once through they were outside the city, marching between well-built tombs, as though through a town of the affluent dead.

Beyond the necropolis, the road was as straight as an arrow. The Tiber was not far away to the left. Between the willows on its banks swallows swooped and dived over the water. Boundary stones lined the road. Some of the plots were farmed as small market gardens by families from the city, others were larger farms. To the right, despite the evident risk of flooding in the winter, stood an imposing villa.

It was good to be out in the countryside, but Paullus thought the land still tainted by the city. Several times they passed noisome wagons from which the foul night soil of the metropolis was being unloaded to be spread as manure. Once there was a pungent stench of piss. Somewhere nearby but screened from view was a textile works with its vats of urine.

It was not long before the Tiber looped across their path. At the Milvian Bridge the press of traffic again delayed them. Over the river the Via Flaminia swung east. Naevius instead led them north along the Via Cassia.

The afternoon was hot, with no breeze. They marched in a haze of dust. Yet Paullus was not suffering too badly yet. Alcimus and he had carried their kit all the way from Temesa to Rome. Although Paullus noticed that Alcimus was limping slightly.

Eventually Naevius called a halt a couple of miles beyond the small town of Ad Sextum.

'Call yourselves soldiers?' As ever the centurion sounded irascible. 'Three hours to cover less than ten miles! You are a disgrace to the standards!'

'But, sir, twice we had to wait,' Tatius said.

'You poor little girl,' Naevius snapped. 'Of course on campaign no one will hinder your progress – not the enemy, not civilians or refugees!'

Tatius relapsed into a petulant silence.

'There is a good reason not to accept recruits from the city,' Naevius said, 'and you, Tatius, are the clear evidence. It was a bad day for me when you passed muster. Everyone fall out for a quarter of an hour. We return at the quick march.'

Alcimus and Paullus divested themselves of javelins, shields and helmets, and sat by the roadside. Alcimus took off one of his boots.

'I am not sure I can make it back to the city.' The heel of Alcimus' left foot was rubbed raw. The blister was bleeding and oozing.

'March barefoot,' Paullus said.

Tatius looked over with no sympathy. 'If Naevius catches you, we will all suffer.'

'Then keep quiet,' Paullus said. 'Alcimus can march in the centre. Naevius will not see.'

All too soon they were back on their feet.

If anything was added to the army quick march, the men would actually be running. Already tired, it was not long before Paullus was feeling the pace. His breathing was torn from his chest in a ragged panting. The bones and joints in his legs ached. His scabbard jarred against his hip. But far worse were his shoulders. The heavy mail coat dragged at them, and the strap of the shield slung over his back cut into the left. Without breaking stride, he shifted the unwieldy thing to his right. It brought only the most temporary relief.

Alcimus at his side ploughed on, occasionally wincing at sharp stones under his bare soles.

'Not far now,' Paullus gasped. 'Just keep going.'

More than one soldier staggered as they went up the ramp of the Milvian Bridge.

'Almost there,' Paullus muttered.

'Silence in the ranks!' Naevius bore the same weight as the men, but, infuriatingly, he looked nearly as fresh as when they started.

The sun was down, and most of the century were dead on their feet, when they reached the Campus Martius and their tents.

'Fall out!'

It seemed unreal that the ordeal was over.

Paullus and Alcimus helped each other out of their mail, left it at the tent, then tottered to the nearest fountain. Paullus bathed his friend's heel. Alcimus was stoical through the pain, as Paullus thoroughly removed every bit of grit, then dried the wound, and applied some ointment.

'Fuck, that was tough.' Alcimus seldom swore. 'Fucking tough.'

'All over now,' Paullus said. 'Let's go and have a drink.'

Paullus knew something was wrong as soon as he entered the tent. Five of the men did not look at them. Tatius was sitting on Paullus' bed, the amphora of good wine at his lips.

For a moment Paullus did nothing.

Tatius lowered the amphora and grinned.

Paullus hurled himself forward. He knocked the vessel from Tatius' hands. It shattered, spilling the dregs. Paullus dragged Tatius to his feet.

'You thieving little bastard!'

Tatius punched Paullus. A short jab to the stomach. Paullus crumpled, the wind knocked out of him.

'What can you do about it, country mouse?'

Alcimus stepped forward. Paullus waved him back.

Without trying to speak, Paullus launched himself up at Tatius. He got him around the thighs. They both crashed into the side of the tent, rebounded to the floor. Paullus landed on top. He drew back his fist and planted it in Tatius' face. Four or five times, he hit him as hard as he could.

Tatius groaned, covered his head with his forearms.

Unsteadily – knuckles hurting like Hades – Paullus got to his feet and turned away.

'Look out!' Alcimus yelled.

Tatius was back up. He had a knife.

Paullus put his hands up, a placating gesture. He started to back off. Tatius came forward, brandishing the knife.

'Not so brave now!' Tatius' face was smeared with blood.

Without hesitating, Paullus leapt at him. Seizing Tatius' wrist with his right hand, he grabbed his elbow with his left. With the weight of his body, he hauled Tatius towards him. Off balance, Tatius nearly lost his footing. Paullus brought his knee up into Tatius' forearm. Tatius clung on to the knife, trying to twist free. Again Paullus cracked his knee into his assailant's arm. This time the blade clattered to the ground. Paullus kicked it away under one of the beds.

A wave of nausea rose up from Paullus' groin. Tatius had his balls in a vice-like grip.

'Neither of you move!'

Both men froze at Naevius' command.

Released, Paullus doubled over, clutching his crotch.

'Stand up straight!'

Somehow, still feeling sick, Paullus pulled himself to attention.

Naevius lashed the vine stick across Paullus' face. He reeled to the side, the taste of blood, like a dirty copper coin, in his mouth.

'Stand up straight!'

Naevius brought the stick across the face of Tatius.

'Don't even think it,' the centurion said. He flourished the vine stick under their noses. 'Touch this and it is a flogging and a dishonourable discharge. Touch me and it is death.'

They both stood mute.

'Who started the fight?'

Not one of the eight soldiers spoke.

'My money is on you, Tatius. A gutter rat from the Subura, you are a troublemaker.'

There was a bright weal across Tatius' cheek.

'Fighting in camp is a crime. If either used a weapon the penalty is death.'

Alcimus looked as if he was going to speak. Paullus stopped him with a glance.

'You two are on extra fatigues and half pay for a month.'

The centurion gazed round at the others. 'You are guilty of doing nothing to stop the fight. All the men in the tent are on rations of barley, not wheat, for a month. Consider yourselves lucky. Any repeat of the behaviour, or any other crime, and you will feel the lash. Do I make myself clear?'

The days of training stretched out to nearly a month. When the whole legion went out, at the end of the march they entrenched a camp. Once the ditches were dug, they filled them in again, and marched home. Naevius gave his century no rest. In the afternoons, when the other legionaries were at ease, he had them throwing javelins at the mark, practising sword drill against wooden posts, or led them on punishing route marches in full armour and carrying their baggage.

Paullus was not unhappy. He had the stamina of an ox, and his skill with weapons earned grudging approbation. He quite liked barley bread. Unlike Alcimus, he was not obsessed with buying whores, so the lack of coins caused him no distress. Tatius had not expressed any gratitude that neither Paullus or Alcimus had told the centurion about the knife. Relations were wary, but not overtly hostile. The other five tent-companions were placid ploughboys from the Sabine country and caused no trouble.

Day after day they toiled under the cloudless sky and scorching sun of an Italian summer.

They were mending their kit one evening when Naevius appeared. The centurion seemed angrier than ever.

The men stood to attention.

'We will march at dawn tomorrow.'

'Where are we going, sir?' Tatius asked.

'Wherever you are ordered. This is not a fucking assembly in the forum.'

Naevius looked at Paullus and Alcimus. 'The senator Lucius Aurelius Orestes is to lead an embassy to the Achaean League in Corinth. We are to provide an honour guard. The ambassador asked for this *contubernium* specifically. Apparently he was impressed by the patriotism of you two rustics volunteering. Your overeager sense of duty has earned us this unwanted task. It might have been better for everyone if you had stayed in Calabria.'

CHAPTER 9

Militia

607 Ab Urbe Condita (147 BC)

IT WAS THE STRANGEST SENSATION. The solid planks seemed to shift and move, as if the wood had a life of its own. At least Paullus was not sick. It was the first time he had ever been on a ship. The sailors had said men often got sick.

The ship was a quinquereme, the largest warship in the Roman navy. More than a hundred feet long, from its bronze ram to the elegant curved stem, it was twenty feet across the outriggers. Below deck three hundred rowers propelled it through the water. It was called a 'five' because each oar on the upper bank was pulled by three men, each one on the lower by two. Down there it was cramped, the air close and fetid. Up here the lightest of breezes – not enough to set the sails – brought the smell of salt and ozone to mingle with the sun-blanched wood and tar and fresh paint of the ship. Of the sailors, only the helmsmen and the lookout were at their posts. The other twenty lounged about the deck with the forty marines. Not a bad life, Paullus thought. All the crew were free men. They might lack the property qualification to join the legions, but they did not have to get footsore marching anywhere. Not a bad life until the weather turned, and a storm blew up. Paullus could not swim.

The quinquereme had been refitted for the voyage. It gleamed scarlet and blue, its decks sanded white, all its metalwork dazzling in the sun. The Achaean League was said to have no fleet. The warship that carried Rome's envoy, Lucius Aurelius Orestes, was designed to deliver a statement of its own.

They had pulled out of Brundisium at dawn. A long day and they should make Corcyra by dusk. From there they would call at Patra, before reaching their destination of Lechaion, the port of Corinth. A galley this size needed to make landfall each night. The rowers had to go ashore. There was nowhere on board for them to cook or sleep or relieve themselves. Lying to at night would be wearisome and unpleasant.

The great banks of oars dipped and rose together, like the wings of a huge seabird. A fine spray drifted back from where the ram punched through the waves.

Paullus walked, still uncertain of his footing, over to where Naevius stood gripping the leeward rail. The centurion looked pale.

'The men are at their station,' Paullus reported.

The honour guard had been assigned a berth by the prow, the dampest place. They would spread their bed rolls on the deck. There were no awnings. If it rained, they would get soaked. Of the embassy, only Orestes and his staff were sheltered. The captain of the quinquereme had vacated his quarters by the stern.

'A Roman should put his hopes in his sword, not miserable logs of wood.' Naevius did not look at Paullus, but kept his eyes fixed on the horizon. 'Let Greeks and Carthaginians do their fighting by sea, but give us land under our feet, solid earth on which we can stand to conquer or die like men.'

A sudden lurch, as the ship breasted a swell, made Paullus grab the rail. Naevius' knuckles were white on the woodwork. The centurion was breathing through his mouth.

'Why are we going to Corinth, sir?'

'To protect the envoy,' Naevius snapped.

'But why is Orestes going?'

'Inquisitive country bumpkin, aren't you?'

Paullus said nothing.

Naevius glanced at him, then swallowed hard and looked back at the horizon. 'As far as I understand, the Achaean League rules the Peloponnese, the southern peninsula of Greece. The city of Sparta wants to leave the league. The Achaeans don't want to let them. Both sides appealed to Rome, and Orestes is going to tell them the senate's decision. When we get to Corinth, we polish our armour and look impressive, while Orestes delivers the verdict.'

'What has the senate decided?'

'How the fuck should I know? Now go away, and leave me alone.'

Paullus went to the prow. Beginning to get his sea legs, he stood with his feet apart, trying to roll with the rise and fall of the deck. The spray on his face, he watched the play of the sun on the sea. This was the way to travel. It beat the long footslog from Rome down to Brundisium. Paullus, the peasant farmer's son from Temesa, was on his way to one of the oldest and richest cities in the world. This was why he had enlisted.

The house overlooking the Temple of Apollo in the centre of Corinth was intended to unsettle the Roman embassy. There were no gates, but an open archway, through which those on the street could see all the way into the atrium. There was no security or privacy. The courtyard itself had no balcony running around the sides. Instead each block had an individual flight of steps. It made it harder to move around the upper floor, and the effect was to give an air of constraint. Less subtle was a statue in the centre of the atrium inscribed with the name Philopoemen. The old Achaean general had conquered Sparta, and was depicted armoured, advancing in a martial pose. The main room also had a mural showing an Achaean army defeating the Macedonians.

The embassy had been received at the port of Lechaion in some style and escorted to their lodgings in Corinth. And there they had been abandoned. In the stoa next to the house were many suits of armour, racks of weapons and great piles of catapult balls. The arsenal was surely meant as a reminder of Achaean military might.

For four days the embassy had been left kicking its heels. When not on duty, Alcimus had slipped off to brothels in the city with Tatius. Paullus had not accompanied them. Relations between him and Tatius had improved on the journey, but were hardly cordial. Paullus thought Alcimus altogether too forgiving.

The envoy himself had bided his time, not rising to what many Roman senators would see as disrespectful Achaean provocation. Orestes had had the soldiers construct a low platform to the rear of the atrium and place on it an imposing chair, fashioned much like a throne. The impromptu tribunal was sited behind the statue of Philopoemen, so that the general appeared to be running away from the representative of Rome. Orestes had done what he could to set the scene for the meeting which finally was about to unfold.

Paullus stood with the rest of the soldiers behind the seated envoy. Naevius had had them burnish their armour until it shone. Orestes wore a snowy white toga with the broad purple stripe of a senator. He was flanked by his two secretaries in equally dazzling tunics.

'Health and great joy, Lucius Aurelius Orestes.' The speaker was the elected general of the Achaean League. Diaeus had heavy jowls and thinning hair. He wore a spotless Greek cloak over his tunic. His right arm was held across his chest, and his hand was concealed in the folds of the himation. Despite the decorum of his attire and pose, there was something truculent and self-important about the general. Diaeus had a reputation as a demagogue, and was said to be no friend of Rome.

'Health and great joy, Diaeus of Megalopolis.' Orestes also spoke in Greek. It was no great concession. Few Greeks spoke Latin, and Greek was the language of diplomacy in the eastern Mediterranean.

One by one the Achaean deputation greeted Orestes, and he replied. There were thirteen men in all. That Orestes knew all their names, and those of their home towns, was impressive. Evidently, he had been well prepared by his secretaries.

The formalities over, Diaeus seized the initiative. 'Sparta is an integral member of the Achaean League and must remain so. There can be no question of withdrawal. It is against the law, and against the wishes of the majority of its citizens. Only a handful of malcontents wish to disturb the established order.'

Orestes let him talk.

'It is unconscionable. The will of the many must take precedence over the ill-considered desires of the few. We are stronger together. How can the Achaean League defend itself if any individual city, misguided by the self-interest of a few politicians, arbitrarily decides to leave?'

In the face of Orestes' sustained silence, Diaeus' bluster came to an end.

'Acting openly, in the sight of gods and men, the senate has considered the representations of both parties.' Orestes spoke sonorously, his delivery pitched to convey the majesty of Rome. 'The conscript fathers deliberated at length, and they have passed a decree, the terms of which they have empowered me to convey to you.'

Orestes paused to give weight to what he was to say.

'The senate decrees that Sparta should be released from the Achaean League.'

There was a gasp of disappointment and anger from the Achaeans.

'Furthermore, having joined after the formation of the league, and having no ties of blood to the league, the cities of Argos, Heraclea on Mount Oeta and Orchomenos in Arcadia also should leave the league.'

Diaeus and his colleagues were open-mouthed with shock.

Orestes continued. 'Likewise the city of Corinth itself.'

'Never!' Diaeus shouted.

Orestes continued to speak, but his words were drowned out by the uproar, as all the Achaeans voiced their outrage.

'We will see what the Achaeans say about this treachery!' Diaeus outshouted the rest. 'Summon the assembly! Tell the people to meet in the theatre!'

Diaeus swept out of the house, the others scurrying after.

Suddenly the atrium was quiet. A dove circled, then perched on the marble head of the statue.

Orestes looked at the bird. 'Probably not an omen,' he said.

Perfectly calm, the envoy turned to Paullus. 'Am I correct in thinking that you are fluent in Greek?'

'Yes, sir.'

'Take off your armour and your sword. Dressed as a civilian, go to the theatre. Listen to what they say. Report back.'

'Yes, sir.'

Orestes waved Naevius to come forward. 'Centurion, secure the entrance. Station two men on the roof as lookouts. A volatile mob is a dangerous beast.'

Before Naevius could execute his orders, another thought struck Orestes. 'Who is the fastest runner in the squad?'

The centurion named one of the Sabine ploughboys.

'Send him back to the warship. Tell him to disarm and make all speed. The captain is to get the quinquereme ready to put to sea at a moment's notice. We may have to make a hasty retreat.'

*

The theatre was no distance, just beyond the arsenal. The streets were already thronged with men making their way to the assembly. Paullus worried how he was to pass himself off as an Achaean. Corinth, Megalopolis, Orchomenos – although Orestes had just named most of the cities of the league, Paullus was struggling to remember them. What if the man who challenged his right to attend came from whichever city Paullus claimed as his native town? And would his accent or attire betray him anyway?

In the event, no one stopped those streaming into the assembly. The theatre was excavated from the natural slope of the hill, facing north, with a view towards Lechaion and the Gulf of Corinth. Most of those entering sought places in front of the stage, the better to see and hear. Paullus found a seat at the east, from where he hoped it might prove easier to slip away.

The theatre was large. Most likely it could hold several thousand. The majority of those present wore the rough clothes of labourers. Paullus was strangely reassured that his neighbours looked better off and respectable.

The throng on the benches buzzed like a disturbed wasps' nest. Paullus gazed at the blue waters of the gulf, and wished he were safe aboard the big Roman galley.

Diaeus came to the front of the stage and raised his arms for silence. The noise died slowly. The mob was in a truculent mood.

'We have heard what the Romans have to say.' The acoustics were good, and Diaeus only had to raise his voice a little. When their general told them the terms of the decree, the assembly bayed its fury, called curses down on the heads of the Romans.

Now Diaeus had to shout. 'Let us take advice from the statesman Critolaus.'

Another man stepped forward. Critolaus was portly. His face was florid and bland, yet somehow full of cunning.

'Does Argos wish to leave the league?'

The crowd roared back that it did not, the Argives among them loudest of all.

'Heraclea ... Orchomenos?' When he named Corinth, most stamped their feet so that the very stones seemed to shake. Paullus noticed that those next to him did not join in.

'The Romans want to dismember the league.' Critolaus was pacing, gesticulating, warming to his own demagoguery. 'When we are defenceless, they will gobble us up. Remember their treachery to Carthage. To trick the Carthaginians into handing over their weapons, they promised them their possessions. Then, going back on their word, they demanded the Carthaginians abandon their city. The Romans are not men, they are as faithless as ravening beasts!'

'Wolves! Ausonian beasts!' Some of the audience stood, the better to shout.

'Rome has no authority over this sovereign assembly of the Achaeans. Reject their arrogant demands. Send them home with their tails between their legs. Only the Spartans wish to leave. Bring them back into line. Ignore Rome, and declare war on Sparta!'

'War! War!' Critolaus had whipped many of his listeners to a frenzy.

Another figure moved to centre stage.

'Sosicrates,' the well-dressed man next to Paullus said. 'Now we might hear some sense from the cavalry commander.'

'Citizens of Achaea!' Only a minority wished to listen to Sosicrates. 'This is insanity!'

Catcalls and jeers greeted the statement.

Sosicrates persevered. 'To declare war on Sparta is to declare war on Rome. Do you think that we can withstand Rome? Learn from the past. Face the realities of the present. Antiochus the Seleucid king brought an enormous army to liberate Greece. At Magnesia he lost that army, and with it not just Greece but Asia as well. At Cynoscephalae the Romans defeated Philip of Macedon, and at Pydna his son Perseus. They conquered Hannibal at Zama. Rome does not forgive or forget. They hounded Hannibal to his death, and now stand ready to destroy his native city of Carthage. No power has defied them. The Romans rule the world from Spain to the Aegean. We stand alone. If you declare war on Sparta, you will bring ruin on our heads.'

Paullus' neighbours were among the few not to yell their contempt for such counsel.

Critolaus almost elbowed Sosicrates out of the way. 'The Romans will not intervene. They are fighting too many other wars, and all are going against them. In Africa the army of Scipio will sit forever before the triple walls of Carthage. This is the third campaigning season, and the Romans are no nearer taking the city. Earlier this summer in Spain the whole force with the Praetor Vetilius was trapped and destroyed in the mountains. The Celts remain unconquered in northern Italy itself. Under the true king, Alexander, son of Perseus, Macedonia has risen, and the legions of Metellus are in full retreat. Should the Romans somehow manage to find men to send against us, we are not alone. Other kings and states share our design. Show yourselves men, you will not lack allies. Show yourselves slaves, and you will not lack masters!'

There was a commotion on the far side of the theatre. An individual had been set upon by a throng. He was trying to get away, but they were grabbing at his hair and clothes, slapping and punching him.

'It is as I feared,' Paullus' neighbour said to his companions. 'They are going to lynch the Spartans. The commoners might not stop there.'

The man had been dragged down. He was lost to sight under the ring of his assailants.

'We should go,' the neighbour said quietly.

Paullus tagged onto the back of the small group of affluent citizens. As they made their way down the steps, the rough working men made caustic comments, even some threats – *your sort are next* – but no one actually made a move to stop them.

Outside, they dispersed. Each rich man hurried away to the comparative safety of his soon-to-be barricaded house.

Paullus did not run. He walked, trying not to move too fast which might betray fear, and not so slowly as to seem to swagger. Best not to draw attention to himself. It did not work. As he rounded the arsenal, he found a gang of a dozen or more toughs loitering.

'And where are you going?' The speaker blocked his path.

'To my lodgings,' Paullus replied.

'Your accent sounds Spartan to me.' The rest moved to surround him.

'No,' Paullus thought fast, 'I am from Syracuse in Sicily.'

'Then you must be a spy for the Romans.'

'No, nothing of the sort. I am a deckhand on the *Eirene*, moored at Lechaion.'

'Never heard of her.'

Before the ringleader could pursue his interrogation, there was an outcry on the other side of the hill.

'A Spartan! A Spartan!'

A lone figure was sprinting towards the sanctuary of the Temple of Apollo. A mob – twenty or more – was baying at his heels. Without a word, those confronting Paullus hared off after the fugitive.

Now Paullus abandoned caution and ran.

The colonnade of the arsenal flashed by on his left. There were armed Achaean soldiers under the stoa. They made no attempt to go to the aid of the Spartan, who was now being kicked and dragged around the square. Where he had been hauled, there was a bright smear of blood on the stones.

Alcimus, Tatius and two of the other legionaries stood, shields locked, across the gateway. They parted to let Paullus through.

Naevius was by Orestes at the rear of the atrium. The envoy was still seated. Unlike his two secretaries, he seemed unperturbed.

From nearby Paullus heard the wailing of women.

'Has the assembly declared war on Sparta?'

Out of breath, it took Paullus a moment to answer Orestes. 'Not while I was there. The mob is hunting all those they suspect are Spartans. They are going to kill them.'

'Yes, we know.' Orestes had admirable self-control. 'Arm yourself, then join those at the gate.'

'We should leave,' Naevius said.

'Not unless we are forced,' Orestes said. 'To do so would not be honourable.'

Paullus had wriggled into his mail coat when Tatius raised the alarm: the mob is coming. Paullus pulled on his helmet. The keening of the women was joined by the crying of children. The noise was coming from within the house. Paullus hefted his shield, took up his two javelins and ran to the door.

The mob must have numbered at least a hundred. They were all shouting at once, something about bringing *them* out.

'Ready javelins!' Naevius ordered.

The four legionaries at the front, gripping one javelin in the hand that held their shield, lifted the other level with their shoulder, ready to throw. The men facing them fell back a pace or two. The fierce, bearded faces continued to yell, 'Bring out the traitors!' The Romans did not reply. The civilians were not armed, but Paullus noticed that there was blood on the hands and arms of some of them. He thought that those at the back were handing out stones.

Time seemed to lose all meaning as the stand-off continued. Paullus saw Alcimus' right arm trembling from the strain of holding the javelin aloft. He felt the sweat running down the hollow of his own back under his mail. His breathing was fast and shallow. There was an air of expectancy about the crowd. The yells had ceased

'They are on the roof!'

At the warning of one of the Roman lookouts, the heads of all the legionaries jerked around.

'Eyes front!' Naevius shouted. 'How many?'

'A dozen, more all the time.' The lookout sounded close to panic. 'They have brought ladders, lots of them.'

'Fucking wonderful,' Tatius muttered.

'Silence in the ranks!' Naevius made his decision without hesitation. 'Fall back on the envoy. Lookouts down from the roof, and join us.'

They walked backwards, eyes and weapons fixed on the Achaeans Only when they were past the statue in the centre of the courtyard did the mob begin to edge through the gateway.

The two legionaries clattered down the stairs.

'Form *testudo* around the envoy.'

Eight shields made an ineffective *tortoise*, and Orestes was still seated up on the tribunal.

'Sir, would you descend?' Naevius asked.

Orestes dismissed the suggestion. It was beneath a Roman senator to cower before a rabble.

From above came the sound of doors being kicked open. The high screams of women followed. Paullus glanced sideways at Alcimus. His question did not need to be spoken.

'They came to us for protection,' Alcimus said.

They were dragged out from their refuge: women, children, one or two old men.

'What will they do to them?' Paullus asked no one in particular.

As if to answer the question a white-bearded Spartan was manhandled to the foot of the statue. He was forced to his knees before the marble image of Philopoemen. One of the Achaeans gripped the old man's long hair, yanked back his head and cut his throat.

'Blood for the ghosts,' the killer shouted.

As if at an inaudible command, the mob began to drag its victims out of the atrium. There was a confused crush in the gateway. A child separated from its mother stumbled and fell. It was nearly trampled under the boots of the crowd. A man reached down and picked it up. The child was only four or five. The man held the infant by its ankles, upside down, squalling. He waited until the press cleared. When he had sufficient room, he swung the child and smashed its delicate head against the stone wall.

And then they were gone. The awful sounds of their progress faded. Everything was quiet in the courtyard. Nothing moved. Paullus could not take his eyes off the stained archway and the small, broken figure.

A flight of doves circled above the house, the clatter of their wings unnaturally loud.

'We will return to the ship.' Orestes got up and stepped down from the tribunal.

'Form two lines of four.' Practical as ever, Naevius seemed unmoved by the horror. 'If the envoy and his secretaries would take their place between the legionaries?'

Naevius looked them over, as if on parade, then went to the front. 'At the military step, march.'

The street was empty, the hill around the temple deserted. Even the beggars had gone. From far away a rising breeze carried horrible cries and shouts, as if the city had been abandoned by humanity and given over to malevolent daemons.

The tiny column turned east. Paullus was at the rear right. A bad position, his back and unshielded side exposed. There was no threat in sight yet. It was not that far to the port. Perhaps the gods would favour them. He looked at the ancient Temple of Apollo. He hoped that he would never see it again.

Ahead was the narrow, steep street down to the Lechaion road. As they approached it, Paullus heard from behind a deep baying sound, like a pack of dogs on a scent. He tried to convince himself that they were not on their trail.

The sound seemed to recede as they entered the dark tunnel between the tall buildings. They had gone no distance when there was a gasp from the men at the front. Their footsteps faltered.

'Halt,' Naevius said.

Paullus looked around the men in front. His spirit dropped. Thirty paces ahead a solid mass of men was wedging itself across the entrance to the Lechaion road. These men were armed – not with military weapons, but long knives and cudgels. Most carried stones.

From behind, the baying of the mob swiftly grew louder. In a moment the other end of the street also was blocked.

'*Testudo*,' Naevius ordered.

Again they bunched together, ringed by the inadequate number of shields.

The curses and imprecations echoed off the facades of the buildings. The sounds made Paullus' head ring. They were working themselves up to a frenzy. Eight soldiers and three civilians against a multitude. There could be only one outcome.

'Above!'

The alarm came too late. The contents of a commode splattered down squarely over Lucius Aurelius Orestes. A turd slid off his shoulder, smearing the snowy-white wool of the toga. From a high window the vessel was thrown after. It missed, splintering into dozens of shards on the pavement.

Mocking laughter, then the first stone was thrown. It whizzed past Paullus' ear. More followed. A hail of missiles rattled off the leather of the shields. Repeated impacts jarred up Paullus' left arm. One stone rang off the side of his helmet.

'Fuck!' A stone had got through. A legionary was hit. Paullus felt rather than saw him reel with pain.

'Be a man!' Naevius was shouting. 'We are going to walk out of this. On my command, one charge downhill and they will run.'

Another legionary yelped.

'Are you ready for war?' Naevius shouted the ritual question.

'Ready!' The response was feeble, no more than a croak.

'What? I did not hear you!'

But Naevius did not put the question again. The rain of missiles weakened, then ceased. Paullus peeked between the edge of his shield and the next. Achaean soldiers were shouldering aside the mob. They wore the same silver-chased armour as the ones from the arsenal. Their curved swords were drawn, and they carried small round shields faced with silver. At their head was a man in a himation and tunic.

Paullus was torn between hope and despair.

The soldiers lapped around the Romans.

The Achaean troops were facing outwards, towards the rioters. And then Paullus recognised their leader.

'Lucius Aurelius Orestes, accept my most humble apologies,' Sosicrates said. 'This is the work of rabble-rousers and the unwashed. Not all of us Achaeans are enemies of Rome. My men would be honoured if you would allow us to escort you to your ship.'

Not all the Achaean soldiers looked as if they shared the sentiment. But they were disciplined and would obey their orders.

And so the envoy of Rome left Corinth and processed to Lechaion in his fouled and shit-stained toga. And, at that moment, the fate of Corinth was sealed.

CHAPTER 10

Patria

609 Ab Urbe Condita (145 BC)

P AULLUS SAT WATCHING THE RAIN. It had rained after the sack of Corinth. People said it was the dead: the damp gases released by the thousands of burning corpses had gathered in the upper air, had formed rain clouds. The rain had put out the fires, laid the soot, turned the streets into tracks of foul black mud. Paullus did not like to think about Corinth, not the first visit – the envoy and the mob howling for blood in the street – and certainly not the second, when everything in which he had believed had been broken.

It was August, two days after the festival of Vulcan. They should have been burning the stubble, but it had taken longer to prepare the stakes for the vines than Paullus had thought. *See that you carry out all farming in good time*, Paullus remembered his father often saying. *If you are late doing one thing, you will be late doing another*. His father had always been ready with a sententious rustic maxim.

They had cut the willows, stripped the bark and were tying them in tight bundles when the unseasonal storm had moved in from the sea, misted the view over Temesa and swept on up the river. Eutyches had claimed that he had known it was coming. The cattle, by raising their eyes skywards, had given him a presentiment of the storm from the smell of the atmosphere. Ants had hastily removed their eggs from their nests. Centipedes had been climbing the walls, and earthworms had come to the surface. When Paullus could endure no more of the old slave's belated prophesies, he had sent Eutyches from the house to muck out the ox stall and the sheep pens.

Now Paullus was alone in the main room with his mother. She had despatched the new maid on some unspecified errand. His mother was working at her loom. They were not talking. Apart from the patter of the rain and the occasional rumble of thunder, the only sounds were the clicking of the loom weights. The silence was not companionable. That morning she had described in detail the virtues of the unmarried daughter of a farmer called Hirtius, who lived along the coast near Clampetia. Tall and healthy, with childbearing hips, not superstitious, extravagant or given to gossip, untouched by any scandal, her virginity assured, she had a biddable nature and was heiress to ten *iugera* of reasonable land, half set with mature olive trees. Eventually, Paullus had told his mother that he did not wish to hear any more.

In rainy weather a farmer should try to find something to do indoors. Some of the wine jars were damaged. Paullus assembled the ingredients to seal the cracks: one pound of wax, one pound of resin and two-thirds of a pound of sulphur. When he had mixed them sufficiently, he added just enough pulverised gypsum to make the consistency of a plaster. His father would have approved. *Remember that even though work stops, expenses run on none the less.* It had been a favoured saying of the old man.

Paullus had not been close to his father. Furius had not been cruel. Paullus had been beaten no more than was usual. Furius had done the best for his son: taught him to farm and to hunt, scraped together the money to send him to the Greek schoolmaster, and at home sought to instil the Roman virtues of duty and respect for the gods. But there had been little affection. Furius had only seemed to approach happiness when drinking and talking with his neighbours, old Severus and Junius. When allowed to attend, Paullus had not been encouraged to speak.

Paullus mended each of the jars carefully, closing the fissures with the paste, then hooping them tightly with thoroughly dried bands of oak wood.

Like all Romans, while his father had been alive Paullus had been completely in his power. Under *patria potestas*, according to the law, a son could own nothing. Anything he might acquire or be given was the property of his father. When he came of age, still he could not marry, divorce or go to law without permission. A father was within his rights to banish or even execute his son. The annals of Rome were well stocked with examples of fathers who had taken the latter harsh decision. In the Greek east Paullus had come to realise that such savage customs were not universal, that other people did things differently.

Paullus set the jars aside. All that remained was to heat the pitch and liberally spread it over the interiors. Later, if he thought it necessary to make the colour uniform after the mending, he could bake two parts chalk with one part lime and paint it on the jars.

Outside Niger started barking – the deep, menacing note that warned of the approach of strangers.

Paullus went out into the farmyard. A procession was leaving the road from town, and coming through the belt of oaks and beech trees. The two annual chief magistrates were at the front. Among the thirty or so landowners who followed, Paullus saw Ursus the priest, and both Fidubius and Vibius. The latter two were accompanied by his friend Lollius and Fidubius' bailiff Croton. There was purpose, even urgency, about the way they all came through the trees.

Paullus whistled Niger to sit at his heels.

'Health and great joy.' It was Ursus who hailed Paullus.

Having returned the greeting, Paullus waited. For some reason, he felt nervous. Perhaps the evident anxiety of the newcomers – the good and the great of Temesa did not cast off their measured dignity to hurry through the countryside without cause – had transferred itself to him.

'Have you seen your neighbour Junius?' Although the magistrates were there, it was the priest who spoke.

'Not since threshing, when I returned his ox.'

'The old witch Kaido said he was dead – murdered.'

'I would not have thought the visions of a Bruttian wise woman would have been given such credence as to bring this company out from town on foot.' Paullus tried to keep any mockery out of his tone.

Ursus sucked in his sunken cheeks even further with irritation. 'She said she had come from his land on the other side of Mount Ixias, actually seen his corpse with her own eyes.'

Paullus looked round. 'Where is Kaido?'

'She vanished.'

'Vanished?'

The priest tutted in exasperation. 'She must have slipped away from the marketplace while we were talking. The most direct route is across your farm.'

'I will come with you.'

Paullus told Niger, who had been winding through Lollius' legs, to stay with a gesture of his hand.

Hunched against the rain, they crossed the first field, their feet treading down the unburnt stubble, the wind whipping the olive branches above their heads. The trunks of the trees were black from the downpour. Picking up the track, the men climbed back and forth up the terraced vineyard. When they were near the top, as suddenly as it had come, the storm was gone. Paullus watched the dark clouds and the trailing curtains of rain driving up into the heights of the Sila.

The sun shone from a blue, washed-out sky. The heat returned to the day. The ground steamed, and there was a rich, loamy smell to the air. They went by Severus' empty house and across the fields that were now a part of the ever- expanding holdings of Lollius' father.

Reaching the hut of Junius, they halted to catch their breath, as if it had been prearranged. Many of the landowners were not young, but they were countrymen, uncorrupted by the indolent luxury of a big city. Whatever their age, these were men who still farmed and still enjoyed taking their hounds into the forest. Not one of them would dream of showing weakness.

Ursus rapped on the door of the hut. There was no answer. The door was locked. At a nod from Fidubius, the slave Croton kicked it open. There was no one inside. Paullus went in and felt the ashes in the grate. They were cold.

'Anything missing?' Ursus asked.

Paullus looked round. 'It looks the same as when I brought back the ox.'

Some innate decency, or perhaps merely a deep-seated belief in the sanctity of private property, prompted Fidubius to order Croton to lash the door shut behind them.

The path over Mount Ixias was narrow. They went in single file, well spaced, so the encroaching brambles did not flick back on the next man in line. The ascent to the ridge was steep, going down the other side no better. They pressed on, although they all suspected that there was no reason to hurry. Paullus got the impression that some of them were certain what they would find.

It took a couple of hours to reach their goal. They fanned out, then halted, every man pausing to appreciate the upland field: five *iugera*, almost flat, facing south and well sheltered. Most of the stubble was blackened, but a patch in the south-west corner was still golden. Just beyond the scorched earth, half a dozen crows were busy, perched on a low, humped shape.

'The old woman was telling the truth,' Ursus said.

The carrion birds rose, cawing their annoyance.

The corpse had not been there very long. It was not yet bloated, but something larger than the crows had already been at the remains – a fox or a wolf. But it was not the work of the scavengers that shocked the men to silence.

Junius lay on his back. In death his eyes did not regard the sky. His eyeballs were gone. Those delicate orbs might have been pecked out. But the birds had not stripped him naked. No wolf had cut out his tongue or hacked off his extremities: his nose, hands and feet. One of the hands was missing. Perhaps a beast had taken that, but only another man would have severed his penis and stuffed it into the bloody ruin of his mouth.

Despite the mutilation and the attentions of the animals, it was obvious how he had died. They were wounds to both arms – Junius had fought – and three cuts to the left side of his chest. The latter were wide and deep, great trenches which had peeled the flesh back to expose the ribs. Most likely they would have killed him before the desecration of his body.

'A butcher's cleaver or a slashing sword,' Ursus said.

Some of the onlookers were ashen faced. The priest was not one of them, nor were Vibius or Fidubius. The latter's big slave

Croton had his head on one side, as if considering the killer's handiwork.

No one moved to touch the corpse. To touch death brought pollution. Those whose calling was to handle the dead lived outside the town, shunned by the citizens except when they were necessary. They would be summoned later.

A swarm of flies rose when Paullus bent to study the body. Close up there was the sweet stench of decay. Careful scrutiny revealed nothing else. None of the others moved to help when Paullus went to turn the body. The flesh was cold and clammy from the rain and decomposition. He heaved Junius onto his side. There was another massive cut to the back of the neck. Mortally injured, Junius had been on his hands and knees when the killer finished him. Before laying the corpse back, Paullus noticed a small puncture wound high on the left thigh. Its edges were ragged from the barbs of the arrowhead when it was removed.

Paullus wiped his hands in the damp earth, then scrubbed them with the stubble. Even so, when he got to his feet, the others stepped away from him.

'The Hero of Temesa has returned,' Fidubius said.

They all looked at Ursus. The priest said nothing.

'In all the stories that was how Polites treated his victims,' Fidubius said. 'It is in the paintings in the temple.'

'Yes,' Ursus said, 'but why would the Hero return after all these centuries?'

'To punish evil men,' Fidubius said.

'Was Junius more evil than other men? Are we worse than our ancestors?' The old priest was unconvinced. 'It is more likely the work of brigands.'

Vibius spoke for the first time. 'Daemon or bandit, the killer must be caught, and caught quickly. If not the peasants will soon be too afraid to work the outlying farms, the land will be abandoned.'

Some of the men put their thumbs between their fingers to ward off evil; one spat on his own chest, as if the words of Vibius would bring about the very thing against which they warned.

CHAPTER 11

Patria

609 Ab Urbe Condita (145 BC)

IT WAS MARKET DAY IN TEMESA. They were held every eighth day. Everyone from the area knew that. There was a calendar inscribed on the wall of the docks for those arriving at the port.

Paullus walked into the forum. The facades of the Temple of Jupiter at the northern end and that of the basilica at the southern were hung with garlands, as were the columns of the porticos that linked them. As ever on the eighth day, the enclosed space was thronged. All the people were clean and well groomed, wearing their best clothes. The bathhouses and barbers had opened early and done good trade. Even the slovenliest peasant from a remote farmstead up in the Sila wanted to look their best.

The previous afternoon, or in the early hours of that morning, many rustics had loaded their produce onto a donkey, or hefted it onto their own shoulders, or those of their wife, and made the trek into town. They brought eggs and cheese and poultry, fresh figs and almonds and chickpeas. With the coins gathered from their sale, they purchased those things they could not make themselves. At stalls set up between the columns, or in the open square, there were traders to meet any conceivable requirements. There were silver- and goldsmiths, potters and stonemasons, confectioners and key-makers, weavers and tailors, cobblers and workers in leather, merchants in ointments and spices, scribes and money-changers.

For the reassurance of body and soul, there were doctors and astrologers. Catering for more transient needs were bakers and innkeepers, the sellers of fast foods and whores.

Elevated at the top of the steps to the temple sat the aediles. These two junior magistrates oversaw the market. They assigned and rented out the pitches, were meant to maintain order and settle disputes. Behind them was a stone table with bowls of various sizes set in recesses in its surface. This was the official gauge of measurements of goods to which anyone could appeal.

Paullus saw that the aediles were unbothered by suspicious customers. Although the forum was crowded, trade was not brisk. Quintus the old ironmonger had fallen asleep on his stool. Babilius the shoemaker stood disconsolate, a suede buskin in hand, all his patter exhausted. No clients sat on the benches which he thoughtfully provided, or perused the footwear artfully arranged on the screen propped between two pillars. Most people stood in small groups talking. There was a larger gathering by the statues in front of the basilica. It was here that official pronouncements were displayed. In the usual run of things, these did not provoke especial interest: lists of candidates for local elections, or copies of decrees of the senate and laws passed by the assemblies of the people in Rome. The former were always from the same limited circle of families, and the latter often of limited effect on the lives of those who dwelt in and around Temesa. Today was different. A man at the front of the crowd was reading what was painted on the wooden boards to those who could not get close, or were illiterate. His audience hung on every word. Paullus did not have to listen. He had read the notice yesterday, when it was posted. It was two days since they had found Junius. The announcement detailed his murder, the hideous mutilation of his corpse, and a promised a large reward for the apprehension of his killer.

To escape the hot sun, Paullus walked into the shade of the colonnade. Some of the others strolling in the dim light glanced at him, then looked quickly away. He stopped at the stall of the fishmonger. At his arrival, two women, empty baskets on their arms, stopped studying the display on the iced trays and moved off. The fishmonger greeted him politely, but without enthusiasm. Mechanically, Paullus chose some sprats, paid for them, said he would collect them later on his way home, and continued on his way.

The winner of the civic crown demanded respect, but a man tainted with violent death was best avoided. Temesa was a small town. Everyone would know that he had been one of those who had found old Junius. Paullus was the one that had actually handled the corpse. Worse, it would be common knowledge that, for some reason, he had not yet seen fit to go to the Temple of Polites for ritual purification.

Back in the sunshine, Paullus paused. Two young children were playing peek-a-boo around the columns of the temple. Their high, clear laughter cut through the hubbub of the market. Paullus could not remember being so carefree as a child, could not imagine ever feeling so happy. An ignoble part of him wanted to shatter their innocence, as certainly as throwing a pottery vessel onto the flagstones.

The old women had not appeared for many days. When he woke in the dead of night, expecting to see their dark, hunched shapes, there was nothing. Instead, just a feeling of hopelessness and impending doom, an almost physical sensation of falling into a pit. There was no way out. To seek purification from Ursus, he would have to tell the priest what had happened in the last house in Corinth, and that was impossible.

The laughter had stopped. From all directions at once Paullus was assailed by the noise of the market. Around him swirled ill-defined shapes and colours, yellow and red and white. The mingled smells of cooking and fish and humanity made his gorge rise.

'Are you alright?'

Paullus realised that he was standing motionless. The vague colours resolved themselves into the brightly dyed clothes of passers-by, the wall of noise separated into the individual sounds of a market day.

'Are you alright?' It was Onirus, the Bruttian camp servant. He spoke in the local language.

'Yes, thank you.' Paullus, unlike many of the colonists, knew the dialect of Oscan.

'You looked unwell.'

'A fever, nothing more.'

Onirus regarded him sceptically. 'If I may say, you have not seemed yourself.'

'I am fine.'

'Well, if you are sure.'

'Very sure, thank you.'

Onirus hesitated before taking his leave. Paullus liked the slim young Bruttian. They had served together. Once, in camp, Paullus had saved Onirus from a beating, and he had given the servant a generous share of the plunder. Yet every time they met the same unspoken question hung in the air. The year before, Onirus had watched Paullus and Tatius and Alcimus leave the precinct of the Temple of Apollo. Only Paullus had returned through the burning streets of Corinth.

Gathering himself, Paullus walked on across the forum. His emotions back under control, he took in his surroundings. From the steps of the basilica a public slave was calling out the names of debtors in case any present would put up the money to secure their release from gaol. It was the sole exception to the ban on public business on a market day. The list was surprisingly long, and no friend or relative came forward. The poor of Temesa had many reasons to hate the rich.

Moving through the crowd, Paullus murmured a good day to those he recognised. There was nothing overt, but few seemed to welcome the greeting. Paullus ignored the incivility. He was struck by the number of well-dressed unaccompanied women. They went about their business unveiled. That would not happen in Greece. They said travel broadened the mind, but it came at the price of making the familiar unsettling.

It was cool and dark in the tavern. Lollius was already there. They hugged each other fondly. Paullus' friend exhibited no reluctance.

Lollius was drinking with an old Bruttian huntsman called Dekis. Lollius kept a fine pack of hounds, and Paullus had heard that Dekis had a beautiful daughter, although he had not seen her himself. Lollius had never done anything that did not serve his pleasures.

Roscius came over with another cup and a plate of salted almonds.

'You two saw him, then?' As always the thickset innkeeper smelt of perfume – cinnamon or cassia.

The young men agreed that they had. There was no need to ask who Roscius meant.

'None of us are safe now the Hero has returned. Only a fool would go into the woods.'

Lollius looked at Paullus. There was an almost supercilious smile on his long, delicate face, as if he was amused by the superstition of the innkeeper.

'The charcoal burners have heard Polites howling like a wolf up in the hills.' Roscius turned to the other customer. 'Isn't that right, Dekis?'

The leathery and deeply lined face lifted from his drink. 'Maybe so, maybe not,' Dekis said. 'For sure they heard wolves howling.'

'It was bandits,' Paullus said.

Roscius shook his head. 'What brigand would mutilate a man that way?'

'One with a malevolent and cunning mind,' Paullus said. 'One that wanted to rest undisturbed at night, maybe to divert suspicion, terrify people so that there was no search.'

The innkeeper made a sign to avert evil. 'What did old Junius have that a brigand would want?'

Paullus had no answer to that.

'A robber would have ransacked his hut,' Roscius said. 'It is like I say, Polites has returned.'

Further discussion was prevented by loud and angry shouting from out in the square.

'It is probably nothing,' Lollius said. 'Let us have another drink.'

'Afterwards.' Paullus got up.

Roscius told his serving boy to mind the inn. If there was trouble, he was to bring the shutters down. The boy, Zeno, pouted. He wanted to come too. Wherever the innkeeper went the delicate youth followed. There was no doubt about the tastes of Roscius. For once the innkeeper told his paramour to stay behind, and then followed Paullus and Lollius out. Intent on drinking, Dekis remained.

A mob of working men had gathered in front of the basilica. Some were townsmen, but most wore the rough clothes of the country-side. They were all shouting at once. The women and children had vanished from the forum.

The uproar brought out the two chief magistrates. The *duoviri* were joined on top of the steps by Lollius' father Vibius, as well as Ursus and Fidubius. The magistrates, *duoviri* and aediles alike, were at a loss. It was Fidubius who raised his hands for silence.

Unexpectedly, the multitude fell quiet almost at once.

'What is the meaning of this outburst?' Fidubius' big round face was solid and impassive, like a boulder. There was an assurance about him that his son, poor Alcimus, had never possessed.

'The Hero has returned! Polites must be propitiated!' the horde chanted, like a well-trained chorus.

'What would you have us do?' Fidubius said.

Everyone knew the old story. The enormity of the thing held them back.

Eventually a lone voice called out what was on all their minds: 'A virgin, offer him a virgin.'

'Who does not want a virgin?' Lollius whispered in Paullus' ear.

But Paullus was not listening. He started to shoulder his way to the front of the crowd. When they saw him coming, they got out of his way. It might have been from respect for the civic crown, or the threat of blood-pollution, Paullus did not care. He went up the steps and turned to face the crowd.

'This is madness.' Paullus pitched his voice to carry. 'Junius was not killed by a daemon. There was an arrow wound in his leg. A brigand shot him from behind, then butchered him with a cleaver or broadsword. The mutilation was to prevent his shade haunting his murderer.'

Ursus came and stood next to Paullus. 'As the priest of the sanctuary of Polites, I record that no portents or omens have been reported. There is nothing to suggest that the Hero has returned.'

'Brigands do not fear the shades of their victims,' Fidubius said. 'They already have too much blood on their hands.'

'This was the work of an outlaw, not the Hero,' Ursus said.

'If Polites has not awakened, then no harm could come to the girl left in the temple.' Fidubius was not yet ready to give up.

'This was the work of an outlaw, not the Hero.' The authority of the priest was not to be set aside.

Fidubius, usually so unexpressive, looked thoroughly put out.

Lollius' father intervened. As ever Vibius was the model of well-bred civility, but he spoke with urgency. 'The killer has to be found before there are more victims. No family will sleep safe in their beds until he has been caught. It is our duty as colonists of Temesa to hunt out all brigands. A posse must be raised, and venture into the Sila.'

'It is the eighth day, and against the law to transact any public business on market day.' Ursus looked to the chief magistrates.

Taken aback by the unexpectedness of events, the *duoviri* affirmed that the priest was correct. They mumbled something about holding an assembly later, on a valid day, when the signs were propitious.

The impromptu meeting began to disperse.

Paullus thought that Fidubius did not seem at all pleased with this turn of events. Oddly, nor did Vibius. Perhaps the latter was dissatisfied with the delay to his proposed expedition against the bandits. Neither man was accustomed to not getting what they wanted immediately.

CHAPTER 12

Patria

609 Ab Urbe Condita (145 BC)

THE FOREST WAS FILLED WITH SOUND. Although the sun would not rise for another half an hour, all the birds were singing. A myriad of trilling voices which lifted and fell, and merged into one song. Paullus loved this time of day in the woods. If you stopped, closed your eyes and just listened, the chorus flooded your senses, made your head reel. Today Paullus had no leisure for any such indulgence. He climbed carefully through the ghostly half-light under the boughs of the oaks. The birdsong would serve to mask any sounds of his approach.

This was not a range of the Sila he knew well, only having been here twice before. But he was a natural woodsman, and it was not difficult to find deer trails heading in the right general direction. Distance was hard to judge, yet he thought that sunrise would find him close to his objective, high on the slope he intended.

The intervention of Ursus on market day had only postponed the decision to raise an expedition against the brigands in the mountains. The very next day popular agitation had forced the magistrates to summon an assembly. The vote for prompt action had been unanimous. Speaker after speaker had stressed the fear of those living in remote farms and working outlying fields. Some were as agitated as women, almost hysterical. But there had been no consensus on the goal of the expedition. All sorts of wild rumours were bandied about: a band of outlaws seen to the north, along the upper reaches of the Acheron river; a secluded camp in the mountains to the south-east above the hamlet of Erimon; a veritable army of them preying on the road to Croton. Several had continued to express the fear that the killing of Junius, if not brought about by the Hero of Temesa, had been the work of a daemon, not a man.

A decision had been deferred. Another meeting would be convened in two days. The citizens were to ready their arms. Paullus had kept his own counsel. The delay would bring no clarity. There was no point in the militia aimlessly wandering the upland trails. Any bandits would note their coming and melt away into the boundless forest. Definite information was needed. Something certain must be obtained, its veracity assured by fear of death and torture.

Dekis had not been in the least bit keen. The old Bruttian was not among those convinced of a supernatural agency. But he was not certain. Best not to meddle in such things, he had said. If it was bandits, the two of them were not enough. The plan was foolhardy. Paullus himself had said Junius had been shot down with an arrow. Dekis was buggered if he wanted the same fate, and what about the mutilation? If you wanted your cock cut off and shoved down your throat, you were welcome. Dekis wanted his to remain just where it was. At the end of their clandestine discussion, Paullus had had to offer him an extraordinarily large sum of money. It was well spent. Dekis was the finest huntsman in the whole region. No one had better knowledge of the Sila. And, for all his misgivings, Dekis was reliable. If they returned, he would not be the man to gossip about Paullus' surprising wealth.

Paullus had told no one, and sworn Dekis to secrecy. Brigands did not just lurk in the hills, waiting for whatever chance brought along. Normally they had informants in the villages and towns, accomplices who would let them know about rich prizes or warn them of danger. Paullus and Dekis had set out after dark, making sure no one had seen them go.

A long march through the night. They took it in turns to ride the mule, the other leading. Paullus had said that he would walk all the way. Dekis had seemed offended by the offer. He was old, not decrepit or an invalid. The complaints reminded Paullus of his mother. In the early hours they had passed the turning to Croton. Not long after, the huntsman had called a halt.

At the first hint of the false dawn, Dekis had outlined the lie of the land. As the darkness slowly receded, he had pointed out the route through the forest that Paullus should take. Looking back at the road, Paullus saw the Bruttian settling down to cook himself breakfast. The idea was that any watchers should know Dekis was coming, and the column of smoke would act as a point of reference to help guide Paullus across the slopes.

The sky was a delicate pink, the few thin bands of cloud under-lit with gold. The sun would soon crest the eastern slopes. Paullus sheltered against the trunk of a thick pine. Through the trees he could trace the line of the road. He thought he was in the right place, but too high on the shoulder of the hill.

There was no hurry. Dekis would not move out until well after sunrise. If the watchers were there, they would not be going any-where. With slow deliberation, Paullus studied the terrain below for movement. A flight of sparrows, the bright flash of a woodpecker; once he half glimpsed a doe. Nothing out of place, nothing human. It was possible that he had paid Dekis to do no more than take a long, nocturnal walk.

The sun appeared over the distant peaks. Its light washed down the slope, casting long shadows through the trees.

Stooping, placing his boots with care, Paullus set off down the incline. He moved silently, bending under branches, keeping to the shadows. From cover to cover, he crept lower.

He was crossing a small glade when the peace was shattered by the harsh cry of a jay. In the open, Paullus froze. *Styx and Hades*, he cursed silently. Then he saw the looping flight of the bird some distance below. He grinned wolfishly. The jay was not shrieking outrage at *his* presence.

Although exposed, he remained still for a time. He was in deep shade, and it was motion that gave you away. When the bird was far off across the valley, he stole forward.

It took him a few moments to find a good vantage point. The roots of a fallen pine fanned out in a natural screen, and a man could just about fold himself into the hole they had left in the earth. He did not have an uninterrupted view along the road, but he was no more than a hundred paces away. The brigands were somewhere between him and the road. He could not see them, but somehow he was sure they were there. Paullus placed the bow he had brought to hand. One by one, he pushed the arrows into the earth. He checked his sword, patted the theta-shaped charm on his belt and settled to wait.

The sun tracked slowly free of the mountains. The sounds of the forest changed. The birdsong was still there, but muted and less exultant. The onshore breeze of morning rustled through the trees. Yet there was a deep quiet in the depths of the Sila.

Many townsmen feared and avoided the wildwoods. Their fear was not unfounded. The forests were the last resort of outcasts, men whose crimes had caused them to be driven out, to be denied fire and water. Consorting with those who worked the woods – shepherds and charcoal burners and loggers – was little safer. They were violent, rough men, and the law was far away and easily forgotten.

Animals added to the dangers. Wolves and bears roamed in the solitude. And the gods themselves still walked through the glades: goat-footed Pan, bestial satyrs and shaggy old Silvanus. Anything could befall the innocent. Inadvertently stumbling across the goddess Artemis bathing, Acteon had been transformed into a stag and torn to pieces by his own hounds. It was in the woods that the women had dismembered Orpheus. The trees themselves posed a threat. To eat or sleep under a yew brought death. Ivy held a particular attraction for cold-blooded, venomous snakes. And everyone knew that dryads inhabited trees. To break even a branch was to invite supernatural retribution.

The forest had to be treated with respect, but it did not frighten Paullus. The woods had been the first home of mankind, providing food and shelter. Roman moralists liked to ruminate on the pristine virtue of their woodland ancestors – hairy and clad in bark, uncorrupted by the evil ways of towns. Even today, when times were hard, peasants around Temesa ground acorns for flour. And the sylvan gods were gentle. Old Silvanus was amiable, Pan only angered if he was disturbed during the siesta, and the satyrs were only troublesome when drunk. As for the yew tree, its poison was easily made safe by driving a copper nail into its trunk. Even easier was to avoid making your bed or taking a meal in its shade.

It was the forest that had brought Paullus home. He had few, if any, strong feelings about the family farm. With the plunder from Corinth he could have stayed in Rome, purchased property – a tenement block, perhaps a shop or two, maybe an inn – lived comfortably off the rents. But the Sila offered much more. Every fifth year the censors in Rome auctioned the rights to fell timber and tap pitch in great swathes of the mountains. There was always a ready market for both, in Rome and further afield. Fortunes were there to be made. The next auction would be in three years. The only question was if Paullus could survive that long in the stifling boredom of his home town.

Waiting, Paullus' thoughts turned to the extraction of pitch. An incision was made into the pine on the side facing the sun, at least twenty inches from the ground. Not a narrow cut; the bark should be stripped for about twenty-four inches. The distillation from the whole tree flowed from the wound. When it stopped, a second opening was made, then a third. Finally the whole tree was felled, then burnt to draw out the last of the pitch.

As his mind ran on to furnaces and copper vats, Paullus wondered at his capacity for violence. At any moment it would be necessary to bring pain and death to this quiet countryside. He had set the thing in motion. There was no stopping it now. If it went wrong, Dekis could be killed; he might well die himself. Yet he felt no apprehension. Instead there was a clarity to his thinking, and his senses were heightened. If anything, there was a pleasurable anticipation. He had been changed by the army. No, not the army, it was Corinth that had altered him forever. Now he craved the release of the fight. For all too brief a time he would be freed from his daemons, lost in the immediacy of life and death close to the steel.

His thoughts returned to the burning of pine trees. The first liquid that flows from the furnace is clear, like water. It is so strong that it can embalm a corpse. The pitch that follows is thicker; mixed with vinegar it coagulates like blood.

A cry, like the hoot of an owl, brought him back to his surroundings. It came from the timber along the road to the south. But it was not an owl. It was a man trying to sound like an owl. Again, Paullus smiled to himself. It was broad daylight. Brigands might have a low cunning, and great ingenuity in cruelty, but they lacked imagination. If they had possessed the latter quality, they would have chosen a profession that did not inevitably lead to being nailed on a cross or thrown to the beasts.

Another hoot answered from just below where Paullus was hidden.

So one of the bandits was stationed as a lookout a little way off down the road, and the other was lurking in the place where Paullus had been ambushed on his way home from the army. It was a good spot. The trees came right down on both sides of the track and there was plenty of cover. All the traffic coming down from Rome, or up from both Temesa and Croton, had to pass through the narrows. Paullus had anticipated the brigands would use it again.

Not taking his eyes off the incline below, Paullus stretched the stiffness out of his joints.

Through the foliage, the old man and the mule came into view. Dekis must be passing where the lookout was concealed. You had to admire the huntsman's nerve. He strolled as unconcerned as if he was in the marketplace at Temesa.

Keeping close to the roots of the pine, Paullus got to his feet. Intent on the trees below, without looking he picked up his bow, and selected and nocked an arrow.

There! A shape emerging from a patch of brambles. Paullus half drew the bow. He only needed one of them alive. It might as well be the lookout. But he would have to wait for him to show himself down on the road.

Another movement. Hercules' arse! A second brigand emerged below Paullus. With the lookout, there were three in the ambush. Paullus calmed himself. A good soldier adjusts his actions to what Fate brings – so Mummius had said after the battle at the isthmus. Paullus had done so then, and he would do so now.

The two bandits went down to the road. They carried drawn swords, but neither had a bow.

Hercules' hairy black arse! Dekis had halted where a thick stand of trees blocked Paullus' aim.

Adjust to what Fate brings. Paullus set off towards the road. He went quietly, not hurrying. When the brigands had Dekis trapped, they were unlikely to kill him straight away. Once they found the golden drinking set, they would want to torture him. A man who owned such a treasure would have more secreted, on his person or elsewhere. They might even think to hold him for ransom.

Taking care with his footfall, folding his body into the gaps between branches, he went down the hillside.

One of the brigands had a sword at Dekis' throat. The lookout had joined the other one, and both had sheathed their weapons. They were engrossed in riffling through the mule's pack. They had found the drinking set. One of them was admiring the engraved wine cooler. Paullus was pleased. Should this turn out badly, perhaps the blood-polluted vessel would infect the brigands.

Standing in the shadows, Paullus drew the string back to his ear and took aim. He was a good shot. It was no more than twenty paces. The target was unsuspecting. As easy as taking a bird limed to a branch. He exhaled, stilled his breathing, and loosed. At the twang of the bow, the brigands started, began to turn. The one covering Dekis was not fast enough. The arrowhead took him in the flank. He doubled up, clutching at the wound and squealing like a pig. For a moment the others were shocked into immobility. They stared, almost uncomprehending, at the blood welling out around their companion's fingers.

Hades! Paullus had not thought to retrieve the other arrows. He dropped the bow, drew his blade and started to run.

It was all over before Paullus had taken a few paces.

The old huntsman had fished out the long knife concealed in his boot. With a speed that belied his age, he had the blade at the neck of the younger bandit. The older had dragged his sword from its scabbard, but was in no mood to fight. He looked wildly round, unsure where to run.

'Drop the weapon!' Paullus was right in front of him. A large part of Paullus wanted him to fight, wanted the cathartic exhilaration.

The brigand let the sword fall.

Paullus damped down his disappointment and kicked the blade away.

'Don't want to watch more than one on the way back,' Dekis said. 'This young'un will talk easiest on the rack.'

Paullus looked at the mop of fair hair and the pale, terrified face. 'You decided not to take my advice, then?'

'No, I was going to,' the youth gabbled. 'It was not easy to get away. I was waiting for an opportunity.'

Paullus pushed the older bandit to his knees. Then he scabbarded his sword and took a rope from the mule's pack. With deft motions, he secured the captive's wrists and tied the rope to the rigging.

'By all the gods, I was going to leave.' The youth continued to plead.

Paullus walked over to the brigand he had shot. The man was quiet now, his life ebbing away.

'You remember what I said the last time we met?' Paullus went back to the youth.

'Please, no, it is not my fault.'

Paullus took him by the arm, gently turned him away.

'I still have the coins. Let me go, and I will not go back to them.'

'A man is nothing if he does not keep his word,' Paullus said.

'I will go north, right now. Not stop until I reach Rome. Start a new life.'

He was still talking, when, in one sweep, Paullus unsheathed his blade and struck. The backhand cut caught the youth in the throat. His head snapped back, and the blood gushed out to splatter on the road.

CHAPTER 13

Patria

609 Ab Urbe Condita (145 BC)

THE PRISONER WAS STRUNG UP naked in the marketplace of Temesa. His hands had been bound, the rope thrown over the beams of the portico, and he had been hauled upright. The whole town had come to watch. Babilius the shoemaker had arranged the benches from his stall at the front, so that a few of the leading men could view the spectacle in some degree of comfort. Obsequiously, he had produced cushions. Somewhat against his will, Paullus had been prevailed upon to take a seat. It was thought only fitting as he was the one who had brought in the brigand. The role of the Bruttian Dekis was quietly forgotten. For the last hour and a half Paullus had sat with the two chief magistrates, Ursus the priest, Fidubius and Vibius.

The audience was accustomed to blood. In every court case the evidence of a slave, whether he or she was the defendant or just a witness, was only admissible after torture, and the process was public. Among the slave owners in the crowd, there would not be many who had not laid open a servant's back with the lash. Blood, human and animal, was ingrained in the patina of life. The necessary worship of the gods demanded cutting the throat of the appropriate beast, slitting its stomach and dragging out its steaming and slimy entrails.

The familiarity with blood was just as well. Temesa was a small town. The torturer, one of the civic undertakers, was no specialist. Lacking the refinements of Rome – having no rack, horse, wheel, pincers, claws or hot irons – he relied on a whip and brute force. The sharp iron knotted into the rawhide had torn the flesh of the brigand and sprayed blood all over the colonnade. It had splattered the flagstones by the feet of the dignitaries in the front row.

The iron smell in his nostrils, Paullus wondered if he was the only one who felt slightly sick.

'Tell us about the mutilation.' Fidubius had asked many questions, this one repeatedly.

The man managed to raise his head a little, but he did not answer. Paullus thought that now he might be incapable of speech.

The captive had been vocal enough at the start. It was an outrage. Only a slave should be tortured. He was a freeman, a Roman citizen, born in Sicily. The latter might be true, but the rest was given no credence. Anyway, a life of brigandage put a man beyond the clemency of the law. At the first bite of the whip, he had protested that he was an innocent traveller. That man there – the one there with the mark of death on his belt – had set upon him in the Sila, had murdered his two companions with the help of a Bruttian woodsman. It was not the first time he had done it: previously he had spared the youth, but not in this encounter. One or two in the crowd stole a glance at the charm Paullus wore. Theta was the first letter of the Greek word for death. Yet no one was ever going to take the word of a stranger against that of a son of Temesa, especially a citizen who had won the civic crown.

The undertaker had not spared himself. It was a hot morning, and soon his torso was running with sweat. After a time Roscius the innkeeper and another bystander had helped him haul on the rope and tie it off, so that the bandit was clear of the ground, all his weight coming down through his arms and shoulders. To increase the agony, a heavy weight was bound to one of the bandit's feet. With a steady rhythm, the whip struck.

The man had begun to talk, but the information gained was generally thought unsatisfactory. Yes, he had robbed wayfarers on the road to Consentia. What else could he do? There was no work. All the estates in Sicily employed slave labour. No, he knew nothing about the killing of a farmer called Junius. He had never heard of brigands mutilating their victims. Yes, there was a band of outlaws in the hills above Erimon, but he had thrown in his lot with those living in the caves beyond Blood Rock. There were about twenty of them, but men came and went. Why would there be brigands on the upper Acheron river? There was nothing there to take.

Fidubius nodded. The torturer threw a bucket of water to bring round the brigand.

'Tell us about the mutilation of Junius,' Fidubius said.

In extremis, with all hope gone, the bandit glowered defiance. 'None of you are any better than me. You rich men drive the poor off their farms, enclose the public land. You embezzle public funds, cheat state contracts. You threaten and you beat and you steal. You rob honest men of their livelihoods and ancestral homes, their freedom.'

Perhaps reviving him had been an error.

'You want a scapegoat for this Junius you say was murdered. Look closer to home. Behind your respectability you are as heartless as wolves. You would mutilate your mothers if you thought there was a profit in it.'

Fidubius signalled to the torturer and the lash swung. A flurry of blows silenced the insolence. Unconscious, the body of the brigand turned under the repeated impacts. The white of bone showed through the ruin of his back.

'Enough,' Ursus said.

The brigand's head lolled forward. Only a fluttering in his chest indicated that he was still alive.

'We have heard enough,' Fidubius said. 'Bandits did not kill Junius. It was the Hero – the daemon has returned.'

'Men will say anything under the pain of the lash,' Ursus said.

'Torture is the touchstone of truth,' Vibius said. 'It is enshrined in law, a thing universally acknowledged. Why should he lie?'

There was a murmur of general agreement at the words of Lollius' father.

'To spare himself further pain.' Ursus was undeterred that most of those present were gripped by the supernatural explanation. 'To admit he had any knowledge of the mutilation would bring further refinements of suffering. At the end he sought to provoke us to earn a quick death.'

Paullus intervened. 'This bandit may know nothing, but Junius was not killed by a daemon, but by a man. Does a daemon use a bow and arrow?'

Fidubius looked at him with detestation. Even the suave face of Lollius' father showed a certain annoyance. Why, Paullus thought, are they so set on summoning up the Hero? Could they not see that it would terrify the populace, open the door to any dark imaginings, that it would lead to nothing but panic?

'Whoever murdered Junius, we have discovered enough to remind us of our duty.' Ursus' furrowed and desiccated face surveyed the crowd, as if the priest himself were some avatar of stern, antique morality. 'The colonists of Temesa are exempt from service in the legions on condition that we suppress brigandage. We have been remiss in our duty. The assembly has already decided to mount an armed expedition. Now we know where it must march: Erimon and Blood Rock. All able-bodied citizens should report here at dawn tomorrow, with their arms and three days' rations. The council will retire to plan the expedition.'

The crowd lingered, as if hoping the entertainment had not ended.

'Are we agreed that nothing more is to be learnt from the miscreant?' Ursus asked.

Everyone accepted that was the case.

'Then have him taken to the main gate and nailed to a cross.'

As the only citizen with experience in the army, Paullus was requested to aid the deliberations of the council. The basilica was shaded and cool. The benches were well padded and comfortable. Servants waited in attendance. Food and drink was placed to hand.

Picking up a cup, Paullus wondered if it had crossed anyone else's mind that out under the hot sun, only a few dozen paces away, a man was being nailed to a cross, the sharp steel cruelly hammered through flesh and tendons. Killing a man was often necessary, and frequently commendable. In war it was unavoidable. Mutilating a corpse to put a daemon off your scent had its reasons, as did the use of torture to obtain the truth. Yet he found it harder to accept the infliction of slow agony merely as a potential warning to others, or perhaps for nothing better than revenge. After all a turn of fate, or a realignment of the stars, and those now at their ease in this elegant room might find themselves hoisted aloft and exposed in public torment. Paullus had lived through the sack of Corinth. He drained the cup in one draught.

Temesa was a small colony. Its council consisted of just thirty men, not all of whom were present. The councillors were the serving magistrates and those who had previously held office. As such, all were of a certain age. Magistrates received no stipend; indeed they were expected to contribute to civic expenses from their own funds. The council was an affluent gerontocracy.

As the leading magistrates, the *duoviri* nominally oversaw the meeting, but official posts counted for less than wealth and force of personality. The same men who had taken the initiative in the forum continued to hold the floor.

'We are not crafty little Greeks or sly Carthaginians,' Ursus said. 'No need for cunning strategies. In the morning, we select the hundred best-armed men, all Romans of good courage. March openly to Erimon, flush out the brigands in the hills, crucify the lot of them along the road. Then we go to Blood Rock and do the same.'

In the gloom silver heads nodded approval.

'Exemplary cruelty serves as the finest deterrent.' As the old priest's head turned to survey his fellows, his scrawny neck reminded Paullus of that of a tortoise Lollius had owned as a child.

'Indeed the punishment of the bandits must fit the savagery of their crimes,' Vibius said. 'Yet a measure of caution may be apposite.'

If not for his old-fashioned manners, Ursus would have snorted with derision. 'Outlaws will not resist Roman steel.'

'Quite so.' Vibius was as emollient as ever. 'And that may be why we should exercise a certain foresight. Once we have dealt with the brigands at Erimon, the news will reach those at Blood Rock. They will disperse, slip from our grasp and escape justice.'

For all his bland exterior, Lollius' father was no fool.

'Let us take advice from one who has been on campaign.'

Paullus was pouring himself another drink. He took his time, collecting his thoughts, then he outlined a plan.

It was agreed that only treachery could unhinge its execution.

The brigands must have seen him coming a mile or more off. Paullus was wearing a bright scarlet cloak, and his mail coat and the fittings on his belt were burnished so that they shone like mirrors in the afternoon sun. Alone, and quite openly, he rode the horse at a steady walk down the road to Croton. The road twisted and dipped. At times the trees of the Sila crowded the track, obscuring the view ahead of Blood Rock and the pass beyond. The singing of the birds, the clop of hooves and the creak of harness, all somehow were small and lost in the vastness of the forest.

Emerging from the final shade, he reached Blood Rock. It was a triangular outcrop of granite. Grey-white, like the rest of the mountain, it must have earned its name from the deeds of men. Paullus did not pause, or turn his head, as he went by. He made no attempt to trace the goat path that Dekis had said snaked up the slope and below the crest to come down above the pass. No one knew the Sila better than the Bruttian huntsman. If he said there was a track, and that it was passable, his knowledge could be trusted.

The road ran straight for about four hundred paces up to the pass. There the slope to the right continued much the same – not too steep, and covered in scrub oaks and briers. But to the left the mountain fell away, as if cut with an axe. The sheer face of the cliff dropped to jagged boulders in a stream far below.

Paullus kept the horse to a slow walk. It chafed against the bit. The big black hunter he had borrowed from Lollius' father was still full of running. It showed no ill effects from the long ride last night, after they had left the main party and doubled back up the road from Erimon. All morning they had holed up in the deserted Bruttian village that Dekis knew was hidden in the hills after the turning to Croton.

Reining in his mount, Paullus halted no more than a hundred paces from the pass. Well within effective bowshot. At this range an arrow could punch clean through the links of his mail. But that could not be helped. Paullus needed to be seen. Shading his eyes, he scanned the incline above the pass and the ridge beyond that.

He moved ostentatiously, like an actor on the stage. If they were there, he wanted them to know that he was expecting them to appear. Nothing moved through the scrub except the occasional darting sparrow or other small bird. Paullus found himself hoping there was no one there. He dismissed the cowardly thought. This was his plan, and he had volunteered himself as bait. When the rest had protested at the danger, he had not revealed his true motives. Paullus had learnt that to put himself at risk kept away the Kindly Ones. Better an arrow in the guts than suffer the attentions of the dark sisters.

Paullus took the hunting horn from his saddle, raised it to his lips and sounded one loud, clear note. The sound echoed away along the slope. If they had not spotted him before, they knew he was here now.

The horse sidled, head down, snuffling for any hint of vegetation. Paullus waited. What he was about could not be hurried. Everything depended on timing.

Flies pestered horse and rider. The hunter swished its tail and Paullus leant forward to brush them from its eyes. There was no breeze, and the sweat was running down between his shoulder blades under the heavy mail coat.

It was still too soon. Paullus swung a leg over the horse's neck and dismounted. He led it to the side of the path, where there was some grass, and hobbled its legs. Then he walked back to the middle of the road.

Paullus stood stock still for a while. Suddenly, he swept back his cloak, drew his sword and began to dance. Two steps back, the blade up to block, three forward, then a lunge. To the left, to the right, his boots raised the dust as they stamped out the time. Cloak billowing around him, he leapt and turned. The blade flashed in the sun as he brandished it high then low in fast, complicated measures. To the Greeks it was the pyrrhic dance, to the Romans the *armatura*, the dance in armour. Any watchers would think him insane, but that was unimportant. The only thing that mattered was that he had all their attention.

He danced until his breath was burning in his chest, beads of sweat stinging his eyes. A final flourish and he stopped. Sheathing his sword, again he stood in the road. His flanks heaved as he fought to catch his breath. Now, surely, it was time.

Walking back, he took a drink before he unhobbled the horse. Gripping the horns of the saddle, he gathered himself and leapt onto its back. It was never easy to mount in armour. The sudden weight coming down on its back, the hunter snorted and bucked. Settling into his seat, Paullus let it circle, caracoling under him, controlling it with just the pressure of his thighs. He was a good horseman. Lollius and he had learnt when they were children in Vibius' stables.

Taking up the reins, Paullus walked his mount into the pass.

Of course they might shoot him down out of hand. That would unravel his cunning plan. And death would bring him no release. Even if they put a coin in his mouth and he crossed the Styx, the Furies would not cease their torment in Hades.

Paullus heard them before he saw them. A scatter of dislodged stones as they came down the scree. There were men behind, as well as in front. Turning the horse to face the slope, he stopped. There was nowhere to go.

They did not run out from the scrub. They were in no hurry. He was surrounded. Eight men to his left, a similar number to his right. They were dressed in ragged finery, the remnants of past plunder. Several had swords. Those that did not carried javelins. Paullus noted that none were archers. Perhaps they remained concealed on the hillside.

Weapons at the ready, the brigands edged closer. Paullus made the horse circle. Its powerful quarters made them step back. When they were stationary, a few paces off, he stopped the hunter. Again he faced uphill, so he could watch both sides of the track.

'Nice horse.' A brigand wearing an elaborate moulded cuirass stepped out from those clustered on the left. There was no doubt he was in command.

'That is far enough.' Paullus raised his palm, as if ordering a hound to stay.

The brigand chief shook his head in mock wonderment. 'You are not really in a position to give orders.'

Paullus did not reply.

'Good quality mail too.' The bandit looked like an astute trader valuing merchandise. 'You must be from a wealthy family.'

'No.'

'So, no one to ransom you.' The brigand leader sounded almost regretful.

'No.'

'Then where did you get them?'

Paullus smiled. 'Their previous owners had no further use for them.'

The outlaw chief laughed, an unexpectedly pleasant sound. 'So your extraordinary display was to get our attention. You have come here hoping to join us.'

'Yes.' Paullus swept back his cloak, so his sword belt could be seen.

It had the desired effect. While the others started and readied their weapons, recognition dawned on the leader's face. 'I know who you are – the theta on your belt.'

Paullus said nothing.

'You are the one who spared the boy.'

'Where is he?'

'Away.'

'A pity, I thought he would serve as an introduction.' It was good that they had not already learnt that the youth was dead.

'He said you were mad. You gave him money, told him to find a new way of life.'

Paullus shrugged. 'That was my plan too. It did not work out.'

'It seldom does for a veteran.' The brigand considered his next words. 'I am not the slave-king of Nemi, always looking over my shoulder, sword in hand, waiting for the next challenger. A band can only have one leader. The brotherhood elected me. Until I die, or they cast votes for my replacement, my word is law.'

'I did not come to supplant you,' Paullus said. 'I came here for sanctuary.'

Paullus thought he half heard something from higher up the mountain. Surreptitiously, he nudged the horse to make it play up. Then, as it stamped and shouted, he made a loud play of soothing it.

The leader waited until he could make himself heard over the sounds of the agitated animal. 'What is your crime?'

'Fratricide.'

'Not much of an inducement to trust you – a man who has killed his brother.'

'Bad things happen. We are at the whim of fate.'

'Your crime might bring us bad luck. Some might fear the pollution of blood-guilt.'

'Then they are in the wrong profession.' Now it was quiet, Paullus was alarmed that he could hear nothing from up the higher slopes.

'Tell me why we should not kill you, and take the fine horse and armour you have stolen?'

Time was running out. Paullus had to keep talking. 'I am a trained soldier. When the boy returns, he can vouch for my skill at arms.'

'He already has.' Again the chief laughed affably. 'Let one of the men take your horse. We will discuss it over a drink. You can take the oath in our camp.'

'No, I will take the oath here.' This was near the end, Paullus knew. It had been a good plan – distract the brigands while Dekis guided Lollius and the others along the trail from Blood Rock to the camp and down to the pass – but it had failed.

'It was not a request. Get off that horse.'

'I don't think so.'

There was a crashing in the undergrowth. Someone was coming down the incline at breakneck speed. The heads of all the brigands jerked round.

'Keep your eye on him!' All affability had gone from the leader's voice.

Paullus forced himself to sit very still. But the hunter could sense his tension. Muscles quivered in its shoulders. Like its rider, it was poised for flight.

The man racing down the hillside lost his footing. He pitched forward and rolled in a cloud of dust.

Any moment now, Paullus thought. Just let him distract them for a moment.

Grazed and bloodied, the man tumbled out onto the road. 'The camp,' he said.

'What about the camp?' The leader snapped.

'They have overrun the camp.' The chief looked at the newcomer. The gaze of the others followed his.

Paullus yanked the bridle. The horse reared up and turned on its rear legs.

'Get him!'

Paullus brought his boots into his mount's sides. It leapt forward. The brigands blocking the way he had come did not want to be run down. They scattered, hurling themselves out of the path.

Paullus felt his spirits soar, and then the shaft punched deep into the shoulder of the hunter. It stumbled, then recovered. The fletchings were bright against the glossy dark hide. The horse lost its rhythm, began to stagger. Blood was rising up around the feathers. The hunter was going to fall. Paullus levered himself out of the grip of the saddle. The horse was toppling towards the slope. Paullus jumped clear the other side.

The surface of the road rushed up, hard and unforgiving. Paullus landed in a jangle of armour. The breath was knocked out of his chest. Pain lanced up his right arm. Thrown out to break the landing, perhaps it was broken. He clattered to a stop, horribly near the precipice.

The brigands did have archers in the scrub, he thought inconsequentially.

Paullus' head was ringing. Shouts and the sounds of fighting seemed to assail him from every direction. He went to push himself up. His right arm gave way.

Amid the chaos, a pair of boots was walking calmly towards him. Their owner wore a cuirass. 'I am going to take you with me,' the brigand chief said in a tone that was almost conversational.

Paullus rolled to his left, scrambled to his feet. He went to draw his blade, but his right arm would not respond. He fumbled the sword out with his left, got it into an inadequate guard.

The chieftain thrust, knocking Paullus' sword straight out of his grasp. Paullus stepped back. He felt the edge crumble under his heels.

'Surrender!'

Lollius and Dekis were closing in from either side. The bandit leader half turned. Paullus lurched away along the edge. Small stones slid out from under his feet, rattling down into the chasm. A few strides and he collapsed behind Lollius.

'Throw down the sword!' Lollius said.

'So you can take me back, kill me at your leisure, make a spectacle of it?' The brigand grinned ruefully. 'I do not say that the stars lie, but the astrologer was wrong. I am not destined to die on the cross.'

Without another word, he stepped off the path.

CHAPTER 14

Patria

609 Ab Urbe Condita (145 BC)

THE FARM WAS QUIET IN THE early morning. Hirtius had sent his wife and daughter into town the day before. They would stay with his sister for the festival of Minerva tomorrow, and return the following day.

Hirtius walked outside. The farmstead on the western slope was still shaded, the sheds indistinct dark shapes, the olive trees silver and ghostly in the gloom. Far below, the mountains threw long blue shadows out over the sea. Further out the water shimmered in the sun. Tiny in the distance, the last fishing boats were putting in to Clampetia. Sunrise always raised the onshore breeze. It moved up the inclines and brought the salt smell of the sea to the smallholding in the hills.

At least it was safe again to work the outlying farms and fields. The brigands taken at Blood Rock and above Erimon had been crucified along the inland road out of Temesa. Well spaced, it was said, they stretched as far as the bridge over the Sabutus. There had been more than twenty of them. It had been only three days, and one or two might still be just about alive on their cross. Hirtius had never really believed the rumours about the daemon. Why should the Hero return after all these centuries? Polites had been soundly beaten, had been driven to take refuge under the sea for eternity. But the murder of Junius, the horrible desecration of his corpse, had rattled Hirtius. Although he had not admitted it to his family, nor to anyone else – not his few and distant neighbours, nor those men he had met on his infrequent visits to town – Hirtius had been scared. The life of a hill farmer was lonely and tough enough without having to look over your shoulder all the time. The flushing out of the nests of bandits had brought a modicum of peace. Yet it nagged at Hirtius that apparently, even under the lash, none of the outlaws had confessed to the killing of Junius.

The shadows retreated from the sea, fled towards him up the slopes, and then the smallholding was bathed in a gentle yellow light as the sun inched over the crest. Hirtius regarded the neat trenches he had dug around the olive trees. They still needed manuring. It was an inconvenient time for his wife and daughter to be away. September was a busy month. The apples and pears were not quite ready to be picked, but it was time to sow the turnips and lupines.

Yet there were not many festivals in September: apart from that of Minerva, there were only those of Ceres and Venus towards the end of the month. If his daughter were ever to marry, she had to be seen. The festivals of September were for women; the men were labouring in the fields. But a man looking for a wife would take the time to attend the celebrations. It was when things often were arranged. For those wanting reassurance, it was legal to consult astrologers at the festival of Minerva.

Hirtius worried about his daughter. She was plain, and not getting any younger. It was a pity that young Paullus had come to nothing. His mother had talked to Hirtius' wife. The girl had not been unwilling. Paullus owned twenty-five *iugera*; with the ten of Hirtius, it would have made a decent holding for their offspring. And there were stories of vast wealth, stores of plunder from the east, buried on his land. Yet something was not right about the boy. Before he went away, he had been wild: always drinking or hunting, or up to something with Lollius and Alcimus. After his return from the wars, he had become quieter but more solitary. There was something haunted about him. The new maid he had bought his mother had told Hirtius' wife that he slept badly, sometimes woke with an inarticulate cry.

The wind stirred the tops of the trees in the woods to the south. In previous years another autumn task would have been cutting leaves. Poplar, elm and oak leaves made good winter fodder, if stored before they were too dry. But that was when it was common land. Last spring Ursus had produced a piece of papyrus claiming it gave him sole use of the woods. The priest was no better or worse than other rich men. They had the money to ensure that the law always worked in their favour. After the enclosure, when Hirtius could no longer let his pigs and sheep forage there, the animals had had to be sold. Now Hirtius had to take in work.

Reluctantly, Hirtius went to light the fire pit. The oak barrels were ranged nearby. Once the fire had caught, he fetched some bundles of straw from the shed. Placing some handfuls in each cask, he took a brand from the fire and lit them one after another. The straw flared and burnt out quickly. He scraped out the embers. It was important that the insides of the barrels were warm and dry.

Pitching casks was a hard and dirty job. The vintner in Temesa had been only too glad to pay Hirtius. Although, like any tradesman, he had haggled the price down. At least these barrels were small enough for one man to manoeuvre, if with difficulty.

Grunting with effort, Hirtius hung the big copper cauldron on the chains over the fire pit. He put in the blocks of pitch to melt. Almost at once the yard was enveloped in thick, acrid smoke. Some said it smelt of incense. Hirtius found the resinous fumes cloying and repugnant.

The pitch needed stirring almost continuously as it came to the boil. When it was liquid and bubbling, came the hazardous business of the ladling. Only one cask could be pitched at a time. It had to be done with the utmost care. Any splash of molten pitch welded itself to the skin, burnt through flesh down to the bone. Once the pitch was in, the lid was hammered down and the barrel turned: rolled from side to side, stood on its top and base to coat all the interior. Finally, a bung was knocked out, releasing a jet of steam, and a tap opened at the bottom, to drain the excess pitch. It was a time-consuming, exhausting and filthy process.

Soon the pitch was viscous. The first big fat bubbles rose to the surface and burst, flicking gobbets of scalding pitch into the air. Hirtius stirred, standing well back, using a long metal pole. The gases caught in his throat and made it hard to breath. The stench was nearly overpowering.

The blow to his back came without any warning. A sharp, stabbing punch that made him stagger forward. Only a desperate thrust of the pole stopped him falling forward into the cauldron and the fire. The liquid pitch sloshed back and forth, threatening to spill over the sides as the cauldron rocked on the chains. Hirtius tottered back a pace or two. Turning his head, he saw the goose feathers, the cane shaft: a hunting arrow. Then the shock and pain welled up. His knees gave way, and he fell to the ground.

Lying on his side, he saw the two figures approach through the swirling smoke. Both wore wolfskins, the masks over their heads. Their naked torsos were dyed the colour of the earth. Was he seeing double? No, the older was broader, the younger carried a bow and was much slighter built.

'Pity,' the younger said, 'I had hoped to have more fun with this one.'

'You are getting a taste for this,' the older said. 'I had a hound like you once. He had to be put down.'

The voices were vaguely familiar.

'Give me a hand,' the younger said. 'Another example is needed.'

As they lifted him, Hirtius felt the barbs of the arrowhead move in his lungs, the ends of his broken ribs grate together. He tried to scream, but the only sound was a low, harsh panting.

They moved forward. Hirtius' head and shoulders were over the bubbling cauldron. *No, by all the gods, no!* He wanted to shout, plead for his life, but his own blood was in his throat.

And then they pushed his face down towards the roiling black pitch.

CHAPTER 15

Militia

One Year Earlier

608 Ab Urbe Condita (146 BC)

No TIME TO WASTE, *break camp at dawn.* Always the same rumour ran through the army. But normally nothing happened. Perhaps this time it just might be different. They were in Dyrrachium, a seaport on the Greek side of the Adriatic.

'The guards at headquarters told me, they swear it is true.'

Paullus and Alcimus did not take much notice of the ex-ploughboy from the Sabine hills. They had heard it all before, and their attention was elsewhere. Tatius was telling a joke. He was good at jokes. Half the bar was listening. It was the one about the man who could not find two fifteen-year-old girls in the market, so bought a thirty-year-old woman instead.

Although it was little over a year since he had enlisted, Paullus now seldom thought about the time before the army. Under the standards every aspect of life was different. Swift justice replaced long-winded appeals to juries, and summary execution the right to retire into exile. The hours of the day were not estimated by the sun, but structured by trumpets and watchwords. With darkness, no longer the domain of sleep or revelry, came the long enforced watches of the night. Words themselves changed their meaning. A vineyard became a covered siege work, and a mouse a mantlet.

A bad camp was a stepmother. Legionaries looked up at the night sky and saw not Orion, but the old sodomite. Fellow soldiers, above all tent-mates, became a new family. They called each other *brother* or *boy*. It was a brotherhood of honourable servitude. Apart from small children, only a soldier or a slave answered to *boy*.

'An idiot goes sailing in stormy weather. All his slaves start screaming. Don't worry, he says, in my will you are all set free!'

Paullus grinned as Tatius wheeled out the old joke. It was amazing how active service could change one's attitudes. After they escaped the mob that had set upon Orestes' embassy at Corinth, on the voyage back to Italy an unspoken truce had come into force between them. Alcimus had helped broker the deal. Over the winter outside Rome – when the legion was dissolved, and then, by a legal fiction, instantly reformed as a *different* unit – they had all become friends.

In the spring the legion had marched down to Brundisium. There they had camped with the other forces assembling to constitute the army of the Consul Mummius. Altogether they waited for almost three months, kicking their heels, impatient for action. No reason was given for the delay. None of the news that reached the legionaries from across the Adriatic was good. The Achaeans had declared war on Sparta, which meant war with Rome. Critolaus had replaced Diaeus as the Achaean supreme commander. The new general was active, and had taken the offensive. The Achaeans had marched north out of the Peloponnese. The great cities of Thebes and Chalcis had joined them. Heraclea on Mount Oeta, which had sought to follow the instructions of Rome and leave the league, had been put under close siege by Critolaus, and was not expected to hold out long.

By the time they had finally embarked, the tent-mates had separated into two amicable groups. On the one hand were the five Sabine farm boys, on the other Paullus, Alcimus and Tatius. The latter had developed the closeness that could only exist among men without women, men who lived and served together, and who, in the face of authority or danger, had nothing to rely upon except each other. It was during that choppy crossing to Dyrrachium that the seasick Centurion Naevius had sourly dubbed them the Three Graces.

'A Sabine heard that a crow can live for two hundred years, so he bought one to see if it was true.'

'Fuck off, you sewer rat,' one of those being mocked said, without any trace of animosity.

The laughter stopped. Naevius had entered the bar. Instead of his customary ill temper, the centurion's face expressed a badly concealed excitement.

'How many of you can ride a horse?'

They all claimed that skill, although with very varying degrees of enthusiasm.

'Good,' Naevius said. 'Then sup up your drinks and follow me. The quartermaster will issue you with your mounts.'

'Do we get a new officer,' Tatius asked, 'now we are transferred to the cavalry?'

'Sordid plebeians like you would never be allowed to join the equestrian gentlemen in the cavalry.'

They all waited expectantly.

Naevius pointed at Paullus and Alcimus. 'This is your fault again. Orestes has asked for you.'

'Jupiter's bollocks, not another embassy,' Tatius said. 'We were lucky to survive the last one.'

'No, not another embassy.' Naevius looked at the other customers. There were civilians in the inn, as well as soldiers from other units. 'I might as well tell you. It will be all round the camp in half an hour. Caecilius Metellus, the governor of Macedonia, has marched south. His legions have crossed Thessaly, and lifted the siege of Heraclea. Somehow he got through the pass at Thermopylae and he has defeated the Achaeans at a place called Skarpheia.'

A groan of disappointment went up from the troops.

'That is right,' Naevius said. 'If we don't move fast, he will finish the war before we even get there. No glory for the Consul Mummius, and no wealth of Corinthian plunder for us.'

Only one or two of the original horses remained, and they were ruined. Twenty-five riders had left Dyrrachium: the Consul Mummius and his legate Orestes, each with one slave, the nine soldiers and the twelve lictors, the ceremonial attendants of a consul. Not all had stayed the course. Both slaves had fallen behind, as had two legionaries. Accustomed to a less vigorous life, no fewer than five of the lictors had lagged behind.

The number of stragglers was unsurprising. They had been in the saddle for almost a month. First they had ridden east, across the wild mountains of Macedon, then south through the green lowland meadows of that recently conquered kingdom and the broad pastures of Thessaly. This was horse-rearing country, and they requisitioned remounts as they went. But the relentless pace broke down men and beasts. Ruthlessly, both were left behind. At Heraclea they learnt that Metellus had captured Thebes and was advancing on Megara, the city at the north of the isthmus, the strip of land that connected the Peloponnese to mainland Greece. Without pause, they had pressed on in the footsteps of his troops.

It was dark in the grove of cedars outside Megara. Paullus sat against a tree, eating air-dried beef and sipping wine. He had fed and watered his mount, but had not rubbed it down. There was no point. The animal was finished. That was the fourth, or was it fifth? A waste of expensive horseflesh, enough to buy a reasonable farm.

The torches of the sentinels on their rounds revealed the camp of the army of Metellus about half a mile away. Like Thebes, the Achaeans had abandoned Megara. Metellus had taken both cities without a fight. Without risking another battle, the Achaeans had withdrawn to the isthmus. The war was not over. The desperate ride from Dyrrachium had succeeded. Mummius had arrived in time. Paullus supposed he should be elated, but he felt nothing except dog tired.

Mummius and Orestes were standing nearby. They talked quietly in the still of the night, but their conversation was perfectly audible. It was not that the enforced intimacy of the journey had bridged the gulf between the senators and those who served them. Paullus remembered a story about a beautiful oriental queen who stripped naked before a servant, because it never occurred to her that he was a man.

'The legions are force-marching,' Mummius said. 'They will not be long behind us.'

'If you dismiss Metellus' men, until they arrive—'

Mummius interrupted Orestes. 'There are the allies from Pergamum, and the Cretans.'

'Mercenaries and Orientals are not to be relied on. If the Achaeans attack, they will be outnumbered.'

'They can camp on the isthmus, hold the narrow pass at the White Cliffs.'

The silence of Orestes was eloquent of doubt.

'It is a risk,' Mummius said, 'but what else would you have me do? Do you want Metellus to add the name Achaicus to Macedonicus?'

There it was, Paullus thought, the true spur that had driven Rome to conquer nation after nation, to bring the better part of the known world under her dominion. It was not the craving for plunder on the part of soldiers like himself, not just the greed for vast wealth on the part of men like Mummius or Metellus. No, it was the intense rivalries among all senators, their relentless desire for military glory.

'We will go in at first light.'

Paullus must have slept. Naevius was shaking him awake. There was a pearlescent light in the sky, and the air was perfumed with the cedars.

'You have a new role,' the centurion said. 'You, and four of the others, are going to act as lictors.'

'I don't have a red cloak.' Paullus was half asleep.

Naevius handed him a folded square of material. 'One of the general's spares. Don't think it indicates your future.'

They were challenged at the *porta principalis*. On either side of the gate was a ditch and rampart, the latter set with sharpened stakes. A runner was sent ahead to rouse Metellus, and they proceeded up the street to the *praetorium*. All Roman camps were laid out in the same way. It was impossible to get lost. Usually the familiarity was a comfort in a strange land. But not this morning. Despite the early hour, legionaries came out to watch them pass. Word of their arrival had flown through the camp. Every soldier in Metellus' army knew why they were here. Nothing was said, but the mood was hostile.

It was a ragged, travel-worn little procession. Twelve men in single file carried the fasces, the axes bound in bundles of rods which symbolised the consul's right to inflict physical punishment or death. Mummius, with Orestes at his shoulder, brought up the rear. Three of the soldiers deputising as lictors lacked red cloaks. Every tunic was dirty, its owner in need of a bath and a shave.

Following a real lictor – *just follow his lead, do what he does* – Paullus wished that he had been left to look after the horses with

Naevius and Tatius. Fourteen men were about to confront a general with over twenty thousand soldiers at his command. Looking at the unwelcoming faces that lined the route, Paullus was reminded of the embassy to Corinth.

Quintus Caecilius Metellus Macedonicus was seated on a tribunal, backed by his senior officers and the standards of his army. His armour was gorgeous – polished leather chased with silver – but his face was drawn and his eyes bleary. As Paullus shuffled into place between two of the experienced lictors, he noted that several of Metellus' staff also looked tired. Perhaps the general and his companions had drunk late, never suspecting the thunderbolt that was about to fall upon their heads.

Metellus did not get to his feet instantly at the approach of Mummius. The delay was not quite long enough to be flagrantly disrespectful.

'*Ave*, Lucius Mummius.' Metellus used neither the consul's third name, nor his title.

Mummius returned the greeting, then, drawing himself up straight, plunged straight to the heart of the matter.

'The senate and people of Rome thank you, and your army, for their service. Now you may return to your allotted province of Macedonia.'

Metellus did not reply at once. He gazed over Mummius' head, as if searching for something that he could not find. The unnatural silence around the headquarters hummed like a taut bowstring.

'That would seem premature,' Metellus said. 'You have no army.'

'It will soon arrive.'

'And in the meantime?'

'The allies will remain.'

Metellus drew a long breath, composed his face into something resembling humility. 'We are prepared to serve under your auspices.'

'The offer is appreciated, but is unnecessary.' Mummius' words were civil, but failed to hide the animosity between the two. 'Macedonia must be settled, your presence is required there.'

'The Achaean war is not finished.' Metellus flushed, but retained his self-control. 'Duty to Rome must come before personal ambition.'

'Do not presume to remind me of my duty!' Mummius was quivering with rage, but he clung to his *dignitas*. 'I am consul, you a praetor. It is the duty of a *junior* magistrate to obey his senior. You will leave for Macedonia!'

Metellus swung on his heel. As he stomped off the tribunal, he flung a last word over his shoulder. 'Best pray things go better for you than they did in Spain!'

CHAPTER 16

Militia

608 Ab Urbe Condita (146 BC)

THE WHITE CLIFFS WERE NAMED without any imagination. A few miles south of Megara the mountains came down close to the sea. Where the rocks showed through the vegetation, they were a pale grey, perhaps even white here and there. The ancient Greeks might have invented philosophy and drama and history, but they had not been so creative with place names.

Three days before, the rest of Paullus' legion had staggered into Megara, footsore and depleted. In the relentless march from Dyrrachium much equipment had been worn out or discarded. On the first roll call it was discovered that no fewer than four hundred soldiers from a strength of over four thousand were absent. Nevertheless the legion had been sent ahead to help guard the isthmus.

The White Cliffs made a terrible campsite. The allies from the Kingdom of Pergamum had already claimed the only area of flat land where the cliffs pulled back from the Saronic Gulf. The tents of the legion were crowded almost on top of each other on either side of the road between the water and the rock face. There was no question of laying out a regular marching camp. There was not enough soil to dig a ditch or build a rampart. The stakes of the palisade were tied together in threes to create an impromptu barrier. But they stood on bare rock, and could be shifted easily.

And the guy ropes of the tents were secured flimsily by piles of stones. Unable to dig latrines, the men relieved themselves in the water. It was hot, and the nearly tideless sea soon stank. If they stayed here long, disease was certain to spread. The White Cliffs were a stepmother of a camp.

'What did Metellus mean about Spain?' Paullus was sitting with Alcimus and Tatius. To get away from the claustrophobic noise and stench, they had scrambled up the cliff to a ledge.

'No idea.' Alcimus yawned. Had he not been so close with his friends, probably he would have been resting in the shade of the tent with the three remaining Sabines. The latter seemed to spend most of their time off duty sleeping. When awake, they were men of very few words.

'But you have no idea about anything, my little backwoods yokel.' Tatius liked to cast himself in the role of the metropolitan expert on every subject. 'A few years ago, when Mummius was praetor, he led eleven thousand men into the far west against the Lusitanians. They got ambushed. Only five thousand got out.'

'But I thought Mummius was awarded a triumph,' Paullus said.

'His was only the latest in a string of defeats in Hispania. The Roman public needed some good news. When Mummius massacred a Lusitanian raiding party across the straits in Africa, he was given a triumph.'

'So Metellus was right,' Paullus said. 'Mummius took a huge risk sending away Metellus' men and relying on the allies to hold the isthmus until the rest of the army arrived.'

'Not at all, my friend. What on earth would you two do without me?' Tatius' delicate lips twitched into a mocking smile. 'The Achaeans lost all the best of their men at Skarpheia. Over a thousand of them were taken alive. Their general Critolaus was never seen again – they say he drowned in the marches. A detachment of another thousand were killed at Chaeronea. When Diaeus took over again, their army was in ruins.'

'So there was no immediate threat?' Paullus said.

'At least, unlike Alcimus here, you learn quickly.' Tatius was enjoying parading his superior knowledge. 'Diaeus got the survivors back to the isthmus, and withdrew the garrison of Megara to reinforce them. But he had to rebuild the army. He issued a summons for all free Achaeans of military age to rally to Corinth. And he ordered the Achaeans to free and arm twelve thousand slaves. To pay for it, he decreed exactions from everyone, women as well as men. It all took time.'

'But now?'

'Now things might be different.' Tatius shrugged. 'Sosicrates, that Achaean who got us out of Corinth, Diaeus had him tortured to death as a traitor.'

'Poor bastard,' Alcimus said.

'Might not be too gentle a war.' Tatius sounded gloomy, but then brightened. 'But Mummius will be alright. He won in the end against the Lusitanians, and it took courage to stand up to Metellus.'

'Not all that much courage,' Alcimus said.

'Your ignorance is sublime, brother.' Tatius grinned. 'The Caecilii Metelli are one of the most powerful families in the nobility of Rome. Mummius' father was just a praetor. He was the first of his ancestors to reach the senate. It took courage to make an enemy of Metellus. If Mummius does not defeat the Achaeans – defeat them utterly – his political career is over.'

'It must be wonderful to be so informed,' Paullus said sarcastically. 'To be born and bred in Rome, and know everything.'

Tatius gazed out over the sea. 'I was not born in Rome.'

The other two waited.

'My father had a farm in the Alban Hills. Nothing much, but it had been ours for generations. When I came back from fighting the Gauls, it was gone.'

'Gone?'

'My father had been run off by toughs from one of the big estates. He had been paid a fraction of its worth.'

Paullus and Alcimus said nothing.

'I swore I would buy another farm.' Tatius looked back at his companions. 'And that is why I will fight like a daemon. The wealth of Corinth will get that land, and nothing, nothing at all is going to stand in my way.'

It was the silence that woke Paullus.

Throughout the night the changes of the watch were marked by the sounding of trumpets. It was comforting certainty. Even in their sleep the legionaries were assured that all was well.

It was time for the third watch, and there had been no trumpets.

The others were still asleep. One of the Sabines was snoring. Paullus rolled out of his blanket. His shoulders and hips ached from the hard ground. Carefully, he stepped over the recumbent figures.

Outside the air was fresh after the fug of the tent. The offshore breeze brought the scent of thyme down from the hills, took the stench of the camp out to sea.

There was no moon, but a lone helmeted figure stood in the starlight.

'Something is wrong,' Naevius said.

They listened in silence. There was just the sound of the wind in their ears.

'I can't hear anything,' Paullus said.

'That is what is wrong. Wake your tent-mates. Shields and swords and helmets, there is no time for armour. No javelins, this will be close work.' The centurion turned on his heel.

Paullus dived back into the tent and scooped up his sword belt. 'Get up! The enemy are in the camp!'

Buckling the belt, he scrambled back out and grabbed a shield from where they were stacked. It was not his, but that was unimportant. Behind him, Tatius was swearing monotonously.

'Trumpeter!' The shout was loud in the night.

A man dragged himself out of a nearby tent.

'Sound the alarm.' Naevius was calm, as if this was just another exercise.

Already other legionaries were groaning into life.

The trumpeter cleared his throat, took a deep breath and put the instrument to his lips.

The brassy note rang back off the cliff face. Hacking and coughing, men hauled themselves into the open, blinking and stupid with sleep.

Naevius was striding off, roaring orders. 'Maniple, eight deep, close order, facing south! Swords and shields, nothing else. Get a fucking move on! We haven't got all night!'

There was no open ground on which to form up. Legionaries tripped over tents, kicked them out of the way, trampled their companions' possessions. They blundered through dead campfires, raising a mist of fine, powdery ashes. Wooden and leather shields thumped and clattered into each other, loose stones rattled out from under boots, and Naevius yelled orders. The uproar swamped any sounds more distant than a few paces.

The Greeks seemed to emerge out of the gloom in silence. Hundreds of them, bearing down fast, like a great wave. Paullus hefted his shield. The Greeks had no weapons in their hands.

'The Pergamenes are running,' someone shouted.

'Of course they are running,' Naevius bellowed, 'our Pergamene allies are fucking Greeks. Get ready for whatever is chasing them!'

The fugitives hurled themselves into the gaps in the nascent line. They shouldered and shoved Romans aside. One, in blind panic, ran at full tilt straight into the shield of a legionary. Both men were knocked to the ground. Out of the corner of his eye, Paullus saw the first Romans throw down their weapons and turn to flee.

'Hold your ground, you motherless fuckers!'

Not everyone obeyed.

As suddenly as they had appeared, the routers were gone. Like a retreating flood, they could be heard sweeping through the camp, spreading chaos.

'Re-form the line!' Naevius was pacing out in front.

But there was no time. The Achaeans advanced at a jog. They had blades in their hands – curved, heavy Greek swords. Their humanity was hidden by bronze helmets and silvered shields. The metal glittered in the wan light. These were no freed slaves, Paullus thought. Not all the best Achaeans died at Skarpheia.

'Get in line!'

But the legionaries did not get in line. Instead, men automatically shuffled towards the shelter of their neighbour's shield. The maniple was broken up into small huddles, too closely packed to properly wield the swords.

Three of the Achaeans went for the isolated centurion. Naevius blocked the first blow with his vine stick. The wood took the force out of the slash, but was sheared through and useless. Drawing his sword, Naevius pivoted and turned the next cut. But the third had got behind him. The steel clanged into the back of his helmet. Naevius went down like a felled tree.

Instinctively, Paullus leapt forward. The Achaean who had downed Naevius had his back turned. A downward chop to the rear of his thigh and the man fell, screaming. The one to the right thrust at Paullus' face. Training kicked in; Paullus caught the steel high on his blade, rolled his wrist, forced the sword wide. Not looking, he punched his shield out in the direction of the other. Whatever he hit, the impact jarred up his left arm, made him stagger a pace sideways.

Off balance, Paullus somehow got his sword in the way of the next attack. The man on his right was persistent, eager for blood. Paullus did not see the blow from the left. It carved a chunk out of his shield, drove him down on one knee. Ahead he saw Naevius stir. Above the centurion another Achaean was bracing himself, legs wide apart, shield slung on his back, getting ready to deliver the killing blow.

Tucked into the curve of his shield, Paullus launched himself up and into the Achaean to his left. Legs pumping, he bundled the man backwards, until he felt the resistance end as his opponent tripped. Swivelling, Paullus was just in time to deflect a downward chop from behind. The momentum of the blow carried that Achaean past. Paullus yelled something incoherent, a mixture of fear and rage, and went for the man standing over Naevius.

Sword high above his head, chest and armpits exposed, a look of horror appeared in the eyes of the Achaean. One moment he was about to despatch a defenceless foe, now this howling fury was upon him. Unable to adjust to the change of fate, the Achaean froze. With all his weight, Paullus thrust his sword through the linen armour that guarded the man's chest. He felt the tip scrape off the ribs, and then it was deep in the soft vitals.

Paullus pushed the mortally injured man away. As the sword came free, there was a horrible sucking sound and the blood gushed hot on his hand and forearm. He stepped over the now groaning form of his centurion. Naevius was trying to get to his hands and knees.

'Stay down,' Paullus ordered. He had no idea if Naevius understood.

The clamour of combat came from all sides, bounced back from the wall of the cliff. There were men coming up behind Paullus. He turned, getting into a fighting crouch. It was Alcimus and Tatius. Beyond them, the Sabines were finishing off the two Achaeans. Only one had a sword – the other was using his entrenching tool to perform the butchery.

And then they were in the calm at the eye of the storm. The Achaeans – preferring the pleasures of cutting down those who were fleeing and offering their defenceless backs – flowed on through the camp like a tide. And like a tide, they left the flotsam of their passing: slumped bodies of the dead, the sobbing wounded, the wrack of broken weapons and discarded possessions. Amid the wreckage, small knots of legionaries who had stood and fought remained like storm-battered rocks.

Paullus shivered in the chill of the night as the sweat dried. He called to the nearest groups to form up on his friends. Stunned by the suddenness of the violence, they were grateful for any leadership. One by one, the bloodied and tired bands of survivors picked their way over.

When about two dozen had gathered, Paullus ordered them to form the testudo. 'All-round defence, this might not be over.'

A legionary appeared carrying the standard of the maniple. The original bearer had been cut down, but its presence lifted their spirits.

Naevius had managed to sit up. He needed help removing his dented helmet. When it was off, his hair could be seen matted with blood.

'We should get up against the rock face, so we can't be surrounded,' Paullus said.

Naevius attempted to get to his feet, but slumped down again. He had not managed to speak yet. Paullus told two of the Sabines to get him up. Brawny arms, used to manhandling livestock, made light work of the task. Together they shuffled like old men to the cliff.

When they got to that illusory safety, some dropped their shields and sat, heads in hands. In the relief of finding themselves still alive, men started to chatter, even laugh.

'Silence in the ranks!'

Accustomed to obey, the legionaries fell silent when Paullus spoke. 'Keep your weapons to hand. Two men from each tent, go and gather your companions' armour and javelins.'

Tatius took Alcimus to see what still remained around the ruin of their tent.

Lost in the dark, from the north came the sounds of continued fighting.

Among the debris, not all the equipment could be found. Those who had armour were pressed into the front rank.

'Fuck,' Tatius said. 'More of them.'

The newcomers were light infantry. Unarmoured, and carrying bows or slings, they slunk up through the pass, sniffing around the Romans like scavenging animals around a sheepfold. They were not looking for a fight, but intent on plunder.

'This might be alright,' Tatius muttered.

No sooner had he spoken than an officer arrived. Mounted on a fine chestnut, and incongruously splendid amid the carnage, he barked out orders. With no great enthusiasm, the skirmishers came to heel.

'Close up, boys,' Paullus said. 'Make sure the shields are overlapping.'

The first volley was ineffective. Some arrows and slingshots thumped off the hedge of shields, but most missed, falling short or pinging off the rocks overhead. The light troops did not want to get too close, and the darkness made distances deceptive, made it difficult to take an accurate aim.

Far from pleased, the Achaean officer spurred through his men, like a huntsman whipping on hounds. Cautiously, they edged a little forward.

The next volley was on target. The missiles rattled on the locked shields like hail on a tiled roof. A legionary yelped in pain as one got through. He was dragged to the centre and another man took his place.

'We can chase the fuckers away,' a voice shouted. There was a throaty rumble of assent.

'No one moves!' Paullus called. 'The first man that leaves the line, I will kill him myself.'

'Who are you to give orders?'

'Do as Paullus says, or you will answer to me.' Naevius was back up. 'Go out there, and they will shoot us all down one by one.'

Another volley scythed in. Another man was hit.

'Keep those shields up,' Naevius shouted. 'Not long until dawn, and they will soon run out of ammunition.'

The second prediction was only partly accurate. Soon no arrows were raining down. But the pass was covered in stones, and the bowmen scurried about collecting them and passing them to the slingers.

Time dragged as the Romans hunkered down, patching up the wounded, enduring the long torment.

'Relief will come at sunrise,' Naevius repeatedly promised. 'Just hold on, keep your discipline, not long now.'

The centurion was unsteady on his feet. He leant on Paullus, whispered in his ear. 'You after my rank, boy?'

Paullus glanced at the centurion's set and bloodied face. He was too tired to answer.

Naevius squeezed Paullus' shoulder, smiled. 'You did well, saved my life. I will see you get the civic crown. If, of course, we live through tonight.'

Perhaps it was after two hours, perhaps three – who could tell? – when they heard the peal of trumpets. Risking a quick peek out between the battered rims of the shields, Paullus saw the stars fading and the nacreous light creeping over the eastern sky.

The incoming missiles, which had slackened anyway, ceased.

They all peered out. The skirmishers were loping off to the south. There was no sign of the bold Achaean officer. A good horse often was an invaluable asset in an encounter.

In the quickening light, the extent of the stricken field became visible. It was untenanted, except by the dead and those too gravely injured to move. A noise like thunder came down the coast from the north.

Like a herd of migrating beasts, put to flight by some predator, the Achaean heavy infantry thundered into view. Now they were in full retreat, all order gone. From behind them came the intoxicating sounds of trumpets and war cries – the trumpets and cries of the legions of Rome.

CHAPTER 17

Patria

609 Ab Urbe Condita (145 BC)

SEPTEMBER WAS A BUSY MONTH for a farmer. Paullus had been manuring the trenches around the vines in the terraced field. To get some peace, he had told Eutyches to gather leaves from the belt of oaks and beech trees down by the road. It had not been necessary to carry out the latter task yet. All the autumn work was well in hand. Paullus could have remained in the house, claiming his right arm was still hurt from the fall he had taken at Blood Rock when the horse went down. It would have been no more than an excuse, as it no longer troubled him, but he could have sent the old slave up the hill. Paullus' mother, however, had found another eligible daughter of a local farmer on whose attractions as a wife she liked to dwell at no short length. At least, Paullus thought, the apples would soon be ripe, and he could find some solitude in the orchard with a ladder and some baskets.

Paullus had been hard at it, spading in the noxious mixture of ashes, straw and sludge from the midden, when the messenger came to fetch him. Pausing to wash in the yard by the well and put on a clean tunic, he had followed the boy down to Temesa. Now he had joined the other notables trudging up into the hills above Clampetia.

It was strange how quickly the body had been discovered. Hirtius' wife and daughter had not been expected to return until after the festival of Minerva, not for another two days. Apparently a slave owned by Fidubius had stumbled across it on some errand to Ursus' neighbouring woods. Paullus had been unaware that Fidubius had any holdings in the neighbourhood. But probably it was unimportant. Rich men like Fidubius were always looking to snap up any land that came on the market.

'Here we are, gentlemen.' The tone of the slave was inappropriate, as if he had conducted a party of thirsty wayfarers to an inn offering refreshment, not to this horror.

Most of the party hung back a few paces. Paullus approached with Fidubius and Ursus.

The fire pit was still smoking, the pitch in the cauldron still warm.

This corpse had not been stripped naked, yet somehow seemed more exposed, as the tunic had been hauled up under the armpits. Hirtius was less mutilated than Junius had been. Only his hands, feet and penis had been severed. The killer had thought the daemon of Hirtius would be sufficiently deterred from seeking vengeance because the ears and nose were blocked with tar, the tongue shrivelled and the eyes burnt out.

Bending over and scrutinising the remains, Paullus could find no injuries except the arrow wound to the back.

'The arrow would have killed him,' Ursus said.

'Not before he went in the cauldron.'

Paullus thought Fidubius was right.

'He could have fallen into the pitch,' Ursus said.

'But then he was pulled out and mutilated.' There was no contradicting Fidubius.

Paullus straightened up and walked away. It was not the smell of the pitch, but the stench of burnt flesh that was making him feel sick. It brought back unwanted memories. After the fire, they had laboured to dismantle the walls of Corinth and tear down many of the buildings in a similar miasma. And after that there had been the death of Diaeus, the Achaean general. That was not something he wanted to dwell upon.

Paullus gazed out to the sea. The surface looked calm at this distance.

Behind him, they were discussing what to do with the body.

The wind was set in the south-west. It brought the salt tang of the water.

Fidubius was for taking Hirtius back to Temesa and handing his remains to his widow. Given the condition of the corpse, Ursus thought better it should be cremated here, and the ashes given to the family.

Paullus shut his eyes and inhaled the clean smell of the sea. He was very tired. Every night since he had returned from the Sila, the Kindly Ones had slumbered around his bed. Since Blood Rock, he had slept just in snatches. Every time he woke, it was to the rasping breathing of the dark sisters, the daughters of Uranus. Last night, in the early hours, when mind and body were at their lowest, he had thought about Orestes. Maddened by the relentless crones, the matricide had bitten off one of his own fingers. All that had stopped Paullus following his example was that it had brought Orestes little respite.

The others had reached a compromise. They would take Hirtius' corpse back to Temesa and entrust it to the undertakers outside the city gates. The family could arrange the funeral. It was up to them if they wished to view the body.

Paullus opened his eyes. The Furies were implacable, like hounds on a wounded fawn. Only mortal danger, and the act of killing, seemed to put them off his scent for a while.

The festival of Minerva was a subdued affair. It could not be otherwise after the finding of the latest victim. The trades of which the goddess was patron had downed tools for the day. There were carpenters and cobblers, school teachers in threadbare cloaks, dyers and fullers. The latter, after an early-morning trip to the baths, were for once not reeking of stale urine. Yet Minerva also oversaw spinning and weaving, and there were far fewer women than usual. And the men were unsettled, forming and re-forming in small groups, talking in urgent undertones.

The obligations to the gods, however, had to come before the anxieties of men, let alone the fears of women. From the Temple of the Capitoline Triad in the forum the procession, stately and dressed in white, had snaked its way through the town and out to the suburban precinct of Minerva. The sacrifices had gone well. When splashed with water, the victims had nodded their heads, as if consenting to their fate. The intestines had shown nothing unpropitious. Now the air was filled with the agreeable scent of roasting meat, and the wine was beginning to flow. It was a pity that the sanctuary of the Hero of Temesa was in direct sight on the other side of the river.

Paullus was dining on the high table, by right of the civic crown. Lollius was next to him, for no better reason than his father was one of the richest men in the town. Like everyone else, they were certain what would happen. At least Paullus was rested. The previous night he had slept well, without any sign of the Kindly Ones.

It did not take long for the wine to give courage to the plebeian participants. The deputation that approached the table of the notables was headed by the hulking figure of Roscius. An innkeeper was not the highest regarded profession, but Roscius was a Roman citizen, a descendant of one of the original colonists. He had every right to speak for the people.

'Everyone is terrified.' Roscius got straight to the point. 'They are all afraid to leave the town, and there is not a man or woman in the farms and villages who can sleep in their beds. The peasants are fleeing their fields and flooding into Temesa. What are you going to do about the killings?'

Vibius took it on himself to answer. 'The magistrates and the council will organise a night watch, send armed patrols out into the country.'

'That will do no more good than it did routing out the bandits.' The innkeeper had drunk enough to cast off any vestiges of respect for his betters. 'They cannot be everywhere, and a few men with swords will not deter the shade of Polites.'

An apprehensive murmur of agreement ran through the crowd.

'What would you have us do?' Often there was a half smile on Vibius' lips, as if he were about to laugh at the follies of mankind, but now he looked serious, and the question appeared genuine.

'Arrest the old witch, Kaido. She has summoned the Hero of Temesa up from the sea.'

The idea obviously had been rehearsed. Those backing Roscius shook back their cloaks and applauded vigorously.

'The Hero did not kill Hirtius.' Paullus had to raise his voice to be heard.

'How can *you* be so sure?' Roscius asked, belligerently. 'Were you there?'

'Like Junius, he was brought down by an arrow. Then it would have taken two men to lift him into the boiling pitch.'

'The Hero has the strength of ten men.' Far from being put off, the innkeeper was full of certainty. 'We must make him an offering, or the killings will continue.'

Again, the suggestion was expected, and there was a roar of approval.

'Ridiculous!' Ursus broke in. 'We are Romans, not superstitious Greeks or barbarians. Romans do not offer virgins to the underworld.'

Some even dared to hoot at the venerable priest.

'But if Paullus is right . . .' Fidubius let his voice tail off. The hubbub quietened, as everyone strained to hear. 'If Paullus is right, the girl will spend a night in the sanctuary and come to no harm.'

'An offering! A virgin to the Hero!' To Paullus' suspicious ear, the chant sounded as if it had been rehearsed.

'She has to be the most beautiful maiden in Temesa.' Fidubius' tone was so dispassionate and reasonable, he might have been discussing the price of wheat.

'Minado,' Lollius spoke up. 'The daughter of the old Bruttian Dekis is the most beautiful unmarried woman in the town.'

Paullus looked at his friend with horror. They had hunted with Dekis since childhood.

'Minado! Minado!' The proposal was greeted with a salacious glee.

'What in Hades are you doing?' Paullus hissed at Lollius.

His friend shrugged. 'Nothing will happen to her. She will get a fright, that is all. You don't believe these old wives' tales any more than me.'

'But the Bruttians do, and they hate us enough already without this,' Paullus said.

'Who cares what they think?'

'She turned you down, didn't she?'

Lollius grinned. 'You would think the bitch would be flattered – a Roman the first between her legs, not whatever stinking Bruttian goatherd she gets given for a husband.'

CHAPTER 18

Patria

609 Ab Urbe Condita (145 BC)

S OME MEN SHOULD NEVER KILL, and some places and days must not witness bloodshed. The commands of the gods were clear. Transgression was sacrilege. A few priests, such as the Flamen Dialis, who served Jupiter, could not touch iron, or even look on men bearing weapons. No human blood must be spilt in any precinct of the gods, or at certain festivals. The festival of Minerva was one of the latter. The injunction about priests was irrelevant, but Paullus was set on breaking the other two. Given the things he had already done, it probably made little difference. At least the bloody actions he intended this night should shake the Kindly Ones from his tracks, if only for a time.

It was dark and still in the grove of wild olives. Their tall trunks showed faintly silver in the weak moonlight. Paullus was utterly alone. The citizens who had locked the girl in the Temple of the Hero had left. Perhaps frightened, or secretly ashamed of what they had done, they had not waited, but had left her to her fate, precipitously making their way back down the hill and over the river into the town.

Paullus had gone with them, making sure his presence was noted, then said farewell and headed home. Waiting until everyone had retired to their beds, quietly he had dressed in a dark tunic and armed himself. As an afterthought, he secured his army entrenching tool to his belt. Given what lay ahead, it might prove useful. Gesturing Niger to silence and to stay, he had slipped away from the farm. At the river he had smeared his face and limbs with mud. Reaching the trees, he had found a point of vantage in the deepest shade, and had settled to wait. It would be best if he entered the temple in the dead of night, when the girl might be asleep.

A gust of wind rolled up the valley. It moved through the gnarled branches and sent fallen leaves scudding along the ground. Tiny waves flowed one after another across the surface of the pool by the spring. Somewhere high in the hills a wolf howled. It was answered by a dog on an outlying homestead. The call was taken up by dogs on other farms. It spread from point to point across the gloomy slopes of the valley, and far off into the depths of the forest.

As quickly as it had come, the wind died. The dogs ceased barking and the silence returned. The water of the pool soon was as smooth as black glass again. In the bare earth by the lip of the water, there were the slots of deer. But tonight none came to drink.

To kill a person in the name of religion was the act of a barbarian. The savage Taurians of the Black Sea sacrificed those shipwrecked on their shores. The Gauls in their northern woods practised divination by observing the death throes of their victims. Until the destruction of their city, only the previous year, the Carthaginians had sacrificed their firstborn to their cruel god.

Yet the Romans themselves were not blameless. A vestal virgin who broke her vows was buried alive. It could be argued that she brought her terrible death on herself. But in times of crisis it was not unknown for the priests of Rome to announce that the gods must be propitiated by the taking of lives. Two couples, a man and woman, one pair Greeks, the other Gauls, were buried alive. No guilt attached to them beyond their race.

Not unduly perturbed by his reflections, Paullus got to his feet. It was about the middle of the night. Time to get moving. Having been quiet for some time, he was reasonably sure that there was no one else in the trees outside the perimeter wall, or those within. He glided down the slope, keeping to the shadows, taking care where he placed his feet. His soft leather boots made no sound. Under his cloak he wore only a tunic and sword belt. So that they neither rattled nor caught the light, he had removed all the ornaments from the belt, even his lucky theta charm.

The outer wall of the sanctuary was not high, more intended to demark the sacred from the profane than act as a physical barrier. Paullus hauled himself to the top, lay there a moment, then dropped down inside. Crouched down, he waited, listening. In the distance a deer barked. Around him, all was still.

Like a ghost, he flitted between the trees until he came to the huge, ancient olive that he remembered from his childhood. Hundreds of years old, perhaps older than the archaic temple itself, the tree overtopped the roof of the building. His cloak would be an encumbrance climbing, so he took it off, rolled it up and secured it under his belt.

The ascent was no more difficult than it had been all those years before, until he reached the top. He was heavier than he had been. The bough that reached out almost to the roof groaned under his weight. He had no problem with heights, but knew that if he stopped it would be hard to force himself to get moving again. Scrambling along the branch like a monkey, there was a sharp crack. The branch swayed ominously and began to droop. Before he reached the end, Paullus launched himself outwards and down.

He landed on his hands and knees on the tiles. The pitch of the roof was not steep, but enough to make him slip. Behind yawned the black drop. It was so far down that it would break his bones like twigs. Finally, his boots found the guttering and stopped his descent. He lay, spreadeagled, waiting for his heart to stop its panicked hammering.

Be a man! He was unsure if he had spoken aloud.

The landing had not been noisy, but in the quiet of the night anyone alert in the temple, or nearby outside, would have heard the impact. It could not be helped. He had seen Ursus lock both doors of the shrine, and breaking them down would have made a noise to wake the dead.

Somewhat calmer, Paullus edged, crablike, along the roof. At every step, he half expected the gutter to give way. If it did, nothing could prevent him falling. It was a long way down. It was hard to believe that he had taken this risk as a child. After an age, he reached the parapet of the facade. The relief left him gasping. But there was no time for reflection. Using the solid stonework, he made his way up to the apex.

The trapdoor was where he remembered. It was locked. The woodwork around the lock was old and rotted. There was no need for the entrenching tool, and Paullus drew his dagger. The soft wood came away in chunks. It took no time to lever the lock open with the knife.

The hinges of the trapdoor squealed, horribly loud, as he pulled it open. Paullus waited, every sense alert. There was no outcry. The silence of the night buzzed in his ears.

Steep stone steps spiralled down. The first few were just visible. Beyond was nothing but blackness. Paullus sheathed the dagger and started to descend. After the first couple of turns, he could see nothing. He put out his hands to touch either wall, and groped for the next step with a boot. There was something primordially frightening about descending blind into the dark. He moved awkwardly, his muscles tense and beginning to lock up with fear. Sometimes divine sanction was not enough protection for the offerings stored in a temple. There were stories that priests set traps: a concealed pit or a missing step. Surely old Ursus was not such a priest? There was little of value in the sanctuary of the Hero of Temesa. Paullus forced himself to keep moving.

Time and distance lost all meaning. Down and down he went, one hesitant step at a time, down through the dark. The air was cool and damp, and smelt of dust and mice. Suddenly Paullus stumbled. He jerked back and jolted his spine against the steps. Reaching out with one foot, he probed downwards. There were no more steps, just a level floor. Finally he was at the bottom, but somehow it was even more frightening than what had gone before. It took an effort of will to leave the security of the solid steps. Paullus inched forward – one hand held out, the fingertips of the other still brushing the wall – half expecting the flagstones to give way with each footfall.

When the outstretched hand touched wooden planks, he recoiled as if he had touched a viper. *Be a man.* This time he knew that he had not verbalised the command. Like a blind man, he ran his hands over the door until he located the handle. It turned, but it was no surprise that this door too was locked. Tracing the hinges, he discovered that the door opened towards him. Unlike the trapdoor, the woodwork was solid.

Paullus congratulated himself on bringing the entrenching tool. Pleasure in his own foresight calmed his nerves. Working by feel, he slid the steel into the gap between lock and doorframe. Once again he was master of his own destiny. Getting the door open would make a noise. There was no way the girl would not know that someone was coming. But there was nowhere she could run, nowhere she could hide.

Using the tool as a crowbar, he wrenched with all his strength. The frame splintered and, at the second attempt, the door swung towards him. The noise echoed away through the cavernous building. Paullus waited until all was quiet. He listened, but could hear nothing. Putting down the tool, he drew his sword. It might be that he was already too late.

Windows high up under the roof admitted the moonlight. After the staircase the main hall seemed nearly as bright as day, although the shadows cast were black as pitch. Wide columns ran up to the rafters around all four sides, creating a walkway around the edges. There were offerings, mainly antique weapons and armour, hung on the walls. Otherwise the space was bare except for statues. There was one of the Hero, larger than a man, in the centre. Smaller marble statues stood between the columns: figures from myth, including the boxer who had driven the Hero into the sea.

The steps had wound down to emerge next to the huge main door. The walkway running off to either side was empty. Paullus could see there was no one in the central area. He walked first one way, then the other, to check the two side corridors. Satisfied that the girl must have retreated to the storeroom at the rear, he went directly across by the cult statue.

As he expected the internal door was unsecured. He pushed it open, then stepped back. There were no windows in the smaller inner room. He paused to let his eyes adjust. This storeroom was crowded with offerings – not just statues relegated from display, but all manner of things. The smaller ones were heaped in piles everywhere. She had to be hidden among them.

'Minado.' In the breathless quiet, Paullus did not have to raise his voice.

There was no response.

'Come out,' Paullus said. 'There is no time for this.'

Again only silence came back.

Paullus rasped his sword down the wall.

As the harsh grating sound died there was a noise, as faint as a mouse, from near the rear door. Paullus went towards it. A stirring in the dead air warned him. He leapt backwards, collided with a stack of amphorae. One smashed, the rest went rolling across the floor. Recovering his balance, he saw the ancient blade she wielded. Her wild lunge had not missed by much.

'No!' Paullus backed off, shards crunching under his boots.

Her eyes wide with terror, and very white in the dim light, she stepped after him.

'Minado, put the sword down.'

She gave no sign of hearing, but gathered herself to strike again.

Paullus took several quick paces backwards. 'Stop! I have not come to harm you.'

'Then why have you got a sword in your hand?'

'I will put it down.' Moving slowly, as he would around a nervous horse, Paullus crouched, placed the blade on the floor and straightened up.

The girl did not move, but her sword remained poised.

'I have come to protect you.'

'With your skin darkened like the Hero?'

'I did not want them to see.'

'Who?'

'The men who will try to kill you.'

The tip of her sword trembled, but she kept her control. 'And who are they'

'I don't know.'

'Why should I trust you?' she said with suspicion.

'You know who I am – Gaius Furius Paullus, a friend of your father.'

'You pay my father to do your dirty work, to risk his life acting as a decoy for brigands. All you Romans treat us Bruttians like dogs.'

'You have to trust me. Whoever they are that want people to believe the Hero has returned will have to come tonight. They will kill you, mutilate your body, make it appear the work of the daemon.'

'You got into the temple,' her tone was decisive, 'so we can get out.'

'It would do no good. People would say that we had cheated the Hero of his offering. I would be gaoled, and you would be returned to the temple.'

'So we just wait?'

'I need proof.'

She snorted with derision. 'Or they kill both of us.'

'There is that risk,' Paullus said, 'but in the last couple of years I have proved very hard to kill.'

She stood, weighing her options. At last she sighed and, as if it had assumed a terrible weight, lowered her sword.

Picking up his weapon, Paullus led her out of the storeroom and across to the stairs. Her decision made, she seemed calm. Paullus guided her to sit where the steps first began to turn. He would be below, by the door. She still had her sword, but, if they got through him, Paullus doubted it would do her much good.

Before settling, Paullus prepared himself. He found the entrenching tool and placed it to hand. Then he took off his cloak and wound it around his left forearm, leaving a foot or two hanging down. Finally, he sat down, placing his blade behind him in the darkness. Now there was nothing to do but wait.

From the light coming through the windows it was hard to judge how much of the night had passed. There must be three, perhaps four hours of darkness remaining. Paullus was certain that they would come.

It was odd, but in the gloom, and the tension of their encounter, he had not really looked at Minado. From a distance yesterday she had appeared as beautiful as Lollius said. Tonight all he had seen were her eyes. But the eyes are the windows on the soul. Terrified as she had been, her eyes had been those of a brave and resourceful woman.

The statue of the Hero loomed in the middle of the hall. He was depicted as a man, but bigger and stronger than any human. The skin of a wolf was draped around his shoulders, the head pulled up like a hood. He was empty handed, but the taut muscled arms and the talon-like fingers, indicated what would have happened to those set upon by the Hero of Temesa. The inscription on the plinth named him not Polites, but Lykas, wolf-man.

The Greeks called the Romans 'Ausonian beasts' – Ausonian from an ancient name for Italy, and beasts from the suckling of Romulus and Remus by a she-wolf. The Greeks were correct. The Romans indeed were the children of the wolf. Just how ravening and insatiable, Paullus had not learnt until Corinth. Perhaps not even then, but later, when he had watched with horror the awful death of the Achaean general Diaeus and listened to his final words.

Paullus thought of the wolves in the Sila. They were padding through the trees with their heavy-shouldered, distinctive gait. Their mouths were open, their teeth white, their lolling tongues the colour of blood.

A nudge. Paullus must have fallen asleep. Minado's foot nudged his back again. Thank the gods! Fresh air drifted through the temple. It brought the smell of the sea, the scent of wild herbs and the rich odours of the night. The back door of the temple must be open. They were here.

Paullus' hand closed on the hilt of his sword. His palm was sweaty, his heart knocking against his ribs. There was no time for second thoughts.

At first he heard nothing. Then there were muffled sounds from the storeroom. The sounds of a man, perhaps two, carefully searching among the accumulated offerings. It would not take them long. And then they must come to where Paullus waited. He would have liked to whisper reassurance to the girl, but it was impossible. Like him, she would have to fight alone in the dark against her apprehensions.

The sharp snap of breaking terracotta, the crunching as it was ground to dust under their boots, showed they had reached the inner door. Any moment now they would come through into the main hall. Paullus grinned, a weight lifted from his shoulders. The Kindly Ones could not touch him now. Kill or be killed. When every other pleasure was vitiated, that was what it meant to be alive.

A movement by the door. An indistinct figure moving beyond the columns and statues, heading away towards the right. No sign of another one. The figure returning, going to check the other long passageway.

Come on, come on, Paullus silently pleaded. There's nowhere else she could be hiding, don't keep me waiting.

The figure emerged into the central space. He walked slowly, but directly towards the steps. The floor was banded with moonlight and shadow, and the man went from one to the other. He was tall and powerful, and clad in the pelt of a wolf; a smaller simulacrum of the statue of Lykas, except in his hand was a broad-bladed Greek falchion.

Seeing the door to the stairs open, the figure paused.

Paullus remained very still, his breathing shallow. He caught the feral stink of the wolfskin and a faint whiff of perfume.

Cautiously, the man stepped towards the black rectangle of the doorway.

Not yet, not yet! Paullus stifled an impatience fuelled by fear.

The broad shoulders filled the doorframe.

In one motion, Paullus rose and thrust. With an agility unlikely in such a substantial frame, the wolf-man pirouetted. The steel missed by an inch. As Paullus drew back to recover, his opponent chopped downwards. With a clangour of metal on metal, Paullus deflected the blow. The heavy curved blade almost slammed Paullus' weapon from his grip. Pushing his free hand to the man's chest, Paullus heaved him away.

They stood a couple of paces apart, both crouching, but balanced. Paullus could not see the man's face. The mask of the wolf was tied under his chin, leaving only the eyes and nose exposed.

The man swung without any preliminary movement. Distracted by the bestial disguise, Paullus was slow reacting. Only swaying back at the last second, he felt the disturbance of the air as the blade whistled by his head.

Watch the blade, watch the blade!

Paullus jabbed towards the face. The man brought his sword up. Paullus pulled the attack and cut down towards the left thigh. The man sidestepped away. Paullus followed up with a thrust to the groin. Awkwardly, the man got his weapon in the way.

The man was quick and strong, no stranger to violence, but he was not a trained swordsman. Yet there was the likelihood that he had an unseen accomplice. Paullus had to finish this quickly.

As if reading his thoughts, the man took a pace backwards.

'Harder to fight a man than murder a girl,' Paullus taunted him. 'Harder still if you are a coward.'

The man took another step away.

'Is that piss trickling down your legs?' Paullus goaded. 'You had better run.'

Quick as a flash, the man jumped forward, angling a mighty overhand blow down at Paullus' head. Catching the blade on the edge of his sword, Paullus rolled his wrist. Grabbing the elbow of his assailant with his left hand, Paullus brought his knee up into the underside of his forearm. The man yelled in pain. His falchion dropped from his grip. It clanged on the flagstones.

Disarmed and in pain, but the man was not finished yet. Fingernails clawed at Paullus' face. They missed his eyes and raked down his cheek. Paullus reared back, and the man had turned and was running.

Paullus raced after him, between the columns, out into the open space. The man only had a lead of a couple of paces.

The missile sliced by Paullus' ear. Then he recognised the thrum of an arrow. Out here he was a sitting target. He hurled himself to one side and dived back behind a pillar. Not stopping, he bundled back into the doorway.

For a split second, he wondered if the girl might not realise it was him. She still had a sword. Instead of attacking, she whispered, 'What do we do now?'

'Listen.'

Low voices from the storeroom. Two men speaking. No words or accents clear.

Then silence.

Paullus' thoughts were tumbling over each other: stay here, keep watch; or stalk after them, they can't get a clean shot in the gloom; no, get to safety up the steps, no arrow can fly around a spiral staircase.

The silence stretched.

'Up the stairs!' Paullus did not wait to know if she heard or obeyed, but started to scramble up the steps. Round and round in the darkness, like a dormouse in a jar, until there was a faint glimmer ahead. He saw her legs disappearing through the trapdoor and dragged himself after her into the open.

The night air was like stepping under a cold fountain – clean and almost intoxicating.

Paullus peered into the dark.

'There!' She pointed.

Two figures glimpsed between the wild olives. One was big and wide, the other slighter and less tall. They were making off into the hills.

CHAPTER 19

Patria

609 Ab Urbe Condita (145 BC)

WHAT IF THEY RETURNED, bringing accomplices? What if there were more of them already in the temple? A third man – any number of men – might have been in the storeroom, and by now be waiting in the darkness at the foot of the stairs.

'Stay here.' Paullus knew what he had to do, and he did not want her to think that he was afraid.

'No, I will come with you.'

He did not argue, for part of him was relieved. The battle at the Isthmus of Corinth had taught him that it was far harder to go back into battle. Sometimes only comradeship could make you put yourself at risk for a second time. She was just a girl, but she had a sword, and already this night had shown her composure and courage.

Again Paullus edged down the spiral staircase. Sword in one hand, he kept his other against the outer wall and felt for each step with his foot before placing his weight. Again the impenetrable blackness and the sheer weight of the surrounding building oppressed him. Irrationally he still feared that the solid stonework would give way under his boot. And at any moment half of him expected to feel the searing pain of an unseen blow.

Nothing could be heard except the sounds of his own furtive descent and the noises the girl made behind him. If some other foe was lurking in the temple, there would be ample warning of their coming.

Finally they reached the bottom. In the moonlight filtering from the high windows in the hall, he could see that no one was lying in ambush. Paullus had to stop and get his breath. It was chill, but he was running with sweat.

'What now?' she asked, almost with impatience.

'Follow me.'

Paullus led her round all four sides of the colonnaded hall. He wanted to be quite certain that no enemy could assail them from behind. Satisfied, he went to the doorway to the storeroom.

There was no getting around the shattered terracotta on the floor of the entrance. He peered into the gloom. Each pile of offerings could conceal a man. They seemed to shift as he stared at them.

Be a man, he steeled himself. *Do not let this girl think you a coward.*

'Stay back,' he hissed.

This time she followed his wishes.

The shards broke under his boots as he entered. The myriad small sounds were incredibly loud in the confined space. Beyond them, he walked on the balls of his feet, poised and ready to spring from one teetering jumble of gifts to the gods to another. He switched direction in the alleyways between the offerings. It was like a small and black labyrinth and, unlike Theseus, he had no thread to guide him.

Eventually he was sure they were alone. He tried the back door. It was unlocked.

'Help me with this table.'

Together they dragged the heavy object tight up against the boards of the door. Determined men could force their way into the temple, but they could not do so covertly.

'What about the front door?' she asked.

They went back across the main hall and checked it was still locked. The distance was too far to manhandle a bulky piece of furniture. Paullus went and fetched an amphora from the store-room. He smashed it on the flags inside the door and spread the shards out with his foot.

Without a word, they made their way to the statue of the Hero in the centre of the hall. They sat with their backs against the plinth. From there they could keep watch on the main door.

'Why did you come?' she asked.

The truth was too confusing, perhaps too frightening: the Kindly Ones haunt me for a terrible thing I did, and only this shakes them for a while from my steps; perhaps, like the men in the wolfskins, I have developed a taste for killing.

'It was the right thing to do,' he said.

She seemed to accept that. 'You are not like the other Romans.'

'You Bruttians hate us.'

'Of course.' She spoke without rancour, as if explaining to a child. 'You massacred our grandparents and stole our best land. Even now we are not citizens in our own country. Our men are conscripted as servants in the armies you send out to bring ruin to yet more peoples.'

It is our nature, he was tempted to say, like the fable of the scorpion and the frog. But he kept quiet.

'Onirus said you were not as bad as the others.'

'You know Onirus?' Paullus was surprised.

'He is my cousin.'

It had never occurred to Paullus that there was a link between the camp servant and her father. He had served with Onirus in the east, had gone hunting many times with Dekis, but now it struck him that he knew next to nothing about them. One was older and heavyset, the other younger and slighter, but beyond that he could not even picture what they looked like. An unsettling suspicion skulked at the fringes of his thoughts.

'You are not like your friend, Lollius,' she said.

'He is not so bad.'

'You are too trusting,' she said with certainty. 'He is selfish and cruel.'

Remembering what Lollius had said about her, Paullus did not reply.

They sat in silence, side by side. Paullus could feel her warmth, smell the subtle scent of her body. He wanted to put his arm around her. But he kept his distance. His own body stank of sweat and the sour reek of fear.

'You are not married,' Paullus said. Most girls were married at fourteen; she was nearer twenty.

'Even you Romans do not force a girl to marry against her will.' Her teeth showed white when she smiled.

'You do not wish to wed?'

'Someone has to keep house for my father, since my mother died.'

'You cannot do so forever.'

'My father is saving to buy a housekeeper. The money you gave him to trap the bandits helped.'

'I am glad a Roman can be useful in some things.'

'And you were generous with the plunder you gave Onirus.'

Paullus made a noncommittal noise. He had told Onirus not to mention the gift, but she was the camp servant's cousin.

They sat, companionably enough, through the rest of the night. Sometimes they talked, mostly they did not. When Paullus turned to her she lifted her chin, but without vanity, and looked into his eyes. In the half-light, he thought that she was the loveliest thing he had ever seen.

When the sky through the high windows paled to the blue-grey of a pigeon, he got up and retrieved his entrenching tool and the weapon dropped by his assailant. It took considerably longer to find the spent arrow. Sitting down again he held out his hand, palm up, to the girl. Without hesitation, she took it. Her hand was small and dry, and callused with hard work. For Paullus it was a rare moment of peace.

At dawn they heard the procession approaching long before the key turned in the lock. As the leaves of the main door swung outwards, they remained sitting. The consternation of the crowd was pleasing. There were gasps of shock, and a couple of men even took a step backwards. Whatever they had been expecting, it was not this.

They were all there: Fidubius and his large bailiff Croton, Ursus the priest, Lollius and his father, Roscius and his young lover, the magistrates, everyone of note in the town. Together they crunched across the bits of broken amphora.

Still holding Minado's hand, Paullus got up and helped her to her feet.

'What are you doing here?'

Paullus ignored Fidubius' question. 'Two men came, not the daemon.'

'Who?'

'I do not know. The one I fought wore the mask of a wolf.'

'What did they look like?' Fidubius was impatient.

'It was dark, and they were disguised. As they left, one appeared taller than the other. The bigger one dropped this.' Paullus held out the sword.

Vibius snatched it from him. The customary refined disinterest of Lollius' father had vanished, but, after turning the blade in his hand, it returned. 'A *kopis*, an old Greek blade, a relic of the war with Hannibal. There are any number in Temesa – almost every farm has one. Some use them for cutting hay.'

'And there was this.'

Roscius took the arrow from Paullus. The innkeeper studied it closely. 'The work of Albinus the fletcher by the forum – everyone buys their arrows from him. Goose feathers, one of his more expensive.'

'They came through the back door.' Paullus turned to Ursus. 'How many keys are there?'

The priest bridled, as if accused. 'Three,' he said stiffly. 'I have one, and my assistant another.'

The man mentioned sidled forward. Overawed by the occasion, he did not speak, but held up a key.

'The third hangs in the senate house.'

Everyone knew that the curia was kept locked. Only the councillors, and a couple of trusted public slaves, had access.

Roscius could contain himself no longer. 'But if it is not the daemon, and it cannot be the brigands . . .' His unspoken question trailed off.

Vibius drew himself up, as if addressing a court. 'Both Junius and Hirtius were Roman citizens. The Bruttians have never been reconciled to their defeat. They want their land back. They are the enemy within.'

Paullus raised Minado's hand. 'Last night the intended victim was a Bruttian.'

'A necessary sacrifice to induce yet more fear,' Vibius said stuffily. His suggestion did not convince all those present.

'Another eastern cult,' Roscius said, 'like the Bacchanalia outlawed by decree of the senate in Rome. Or the deadly superstition of the Jews. Or the Carthaginians – they sacrificed their own children. Thousands of them were abroad when Carthage fell. They want revenge.'

'There is no evidence of foreign cults in Temesa,' Ursus said. The words of the priest carried authority, but some men looked sideways at each other. Anything was possible with easterners.

Lollius walked forward with the usual slight overconfidence he employed, even when it was not necessary. 'Both the victims owned land. Their killing could be inspired by the envy of the propertyless poor.'

'Some hounds acquire a love of killing,' Fidubius said. 'It is the same with some men.'

Lollius looked at Fidubius. 'Whoever they are, this is not over.'

'For today it is,' Paullus said. 'I will return the girl to her father. And Kaido must be released. The old wise woman did not summon the Hero.'

The throng parted as Paullus led Minado by the hand out of the temple. Several men gave him odd looks. Since his return from the east they knew he had changed, and he had killed several men. The realisation came to Paullus that he was an object of suspicion, perhaps had been from the start. Only he and the girl could swear to the truth of what had happened last night. The others had just his word.

CHAPTER 20

Patria

609 Ab Urbe Condita (145 BC)

IT HAD BEEN ALMOST A MONTH since the night in the temple. There had been no more killings. One or two stories had circulated of sightings of wild men clad in the skins of wolves roaming the remote pastures and the depths of the Sila. While each one had, on investigation by the magistrates, turned out to be no more than unsubstantiated rumours, they were the product of the palpable sense of fear that still gripped the territory of Temesa. No one, if they could avoid it, went alone to out-of-the-way places, especially not after dark.

A hunting party, however, was the opposite of a solitary pursuit. A huge wild boar had been seen on land owned by Vibius along the upper reaches of the Acheron river. Initially Paullus had been unenthusiastic when Lollius had come to ask him to join them. It was October, the days were getting shorter and there was much work to be done. The grapes had to be gathered and the pears were ready for picking. When not labouring in the fields, Paullus had taken to spending his time with Minado.

Her father had thanked him with formal courtesy when he returned her unharmed to his smallholding. Yet since then, old Dekis had been oddly distant. Although his behaviour had changed, it was nowhere near enough to give any credence to the hint of suspicion that had snaked through Paullus' mind in the temple. While it was not beyond the bounds of imagination that the Bruttian huntsman might have wanted to murder Junius and Hirtius, or any other Roman, it was inconceivable that he would have plotted to kill his only child. Perhaps his frigid demeanour merely indicated that, quite rightly, he blamed the Romans for the ordeal of his daughter, and a portion of that blame had somehow stuck even to her rescuer. Still, it encouraged him to leave them alone.

Sitting with her in the evening, watching the bats flitting over the river, gave Paullus a happiness he had not known in the last year, perhaps ever. He did not touch her. He wanted to, but the behaviour of Lollius was always at the back of his mind. Sometimes she took his hand. Minado talked about her family and her friends, and told tales about the townsfolk to entertain him.

'You know Zeno, the little serving boy of Roscius, the one who is always arranging his hair with one finger? He is unhappy with the innkeeper. They say he is now also the lover of Croton, the brutish bailiff of Fidubius. Croton lives alone at the edge of the farm so he can indulge unobserved in his vices. But Roscius is a brute too. It will end unhappily.'

'How old are you?'

'Nineteen.'

'And how does a nineteen-year-old girl know such things?'

Minado laughed. 'People talk, your maids and servants talk. You Romans do not trouble yourselves about what you say in front of Bruttian servants, any more than they would in front of their cattle. We know more about you than you do yourselves.'

She talked happily and unselfconsciously. Mostly Paullus was silent. He wanted to talk to her, wanted to tell her about the death of the Achaean Diaeus, and, above all, wanted to tell her the thing he had done in Corinth. But he did not. Even if she were not repulsed, she would not understand. No one could understand who had not been there. And it would be unfair to put that burden upon her.

Paullus had been more reluctant to forego another evening with Minado than he had been to leave the grape harvest to old Eutyches. But Lollius had been insistent. His father particularly wanted Paullus to join the hunt. Vibius wanted to talk to him in confidence. It was a matter of importance. Fidubius wanted to talk to him as well. Paullus had let himself be persuaded. He liked hunting, and he was intrigued as to what this matter of importance was. Paullus had his suspicions, and it would be interesting if they were confirmed.

The hunting party had crossed the river and climbed up into the hills the day before. They had followed the course of a shallow mountain stream that ran down to the Sabutus. Its waters were as grey as the rocks, and trees leant across its surface at improbable angles. The going was tough, but they all walked. Vibius and Fidubius set the pace. For all his sleek urbanity, Vibius was as hard in mind and body as Fidubius. Age had not weakened the teak toughness of either. The servants had struggled to keep up. Although, of course, they were burdened with the baggage.

In the afternoon they had come out into the high country of the upper Acheron. It was a land of open, broad meadows, but always ringed with woods, and always with the mountain peaks on the sky-line. They made camp in the lee of a stand of holm oaks. They ate and made conversation, but nothing of importance was raised.

The sleep of Paullus had been undisturbed. There had been no sign of the Kindly Ones since he had met Minado in the temple. In the morning he had worried that he was treating her as a talisman to keep the old women from his heels. Without thinking he had touched the theta charm on his belt.

After the sun had risen, they had eaten porridge and drunk a little warmed wine. This was not an outing of sybaritic nobles, but of men still close to the soil, and there was a bite to the autumn air. When they had finished, a shepherd of Vibius had led them to the valley where the boar had most often been seen. A single hound had been released. The Spartan bitch, tawny and alert, had quartered the ground, nose down, at a half-run. There were many scents. When she got on the freshest, they had followed in single file. Soon they had seen the signs: broken branches, tusk marks on the trees.

The bitch came to a thicket, close by a tiny tributary of the Acheron. Boars liked such places: well watered, and warm in the winter and cool in the summer. True to her training, the bitch did not enter the undergrowth, but gave tongue. A huntsman whistled her in, and tied her up with the others at a distance from the lair.

The boar had not been roused by the baying, and the hunt was arranged in silence. The nets were strung across a narrow place down the valley. The meshes were thrown over the forked branches of trees, the rings well pegged to the ground. The inside was propped with twigs, so that the interior should seem as light as possible to the onrushing boar. The skirting lines were fastened to strong boughs, and even the places with bad footing were blocked with brush, so that the boar could not escape to the side.

Vibius, Fidubius and a pair of huntsmen took their stance behind the nets. They had bows as well as javelins and boar spears. The younger hunters got into line uphill of the thicket. Paullus was in the centre, with Lollius to his left and a youth called Solinus to his right. There were two others, like Solinus, relatives of the older landowners, one on each wing. Respectfully, the huntsmen took their place a few paces to the rear. Paullus noticed Fidubius' unlovely bailiff Croton was behind him.

'Are you ready for war?'

Paullus swallowed his contempt for the words of Lollius. A boar hunt held its dangers, but it was not war. Nothing else was like war. Lollius had no idea of what he spoke.

'Ready!' the others chorused.

Old Dekis brought up the hounds. Whatever the Bruttian's feelings towards Lollius, he needed the money to buy a housekeeper, and Vibius would be paying well.

The hounds were Molossian: eight great black beasts. They were silent but twitched with impatience, white teeth showing and eyes popping. They wore iron studded collars, useful against wolves, but offering no protection against the tusks of a boar. So great was the strength of a boar that when provoked his tusks became red-hot. They singed the coats of hounds they narrowly missed. If you placed a hair on a tusk, as soon as the boar was killed, it would shrivel with the heat.

'Let them go, Dekis.'

They were on slip leads, and went away smoothly. As soon as they were released, they raised a terrible clamour and rushed into the thicket. Paullus could hear them working through the undergrowth. Then something much larger was crashing through the bushes.

The boar was larger than any Paullus had seen, like something out of myth. One hound, discretion forgotten in its frenzy, attacked it from the front. A sweep of the enormous head and the hound was tossed aside, a horrible scarlet rent in its flank. The others closed, but with more circumspection, darting in, snarling and nipping. The boar ran, with its stiff-legged, scuttling gait, downhill. The hounds were snapping at its heels. The hunters jogged after.

This was an old boar, long schooled in cunning. An instant before it would have entangled itself in the net, it skidded to a halt.

It swung around to confront its tormenters. More hounds would be maimed. Dekis used his hunting horn to call them off to safety behind the line of hunters.

The tiny piggy eyes regarded the puny figures of the hunters with malice.

One of the older men behind the net loosed an arrow. It flew wide. Someone shouted a warning. No more missiles followed. The danger of hitting one of the younger men was obvious.

With unknowable bestial calculation, the boar picked its victim. Its acceleration was improbable for such a heavy animal. Head down, it charged straight at Solinus. The youth met it bravely, spear well out. But his stance was not right. The tip of his spear gouged along a slab of a shoulder, but did not stop the beast. The shaft twisted and snapped. A second later, the impact of the boar smashed Solinus to the ground. The beast swung around, all thoughts of flight overtaken by the desire to kill.

Solinus was groggily sitting up.

'Get down!' Paullus yelled. 'Lie flat! Dig your hands into the earth!'

Solinus rolled over, hugged the ground.

Sure enough, the boar was using its tusks to pry him loose. If it succeeded, nothing could stop him being gored.

Paullus glanced at those nearest. Neither Lollius nor Croton was moving.

'Draw it away!' Paullus shouted.

Still the other two remained motionless. On the face of Lollius was a mixture of fear and excitement. Croton appeared indifferent.

Failing to lever the man from the soil, the boar began to trample him.

Paullus jumped forward, shouting.

The porcine eyes flicked to this annoying newcomer.

Paullus made as if to throw his boar spear.

That was enough provocation. The beast lowered its tusks and charged.

Hold the spear with the left hand forward, the right hand back. The instructions from his childhood filled Paullus' mind. The left guides, the right thrusts. Left foot first, following the hand, the right grasping firmly. Legs bent and braced, no further apart than wrestling.

Look straight into its eye, straight into the eye!

The boar was on him. It jerked its head. Paullus' left hand followed, guiding the tip of the spear.

Thrust inside the shoulder, deep into the throat. The thought was the master of the deed. The strike was clean, near perfect. Even so, Paullus was driven back – three, four paces. And the boar was not done. Blind to the agony in its vitals, it was using its great strength to push itself up along the shaft of the spear, its teeth taking chunks out of the hard cornel wood. It reached the jutting wings of the spear. Paullus could feel the heat of its breath.

Someone else drove a spear in behind its right shoulder. Solinus had not dishonoured himself. He had got to his feet and closed with the beast again. With one last breath, and a great shudder, the boar's legs gave, and it collapsed dead.

The huntsmen, servants and shepherds had built a huge fire and butchered the boar. They had the animal turning on a spit brought for the purpose. Their betters had made an offering to the deities of the woods and were reclining on rugs at a distance.

Paullus, exhilarated and flooded with relief, was trying not to drink too much.

Lollius was holding forth. 'What pleasure can a civilised man get when a noble beast is pierced through and through by a hunting spear? Does one hunt for profit or pleasure? If profit, the motive is ignoble. If pleasure, go to the games, and keep your legs whole, instead of scratching them to bits on brambles as you scramble through the wilds.'

Fidubius was having none of this. 'Hunting wins a reputation for courage, improves your health, your muscles, your circulation. That was the way of the old heroes of Rome. Nowadays the idle rich build walled parks and slaughter animals that are almost tame. Even worse are those who just sit in comfort and watch trained slaves massacre beasts for the amusement of the vulgar. But not all antique virtue is forgotten. Scipio, the conqueror of Carthage, made his name in the hunting field.'

Lollius looked sulky at the implied criticism of himself.

The meat was carved and served on rounds of flatbread. The aroma was mouth-watering, the taste just as good. Paullus had not been hungry, but now was starving. All manners set aside, he ate as if he were back in an army camp.

Vibius turned his long, intelligent face to Paullus. 'Living with a woman is a trial, but living without one even worse.' He smiled a courteous smile. 'Have you yet thought of taking a wife?'

Paullus looked up, grease smeared on his chin.

'My cousin, down near Terina, has a daughter. It is not too far,' Vibius continued.

Paullus wiped his face on a napkin. 'I am honoured, but I already have a wife in mind.'

Vibius nodded smoothly. Lollius sniggered.

Paullus wanted to punch his friend.

Fidubius tried an affable smile. It sat unnaturally with his heavy, disapproving looks. His mouth was too small for his big round head. 'The prefect of the Bruttians will be visiting Temesa in December. In the past Lucius Aurelius Orestes has done me the honour of dining in my house.'

Fidubius said something else, but Paullus was not listening. It would be good to see Orestes again. Naevius would be with him, commanding the soldiers of his bodyguard. Even better to be reunited with the old centurion, to talk to a companion who had shared so much on the Achaean campaign. December, not long at all.

'Paullus?'

'Sorry, my mind was wandering.'

If Fidubius was irritated, it did not show on his stony features. 'I was saying that, as your old commander, I am sure Orestes would be delighted if you could join us.'

'That is very kind,' Paullus said. And very unexpected, he thought. And heartless. You blame me for the death of Alcimus. Do my links to a powerful man outweigh your grief for your son?

Fidubius was not finished. 'In three years' time the censors in Rome will again auction the rights to collect pitch and fell timber in the Sila. You know that Vibius and I have the contract for the current five years in the area around Drys and the pass of Laboula. Obviously we will bid for that again, but we have our eye on the forest around Sestion. Additional funds will be required, and we thought you might care to join us.'

'And let us be honest.' Even Vibius' interruption was polished. 'In Rome it is spoken of as a certainty that Lucius Mummius will be elected as one of the two new censors. The general who awarded you the civic crown might look favourably on any bid which included you.'

'I am not sure that I have that sort of money,' Paullus said.

Vibius smiled, showing neat white teeth. 'Corinth was the wealthiest city in the world. Only a fool would not have made a fortune there, and no one would mistake you for a fool, my dear Paullus.'

Paullus took a drink. 'Three years is a long time.'

'And here and now there is profit to be made,' Fidubius said. 'Of course the killings are a tragedy, but they have made land cheap.

Marcellus has some good fields up the Sabutus from you. His heart is not in working the land, and he is a man of no account – no family and few, if any, friends. With the right persuasion he might sell up for a reasonable price. If a veteran such as yourself put it to him – put it to him forcefully – we would be happy to divide the farm three ways.'

'No, I think not.' Paullus might have answered too abruptly, but he was appalled by the idea.

CHAPTER 21

Militia

One Year Earlier

608 Ab Urbe Condita (146 BC)

T HE DAY AFTER THE AMBUSH AT the White Cliffs was the worst of Paullus' life. It was not the enemy. The Achaeans had fled away to the south, for the moment thoroughly defeated. It was the fear of decimation. The legion had broken, almost every soldier had fled. In the chaos of the night, it had been hard to tell the few who had not been guilty of desertion. A legion that had run was summoned on parade. After a coruscating reprimand, lots were drawn – one man in ten. The commander took a cudgel and, walking through the ranks, lightly touched each condemned man. Most stood overwhelmed. Some tried to run, but it did them no good. They were hunted through the camp with clubs and stones. Their own tent-mates beat them to death.

The legion had been withdrawn to Megara. Now it was preparing to meet its fate. Paullus was scouring the links of his mail with sand. Almost every legionary was attending to his kit, as if it might make some difference. Cross-legged, cleaning his helmet, Tatius called for a drink. Although the camp servants ran no risk of decimation, the tension had got to them. Onirus was clumsy. Some wine spilt onto Tatius' tunic.

'You stupid . . .' Tatius leapt to his feet. His first punch caught the Bruttian in the mouth. Onirus staggered back, covering his head. Tatius followed, fists busy.

After a stunned moment, Paullus was up. He grabbed his friend. Tatius spun round. The blow to the eye took Paullus off guard. Tatius – eyes wild – had him by the throat. The fingers were digging into his flesh, throttling him.

'Stop it!' Alcimus dragged them apart.

For a moment Tatius continued to glare.

'We are brothers,' Alcimus said. 'We will face this together.'

The madness drained out of Tatius. 'Sorry.' He looked sheepish. 'If it is decimation, and I am one of the chosen, that will motivate you.'

The others did not laugh at the attempted joke.

The trumpet sounded. It was time. They began to help each other arm.

Paullus stood in the front rank of the *hastati* with Alcimus and Tatius. Centurion Naevius stood out in front. The wind raised little dust devils on the parade ground. Paullus' left eye hurt. It was beginning to swell.

The Consul Mummius joined Orestes on the tribunal. The tension was almost unbearable as the silence stretched. And then Mummius spoke gently to them. He did not mention the five hundred shields that had been thrown away in the panic and captured by the Achaeans. The temporary reverse had been the will of the gods. In the dark and confusion there had been no chance to form a battle line. There had been individual acts of heroism. And then Paullus, and three other legionaries that he did not know, were summoned to the tribunal. Before the assembled legion they were crowned with the oak wreath of the *corona civica* for saving the life of a fellow citizen. The consul praised them as an example to all. With such soldiers the legion would acquit itself well in the coming battle. As a token of his trust, and to restore its reputation, Mummius announced that it would lead the advance to Corinth.

Two days later they marched down the east of the isthmus. They passed by the White Cliffs. There was little to see apart from the ashes of the pyres. The bodies of Romans and Achaeans alike had been cremated. There was little other debris. The battlefield had been picked clean. Greece was a hard and poor land. To the local peasants even a broken belt buckle or a shattered sword had a value.

The legion led the heavy infantry, but, as military prudence dictated, it was preceded by the light troops. If there were another surprise attack, it would fall on the mercenary archers from Crete and the cavalrymen from the allied kingdom of Pergamum. They were expendable. Their deaths would buy the necessary time for the Roman citizens of the legion to make ready.

They took it in easy stages. The first night in camp the mood of the legion had been euphoric. Far from being decimated, they were not even eating the barley bread of punishment rations. Those legionaries painting their names on their hastily issued replacement shields had responded good humouredly to the teasing of their comrades. Even Naevius seemed relieved. Men from other maniples had come to pass the time with Paullus, as if some glory of the civic crown might reflect on them.

In the morning, not long after they had broken camp, the word came back down the line: the Achaeans were in the neck of the isthmus, drawn up for battle. The legionaries sang as they helped each other arm.

They were still singing as they came out onto the plain.

> *Then awake and beware, for the foeman is near;*
> *He is laying an ambush to cut off your rear.*
> *Look alive and take thought how to counter the host,*
> *Do not sleep at your ease, there's no time to be lost.*
> *Make a march, intercept him, get up men and doing,*
> *Outflank the invader and save us from ruin.*

The legion turned due west and halted about five hundred paces from the shining waters of the Corinthian Gulf. The cavalry and the Cretans had formed a screen to the south, and the dust they raised obscured the view of the enemy.

Orders were barked, trumpets sounded, standards inclined. The legion wheeled left and got into battle array. The manoeuvre went smoothly. The gods knew, they had practised it often enough. Paullus was in the front rank, near the extreme right – the position of greatest honour, the position of greatest danger. The Sabines formed the first three of the file to his left; Alcimus and Tatius were to his right. As ever Naevius was strutting about in front.

The legion was set out in three lines, each of ten maniples, the *hastati* to the fore. In each line there were gaps between each maniple and its neighbours, each about as wide as its own frontage. The *principes* covered the gaps in the *hastati* at the rear, the *triarii* those in the *principes*. The chequered formation was reminiscent of the pieces on the board of the game of *latrunculi*. The light armed *velites* were somewhere out ahead in the dust with the Cretans and the cavalry.

To leave enough room for the cavalry to wheel and turn on the narrow plain of the isthmus, the legion was ordered to form up sixteen deep, double the normal depth. None of the maniples were that deep. Those of the *hastati* and *principes* should contain one hundred and twenty men, those of the *triarii* sixty, but the forced march and the White Cliffs had taken their toll, and every maniple was well under strength.

Although unable to see, Paullus knew the formation was repeated across the army. The legion occupied a quarter of the battle line. To their left was the other legion of Roman citizens, beyond them the two legions of Italian allies – according to the muster rolls, some sixteen thousand fighting men. The infantry of the Pergamene allies, having performed so badly at the White Cliffs, had been left behind to guard the camp.

A wave of cheering rolled along the army, and out of the haze rode Mummius and his staff. In Greek history books a general always made a long and rhetorical oration to his whole army. In reality distance and time intervened. How could all the men hear, and would the enemy remain inactive? But literature did more than reflect reality, it shaped expectations. Mummius would have already addressed a few words to the other three legions.

Mounted on a suitably heroic grey stallion, Mummius pointed towards the enemy. The gesture was somewhat vitiated by the pall of dust which hid them. 'Soldiers, some of you will have heard that a pike phalanx is unstoppable on flat ground like this plain. That is nonsense. A phalanx is only formidable when its line is unbroken. When you throw your javelins, those *pila* will break their line. Once you are among the enemy, they will be helpless. Their short cutting swords are useless against your sturdy shields. Their flimsy little shields cannot withstand your thrusting swords. You will scatter them like wind sweeping up leaves or lifting thatch from a roof!'

At the front, Paullus could hear well, but he was not totally reassured.

'Our cavalry outnumbers theirs by more than five to one. Once their horsemen have been chased from the field, their infantry will be surrounded. No phalanx has ever stood when hit in the flank and rear.'

That was more encouraging.

'These are the Achaeans that Metellus defeated at Skarpheia and Chaeronea. They are accustomed to defeat, because they are Greeks, and we are Romans. Now in desperation their numbers are made up, not of freemen, but of slaves. A slave should not wait for the hand of his master. A life of servitude, of the bite of the whip, does not prepare a man for the battlefield. They will never stand close to the steel!'

That was more like it, and the legionaries cheered lustily.

'Never forget that our cause is just. The Achaeans declared war on the Spartans. We are bound by sacred oaths to defend our allies. The gods favour our cause!'

This was slightly less rapturously received. The Spartans meant nothing to the legionaries.

Mummius made his steed prance as he struck a martial pose to end his speech. 'Only a rabble of slaves and effeminate Greeks stands between you and Corinth, a city overflowing with silver and gold. Sweep them aside, and it is yours! There is not one soldier in the ranks who will not return to Italy a rich man!'

As Mummius rode away through the maniples, back to his position at the rear of the centre, they cheered him to the skies.

'Gold and silver are no use in Hades,' Alcimus muttered.

'Stick with me, and no Greek is going to kill you,' Tatius said. 'Nothing and no one is going to stop me getting my hands on the plunder of Corinth.'

Trumpets rang out, and the Pergamene cavalry clattered off to take station on the right wing. Once they had departed, the enemy began to become visible through the slowly dispersing dust. A forest of spears, their tips flashing in the sun, could be seen above the roiling clouds. Here and there below them pinpoints of shields and armour glinted through the remaining murk. And then, like the breath of a god, a breeze sprang up in the west. It pulled aside the gloom, and revealed the enemy.

A low sigh came from the legionaries. The phalanx was about four hundred paces away. It was arrayed on the far slope of a previously unseen shallow dip in the ground. The phalanx stretched for more than half a mile. Solid and deep, like a huge armoured beast, it ran all the way back to the Saronic Gulf. The shields of those opposite the legion blazed in the sunshine.

Paullus felt his heart rise, and choke him. No power on earth could break through that mass of armed men. There were thousands upon thousands of them. They would walk forward and spit the Romans on those long pikes like quail.

One of the Sabines whimpered with terror. The crotch of his tunic was wet, piss running hot down his legs. A man in the rear ranks retched. Paullus felt his stomach turn at the smell of vomit.

'What the fuck is wrong with you!' Naevius bellowed. The blow to the head he had taken at the White Cliffs had done no lasting damage, but it had not improved his temper. 'What were you expecting, a flock of sheep?'

'They aren't slaves,' Alcimus said.

'Who gives a fuck about their parents?' Naevius roared. 'They are Greeks, and they are going to die. You know why they are going to die? Because you have been trained by me!'

The centurion jerked a thumb at the enemy. 'See those spear points wavering like a field of wheat? The men holding them are quaking. They are scared shitless of you! Although the gods only know why,' he added.

It broke the spell. The men laughed.

'Now put your shields down, rest them against your legs. I don't want you delicate girls tiring yourselves out,' Naevius said. 'Any of you got any wine in your flasks, pass it around. It will be an hour or more before the light infantry stop swanning around.'

Now the dust had cleared, Paullus could see a line of wagons beyond the Achaean phalanx. The tiny figures of women and children were visible. Were the Achaeans so confident of victory that they had brought their families to witness their triumph, or did their leaders think they would fight better under the eyes of their loved ones? Either way, it blocked their retreat. It was madness.

Someone gave Paullus a drink. The wine was unmixed and rough. It burnt as it slipped down his throat, but it warmed his belly. There was no way that he would let Naevius or his comrades down.

The prediction of the centurion was accurate. The light troops of both sides swarmed about in the hollow. They went in twos or threes, running forward, jinking and dodging, ducking back, the javelin men to the front, the bowmen hanging back. Missiles whirled through the air. Few found a mark, and no one came to close quarters.

'Here we go,' Naevius said.

From the right came a peal of trumpets and the tramp of horses. As if by mutual consent, the cavalry of the Achaeans and the allies of the Romans began to pace towards each other. At first they went at a walk, squadron after squadron, all in order and richly apparelled. It was obvious at a glance that there were far fewer Achaeans.

The trumpets sounded a sharper note. The troopers on both sides kicked on. The ground trembled beneath thousands of hooves as they moved to a canter. The air rang with the shouts and the rattle of their equipment.

The thunder of the charge reverberated in Paullus' chest. He found he was holding his breath.

An instant before the clash, just before they collided and the foremost riders and their mounts must be dashed to ruin, the Achaeans could be seen hauling on their reins. Their horses skidded about, some bored into each other, some men were unseated, a few horses went down. In a dozen heartbeats, the proud formation was transformed into a panicked herd, fleeing back the way they had come.

A full-throated roar rose from the watching legionaries.

The Achaeans raced past the flank of their phalanx. The Romans' Pergamene allies spurred in pursuit, cutting the rearmost from the saddle.

The roar of the legionaries faltered.

The Pergamene horsemen did not slacken their pace.

The legion fell silent.

All the cavalry – allied and enemy – pounded away out of sight to the south.

'Fucking Greeks,' Tatius said. 'No better on our side than the other.'

'Fucking cavalry,' Naevius said. 'Once they charge, there is never any getting them back. Still, no matter. Now we will have to earn our pay.'

The Cretan archers hared back through the gaps in the maniples. They were mercenaries. Only interested in their wages, they had no intention of being caught between the battle lines. The legion's own *velites* jogged off to take the open ground vacated by the horsemen. The Achaean light infantry moved in parallel. Doubtless they would continue their inconclusive skirmish.

'*Hastati*, form line!' Naevius ordered.

Even as the trumpeters relayed the command, the rear ranks trotted around to fill the spaces between the maniples. In no time, a continuous line of *hastati* faced the phalanx. But, looking over his shoulder, Paullus realised how much thinner and more fragile was the Roman formation. He would have given anything to be with the *principes* or *triarii*, safe behind the front line.

Roman trumpets gave the order: *prepare to advance.*

'Right, boys,' Naevius shouted, 'silence in the ranks. Listen for your orders. No one throw his *pila* until I say. Raise the war cry when you are in their faces.'

The men mumbled they understood. Paullus hoped his training would get him through this, prayed he would not let those around him down.

'You ready for war?' Naevius' voice carried through the maniple.

'Ready!' they bellowed back.

Three times came the call and response. Paullus felt it raise the hackles on his neck.

'At the slow military step, advance!'

The ground sloped a little, but it was not hard to keep place. Paullus could hear nothing but the rattle and clatter of armed men moving. He saw a swallow swooping low across the land ahead. Many men were about to suffer and die, but it was nothing to the graceful bird.

The Achaean phalanx was moving too. Very slowly, at little more than a shuffle, it edged down the slight incline. Its approach might be ponderous, but it was silent and somehow inexorable. The two forces would clash on the floor of the gentle valley.

Three hundred paces, two hundred. Dear gods, Paullus thought, how can anyone go through this more than once? He fought down an urge to break ranks, to run forward, get this over one way or another. Beside him, one of the Sabines was swearing continuously under his breath.

When they were about a hundred and fifty paces off, the Achaeans halted. Officers could be seen and heard trying to dress their ranks.

Moving in formation would be harder encumbered with an enormous heavy pike like a bargepole, twenty feet or more long.

The Romans maintained their slow pace.

When they were within a hundred paces, the pikes of the Achaeans swung down. The points of the front ranks bristled out like a hedge. Those to the rear sloped over the heads of those at the front. The phalanx resumed its steady advance.

The Achaeans were packed close, much tighter than the Romans. There was about six feet between the shoulders of the men on either side of Paullus. He would be facing two files of the enemy, the points of ten pikes. He looked at the faces of the leading Achaeans. The cheekpieces of their helmets were fastened. Only their eyes and noses could be seen. They revealed no humanity.

Fifty paces.

'First *pilum* ready!'

Paullus transferred the lighter of his two javelins to his right hand. The heavier remained in his left which gripped his shield.

Thirty paces.

'And ... throw!'

Three quick steps, half turned, right arm back, and Paullus hurled the *pilum*. Watching its flight, he got the heavier missile ready. The rain of javelins pelted down into the phalanx. He did not see his land, but here and there an Achaean went down, and a pike dropped to the ground.

'Second *pilum*, throw!'

Three more steps, right arm following through, then recovering balance, yanking out his sword.

The range was closer, the javelins heavier, and more Achaeans fell. But not enough, not nearly enough. Holes appeared in the barricade of spears, but they were filled as men jostled to take the places of those hit. Mummius was wrong. The *pila* had not broken the jutting barrier of steel that guarded the Achaeans.

'Draw swords! Charge!'

It was like running into a wall. Spearheads rammed into the leather and wood of Paullus' shield. They jarred him to a halt. Shield held low, the bottom rim almost on the earth, he hunkered down. The tip of a pike sliced by his shoulder. He slashed at it with his sword. The blade hacked a chunk out of the wood, but did not shear through the shaft. Another got under his shield, narrowly missed his boot.

A terrible scream, like a pig at the slaughterhouse. The leading Sabine was clutching at the pike that had run him through the stomach. The legionary following stumbled into his back. Another pike took him clean in the throat.

Paullus stared in horror. The inattention almost was fatal. A pike thrust harder than seemed human punched clean through his shield. The razor-sharp tip missed his face by a hand's breadth. And then he was fighting like a madman. All fear forgotten, swept away by the desire to survive. He chopped off the shaft poking through his shield. Bending low, he tried to force the pikes up and out of his way. To turn and run would open his defenceless back to the enemy. It would invite death. The only way out was through those ahead.

'Three paces back!'

The words meant nothing to Paullus. Using his shield as a battering ram, he forced his way into the furious heart of the pikes. Twisting and turning, lopping off spear points, he wormed his way deeper.

A strong hand caught the back of his mail coat, hauled him out.

'You fucking deaf, boy?' Naevius dragged him back. 'I give an order, you obey.'

Six or seven paces separated the wall of pikes and the panting line of legionaries. Both sides were stationary. Achaean officers were yelling, getting their men in order, working them up to cross over that space, to go back into the storm of fighting. The respite would not last long.

Paullus straightened up, and slipped. There was mud under foot. It had not rained. The mud was red. The ground was greasy with blood. Paullus was exhausted, his limbs shaking. He knew he could not face that again. Glancing at Tatius on his right, he saw the battle madness draining from the face of his friend. Alcimus looked no better. They were still alive, but they were spent. This time they would all run.

'We are done, boys,' Naevius called. 'Get ready to fall back, our battle is over.'

CHAPTER 22

Militia

608 Ab Urbe Condita (146 BC)

'AND ... RUN!'

Somehow it was harder to run than to remain facing the enemy. To run was to turn your back, to open your shoulder blades to the fatal thrust. The wicked tips of the pikes were only a few paces away. There were hundreds of them. It would be so easy for the men wielding them to charge forward. No one had a problem stabbing a fleeing man. It would be easier than spearing a fish.

'Fall back!'

Paullus glanced at Alcimus and Tatius. They looked as scared as he felt. None of them could summon the courage to move.

Naevius rapped Paullus across the shoulders with his vine stick. 'You fucking deaf? I gave you an order!'

The blow stung. Paullus turned and ran. Alcimus and Tatius came with him.

The first few steps were the worst. At any moment he was expecting the lancing pain as an Achaean pike snapped through the links of his mail, drove deep into his body, punched out through his chest.

All order was gone. The legionaries jostled into one another, got in each other's way. They fled like a herd of timid but clumsy animals with a lion at their backs. Paullus stumbled, nearly lost his footing. Alcimus must have sheathed his sword. He grabbed Paullus by the belt, yanked him back upright.

It was difficult running carrying a big heavy shield. Paullus wanted to throw the thing away. But if he did, he would have to face the wrath of Naevius. Civic crown or not, the centurion would not spare him. He blundered on with the awkward thing dragging at his arm and banging against his legs.

Then they were funnelling between two maniples of the *principes*. The Achaeans had not pursued them. Paullus was safe. By all the gods, he was not going to die – not now, not yet.

The *principes* did not call out any reproaches. The older men had seen battle before. They knew what was happening. Maybe they had hoped they would not have to fight, but their faces showed they were set on the grim task ahead.

The crush lessened and the stampede slowed. Paullus looked back. Already the rear ranks of the *principes* were trotting around to fill the gaps and present a new, unbroken line to the enemy.

Safe for the moment, the *hastati* jogged back between the *triarii*. They kept going for a hundred paces or more beyond the third line of veterans. Part of Paullus never wanted to stop – just keep running, back to the camp, to Megara, anywhere but here.

'Rally on the standards!' Paullus did not recognise the centurion who gave the command. The maniples of the *hastati* were all jumbled together.

Paullus saw the wolf standard of Naevius' maniple off to the left. Together with his friends he walked over. They moved stiffly, like old slaves, overworked and much beaten. When they got there, Paullus dropped his shield and sword, doubled over and threw up. He had eaten this morning – they had not known they would have to fight until after they had left camp – but now he brought up only bile. It was thin and acid in his mouth, and burnt in the back of his throat.

Tatius gave Paullus a wineskin. He rinsed his mouth and spat, then took a long pull. Suddenly he was very hungry. Alcimus produced some air-dried beef. Paullus tore at it like an animal, swallowed it barely chewed, much like Niger would back on the farm.

The blaring note of trumpets called their attention back to the front. The *principes* were going into action. Two volleys of *pila* – in quicker succession and better grouped than the earlier efforts of the *hastati* – arced down on the Achaeans. Their effect could not be judged. The backs of the *principes*, and the tall feathers nodding above their helmets, blocked any view of the enemy phalanx.

Actually it was getting hard to see anything. The breeze still blew from the east, but it had decreased. It no longer snatched away the dust, but pulled it slowly in great thick banks across the battlefield. Only to the right, where the wind came ashore from the Corinthian Gulf, could things be made out clearly. There the light infantry of both sides kept up a desultory pretence of combat. Having run out of javelins, occasionally two or three men would dart forward and throw a few stones. They were easy enough to dodge. No one ever seemed to get hit. They all knew the battle would be decided elsewhere, and probably considered that there was no point in risking their lives for nothing.

'On your feet, boys.' Naevius appeared as unmoved by the carnage as if he were at the theatre. 'Get in line.'

Numb from what they had experienced, the *hastati* shuffled together. Naevius took the roll call. The centurion consulted no written record. He knew all one hundred and twenty men by name. He knew who had been present this morning, and who was now among the fallen. Despite the savagery of the combat, only ten were missing – although all three of the Sabines were among them – and just four were too badly wounded to continue. The latter were to be helped to the aid post to the rear.

The *principes* were still fighting up ahead. The noise was oddly muted, like a distant storm. If they did not break the phalanx, it would be down to the *triarii*.

Realisation came to Paullus with another surge of nausea. The three lines of the Roman legion, the system of battlefield reliefs, was a perfect stratagem for a general. If the enemy broke ranks and chased those retiring, many legionaries would die; men like Paullus himself would be cut down as they fled. But that was a small price to pay for victory. The enemy would rush forward as a mob of individuals, and they would be easy pickings for the next line of Romans waiting in their disciplined maniples. If, like just now, the enemy stayed in line, they would have to steel themselves to go into combat again, not once but twice.

Paullus doubted that Naevius, or anyone else, could ever force him back into that storm of spears. To Hades with the high-flown talk of true Roman *virtus*, the innate manliness of the sons of Romulus. Courage was like a grain store on a farm. It contained only a finite amount. You could take grain out, but never put any back. Sooner or later, it would run out. And you could never tell when that would happen.

'Bollocks,' Tatius muttered.

The *principes* were falling back. Again the Achaeans must have maintained their discipline. No pursuit could be seen through the murk. The *principes* were re-forming in front of the *hastati*, and the *triarii* were getting into a continuous line.

'If only the fucking cavalry had not fucked off,' Tatius said. 'This would have all been over an hour ago.'

'Courage, boys,' Naevius said. 'We are not finished yet.'

'But it's down to the *triarii*,' Tatius said. It was a proverbial expression: the third and final throw of the dice. It was all or nothing now.

The *triarii* were armed with spears, not javelins With a brave shout, they levelled their weapons and surged forward. The sound of the clash rolled back like a clap of thunder.

The *triarii* knew their trade. They had stood close to the steel many times before. But they were massively outnumbered, and their spears were outreached by the Achaean pikes. Paullus knew that this was a fight they could not win.

'Sir.'

Naevius was studying the battle. He was beating his vine stick against his thigh, as if exorcising a daemon, or beating out an obscene thought.

'Sir.'

'What the fuck is it, Paullus?'

'We could do what the horsemen failed to do, sir.' To Hades with his empty store of courage. Something had to be done, or they would all die on this windswept plain between two seas.

'What?'

'Lead all the maniples of the *hastati* around to the right, sir. You are a senior centurion, they will follow you. The Achaean light infantry will not delay us. The general himself said no phalanx has ever stood when hit in the flank.'

'We obey orders. That is Roman discipline. Never leave the line. That is why we win. Mummius ordered us to stand and fight here.'

'But sir—'

'You know better than the consul, do you?'

'No, sir, but the dust – the general can't see. He has no idea what is happening here.'

Naevius turned his back on Paullus. He gazed out at the dust-shrouded battle line. The rear ranks of the *triarii* were giving ground. They were not ready to turn and run, but step by step they were being driven back.

'Fuck it!' Naevius shouted. 'Right face! Form column!'

He bellowed to the centurion of the maniple on the left to follow him, pass the word down the line.

It was almost joyous to be doing something, not just watching helplessly.

Naevius brought his face very close to that of Paullus. 'If this does not work, and we are punished for disobeying orders, for leaving the line, I will make sure that you are executed with me.'

Before Paullus could frame any reply, Naevius stalked off to the head of the column.

'At the quick step, forward!'

There was no time to lose. The *triarii* might break at any moment. They almost jogged towards the blue water, before wheeling to the left. Paullus felt exhilarated, but also bone weary. One last effort would decide this day.

Seeing them coming, the *velites* did more than cheer. Most attached themselves to the column. The Achaean light infantry took one look and fled away to the south.

'Keep moving!' Naevius was bellowing. 'At the run!'

They were pounding past the fighting line. The Achaeans in the rear ranks looked over with horror. The front fighters were too busy trying to stay alive.

'Halt!' They were no further from the flank of the phalanx than a boy could throw a stick. 'Face left!'

Paullus felt as if a rope had been tightened around his chest. Each breath was like inhaling smoke.

'Swords!' Naevius shouted. 'Thrust at the face or the crotch!'

Paullus realised that his sword was not in his hand. He must have sheathed it without knowing. He dragged the blade from the scabbard.

'Charge!'

The outer files of the Achaeans were trying to turn and bring their pikes to face this unexpected threat. The great long shafts were getting entangled.

Paullus set off with the others.

There were only two spear points facing him. He caught them on the face of his shield, deflected them to the side. But then a third jabbed at his chest. Paullus pivoted. But he was not advancing any more.

A blade smashed down and lopped off the head of the pike that was groping for Paullus. Dropping his shield, Tatius dived forward and rolled under the spears. Coming up, he stabbed the nearest Achaean in the groin.

'With me,' Tatius yelled.

Awakened from his daze, Paullus shoved the other two pikes aside and rushed into the fray.

An Achaean let go of his spear and fumbled for his sword. Paullus punched the tip of his sword into his face. With a backhand blow, he cut another man down.

Tatius was fighting like a man possessed. He was in the midst of the enemy, his sword moving like lightning. Paullus tried to reach him. Another Achaean got in the way. With two swings, Paullus chopped the man's small shield into firewood. The silver decoration offered no resistance. The general had been right – man to man the Achaeans were helpless against Roman arms.

And then the Achaean gave up. His arms fell to his sides. From the right, Alcimus slashed open the man's thigh. The Achaean fell to his hands and knees. Paullus killed him with a blow to the back of the neck.

And then it was over. Like a huge tree hollowed out by termites, the Achaean phalanx collapsed. Where there had been fighting men was now a panicked throng. They shoved and clawed each other out of the way. Thousands of men were streaming away to the south. But their escape was blocked by the wagons containing their women and children. This was going to be a massacre.

Paullus stood, mind empty of any thoughts. He leant on the top of his shield. It was the only way he could stay on his feet. There was a cut he had not noticed taking on his thigh. There was blood and gore on his blade, on his hands, up his forearms. So this was glory.

Tatius was bent over, searching the corpse of the man Paullus had butchered.

'He was mine,' Paullus said.

'Too late, brother,' Tatius replied. 'You have a farm to return to. The wealth of Achaea is going to earn me one. My need is greater than yours.'

CHAPTER 23

Patria

609 Ab Urbe Condita (145 BC)

THE SHARE BEAM WAS OAK, the plough beam holm oak, and the poles and stilt were made of elm. Paullus was ploughing the top field, the one over the crest on the far side of the Sabutus. As the field was on a hillside, he drew the plough across the slope, with the share alternately pointing uphill and down. The furrows ran smooth and straight. Their ordered rows reminded him of the files of the Achaean phalanx at the isthmus, before the latter had collapsed in mortal panic. The memory did not trouble him. It was better to think of the battle than what came after.

The metal blade of the share caught on a thick root and he halted the oxen. They were a new pair. Nine years old, in their prime, they were accustomed to the yoke and to each other. They would not fight in the furrow. Paullus had not wanted to spend the money. It was not parsimony, but a reluctance to give credence to the rumours about his hidden wealth. After the unsettling conversation with Fidubius and Vibius at the hunting party, he was very sensitive to the stories that he had brought a fortune back from Corinth.

Paullus took down the billhook from where it hung on the stilt. Bending to the work, laboriously he sliced through the tough root. Twice he had to stop with a fit of coughing. The fever had come on him after the hunt. It had lasted only four days, but had left a persistent racking cough. Finally the task was done. It was worth the effort. Better he work up a sweat than tear the root out with the plough and risk either breaking the share or straining the oxen.

Rehanging the billhook, he stood and stretched his aching back. There was a bitter wind. It blew over the crest, down the wild, rocky cliff, through the olives and vines, and then out across the open plough land. It was cold enough to flay an ox. Paullus rubbed his hands together. His cloak and sword belt would have got in the way, and he had left them with his lunch by the water trough at the lower side of the field. In this weather it was better to be moving. He gathered the whip and reins, and stirred the beasts back into motion.

Paullus cast a lonely figure as he plodded behind the team, crossing and recrossing the windswept hillside. Pastor had driven the flock down from the Sila ready for the winter, and Paullus had left Eutyches with the shepherd to settle the sheep into their sheds. Paullus had wanted to be on his own. The eternal rhythm of ploughing, the rich, clayey smell of the turned soil, helped him think.

Perhaps it was the lingering illness that had made him more taciturn than usual with Minado the previous evening. But he had much on his mind. Four or five nights ago there had been an intruder on the farm. Paullus had been the last to leave the barn and the first there in the morning. He had noticed at once that some of the implements were not exactly where he had left them. Nothing had been stolen, but someone had been there. Paullus had questioned Eutyches and Pastor. They said they had not stirred from the slave quarters all night. There was no reason to disbelieve them. A stranger had crept into the farmyard. It was strange that Niger had not barked. But the hound was getting old, and he slept a great deal.

Two mornings later, the theta charm had been missing from his belt. It had been hanging with his armour by the fireplace. His mother had accused the new maid. The girl had denied the theft. The ornament was copper. It had no value. Of course, it could have been lost the day before, fallen off somewhere in the fields, but Paullus was certain that he would have noticed when he took off the belt. From then on Paullus had locked the farmhouse door at night.

And then last night the Kindly Ones had returned. There had been no hint of their presence since the Temple of the Hero. Paullus had dared to hope that saving Minado had been some sort of redemption. That fragile optimism had been shattered when he awoke to hear their rasping breath and smell their foul corpse odour. All three sisters had been standing in the dark at the foot of the bed. The old women did not speak to him, but murmured to each other. Their words were inaudible, but their demeanour was that of a jury considering the verdict.

'The past cannot be undone,' Paullus had said. 'What happened in Corinth was not my fault. I did not wish it to happen. I should not be cursed.'

They had not replied, but regarded him with deliberation. And then they were gone.

Paullus pulled the oxen to a stop and cleaned the share with a stick tipped with a scraper.

Sometimes he wondered if it was all in his mind, if what he had done in the last house in Corinth had permanently unhinged some delicate mechanism that ordered his perceptions. He would not be the first man driven mad by guilt. Hercules had locked himself in a dark room, shunning all contact with humanity after he had flung his own children into the fire. Alexander had tried to starve himself to death when he had drunkenly murdered his friend.

Paullus checked the oxen were yoked as tightly as possible. It kept their heads up and prevented their necks getting chafed.

The Macedonian army had begged Alexander to eat and drink, to preserve himself for them. Hercules had been told the road to redemption by the Delphic Oracle. No deity or army was going to intervene for Paullus. Deliverance could only come from within.

The team was nearing the plantation. Wheat would be sown between the rows of olive trees. Paullus fitted the oxen with muzzles of soft basketry to stop them nibbling the leaves.

Deliverance could only come from admitting what he had done.

Paullus cracked the whip above their heads, and the great strength of the oxen took the strain. As the plough got moving, Paullus doubled up coughing.

It saved his life.

The arrow hissed through the air where his neck had been. It was close enough to feel the wind of its passing. Instinctively, Paullus threw himself to the right. He rolled, then scrambled to his feet, getting the team between him and his assailant.

Leaning against the broad shoulder of the near ox, he was paralysed with shock. Someone was trying to kill him. Not in Corinth, but here in his own field. Not a foreigner, but one of his own fellow townsmen. Someone he must know was trying to kill him. The thing was incredible.

Think, you fool. Think, or you are dead.

Paullus risked a peek around the beast's head. The arrow had come from down the slope, from somewhere near where he had left his belongings. He saw movement behind the drystone boundary wall of the field.

Stay here, and the bowman will shift his position. Easy enough to work round the edge of the field, get a clear shot and pick him off. The plantation was only some thirty paces off uphill.

Paullus set off. He ran as fast as he could, trying to keep the oxen between him and the archer.

Twenty paces to the safety of the olives and vines.

Another arrow. This time from ahead, and off to the left. It seemed to accelerate as it closed. Paullus threw himself down. Stones grazed his arms, mud splattered his face.

Before his mind had accepted that the shaft had missed, he was up again. Now he angled to the right. It took him away from the lee of the oxen. Both bowmen could take a shot. He jinked and sidestepped. To the left, then to the right, then to the right again – anything to throw off their aim, to avoid a predictable pattern.

He heard rather than saw another arrow. It thrummed behind his back. Another whipped past his face.

Ten paces to the treeline. The damp earth was pulling at his feet, weighing down his boots. Paullus felt his luck running out. He dived forward, hit the ground, rolled, then scrabbled like an animal on all fours into the plantation.

The olives were in widely spaced rows. The vine trellises ran between their trunks. They made it hard to see up the slope, but looking from side to side there was nothing but lanes of bare earth waiting to be ploughed between the trees.

Paullus crashed through the first row of vines, snapping the thin poles, trampling the tender plants. He dashed across the open space and burst through the next line. They could track his progress by the noise. But that was less important than getting deep into the trees.

Seven or eight rows in, he risked turning and running down the avenue between the trees. He ran for forty paces, then worked his way quietly through the next trellis uphill. Panting, he cowered against the silvery trunk of an ancient olive.

He turned and peered back down through the foliage to the ploughed land. The oxen stood passively, untroubled by this human activity that meant nothing to them. Then Paullus glimpsed what he had expected. The first archer was crossing the field. A slight figure in a dark tunic, limbs blackened, face disguised by the mask of a wolf. Bow in hand, arrow nocked, he was scanning the plantation, but moved confidently, without hurry. There was something familiar about his gait, but there was no time to dwell on that.

The other bowman now would be somewhere off to Paullus' right. He would be sneaking up through the trees, seeking to finish what they had started. This was the time for Paullus to act, while the two men were separated. Ghost up to the one in the plantation. Turn the hunter into the hunted. Get in close, so he could not use the bow, and kill him. It did not have to be done quietly. Once he was dead, Paullus would have his bow. If the slender figure in the field did not flee, Paullus could shoot him down.

But Paullus had no weapon. Not even a knife. That was on his belt with his sword. The billhook! Hades, he was a fool. He had forgotten the billhook. It was still hanging on the stilt of the plough.

If he could not fight, then he must hide.

This was no good. In a forest he could have concealed himself. But not in the ordered lanes of this plantation. All the second bowman had to do was move upslope, carefully checking each open avenue, and sooner or later he would run his quarry to earth. There was nowhere to hide among the olives, and above was only the cliff. Dotted with wild junipers and brambles, it offered no cover. The hopelessness of utter despair. There was nothing he could do.

The brambles! Of course, the brambles on the rock face above that screened his childhood hiding place. All he had to do was reach the tiny cave unseen. No one else knew it was there.

Now Paullus went with more caution. The cave was uphill and to the right. Thank the gods, it was away from the bowman already scouring the plantation. Paullus scurried down each avenue until he spotted a gap in the vines where he could crawl through without making a sound. His ascent was noiseless, but painfully slow. A rising tide of panic urged him to haste. At any moment the point of an arrowhead might punch into his defenceless back. Fighting down the fear, he continued his stealthy progress.

Eventually – it seemed an age – he reached the final line of trees. He had come out where he intended. There, not twenty paces away, at the foot of the cliff, were the bushes that obscured the entrance to the cave. The incline to them was not steep, but it was completely bare. And there were loose stones. Paullus hesitated in an agony of indecision. Cross the exposed rock fast and risk being heard, or slowly increasing the chance of being seen?

Somewhere close behind a branch snapped.

Paullus went up fast, but watching where he placed his feet.

There was no cry of alarm.

The gap between the brambles and the rock was narrower than Paullus remembered. The bushes had grown, or he was bigger. He used an arm to sweep back the wiry branches, ignoring the barbs tearing his skin. Sideways he forced himself through, shielding his face with his other arm. And there was the entrance. It was only half as wide again as his shoulders. He wriggled into the dark.

The floor of the little cave ran upwards. It stretched no more than eight feet into the cliff. There was no room to turn round. Paullus wedged himself as far in as possible, drew up his legs.

There was nothing to but wait. There was no point in praying. The gods did not listen to men like him. The odds against some neighbouring farmer coming to this remote place were enormous.

Once his eyes became accustomed to the gloom, and his body was blocking most of the light, he looked with wonder on the small relics left from his childhood. His name scratched in the wall, the letters lighter than the rest of the rock. A small, crudely carved toy soldier. He had whittled it himself, an image of the man he had always wanted to become. He had become that man, and it had brought him wealth, but nothing else that was good. And now he was reduced again to hiding in the dark, like the child he had once been. Except now he was hiding from much worse than his father's disapproval and the lash of his belt. There was no way out of here. If they found him, he would be dragged out feet first, and butchered.

Paullus heard the stones sliding out from under boots. Each step produced a small cascade. They were getting closer. Had they seen his furtive scurry up to the cave?

The footsteps were very loud, the chink and scrape of each pebble audible.

Paullus stilled his breathing.

The footsteps stopped by the bushes.

The scratches on Paullus' arm were stinging. Dear gods, was there blood on the brambles? Would they see?

Moving inch by inch, Paullus craned his neck and looked down over his huddled body. In the sunlight beyond the undergrowth, he could see a pair of boots. The man was standing right there. The boots were solid, workmanlike, the boots of a countryman. The figure was so close Paullus could smell him: the feral reek of the pelt of a wolf, human sweat and something sweeter, cinnamon or spikenard.

Suddenly Paullus felt the tickling in his throat, the desperate need to cough. He tried to swallow. The sensation was worse. He buried his face in his arm, breathed very shallowly through his nose. At any moment he would lose the unequal fight.

And, like a miracle, the boots moved off. Coughing forgotten, Paullus lay in his lair and listened to the receding crunch of the footsteps.

After a time they were gone, but there was still nothing to be done except wait.

CHAPTER 24

Militia

One Year Earlier

608 Ab Urbe Condita (146 BC)

REVENGE WAS A SACRED DUTY. It had to be proclaimed and enacted in public. Rome would never shirk the duty of revenge. Any show of compassion would be interpreted as weakness. Enemies would be emboldened, and the safety of Rome threatened. Even after the bloody sack and burning of Corinth there had to be yet more dire punishment.

'Father Dis, Veiovis, Manes, or whatever name it is right to call you, may you fill the city of Corinth with dread. May the people who live in this place, in its fields and regions, be deprived of the light of the heavens.'

Paullus watched the Consul Mummius pronounce the curse on those captured in the taking of Corinth. The survivors had been herded together outside the city, between the long walls that led to the port of Lechaion. Despite the slaughter, there were many thousands of them. They came from all over the Peloponnese; Corinth had been the capital of the Achaean League. The captives were surrounded by soldiers. Additional legionaries had filed in without display, but they had been seen. Clinging to one another, the prisoners were terrified – men, women and children alike.

'May you judge this city and its fields, and its people's lives and lifetimes cursed and execrated according to those laws under which enemies have throughout time been cursed.'

A thin keening rose from those who expected to die.

'I call on you, Mother Earth, and you, Jupiter, as witnesses.'

When Mummius mentioned Earth, he touched the ground with his hands; when he mentioned Jupiter, he raised his hands to heaven; and when he took the vow, he touched his chest with his hands.

The ritual complete, Mummius regarded them dispassionately.

'By the laws of war, all your lives are forfeit. But the clemency of Rome is infinite. Only those *most* guilty will suffer.'

The wailing stopped.

'Half a century ago, a Roman general, Titus Quinctius Flamininus, stood before you and proclaimed the freedom of Greece. You and your fathers repaid him with intrigue and treachery. Violating your oaths, you declared an unjust war on our sworn ally Sparta. Despite your sins, I reaffirm the proclamation of Flamininus. You will all go free!'

There was a stunned silence. Before it could be broken, Mummius continued. 'Except for those slaves wrongly freed to bear arms against Rome. They will once again return to bondage. And there will be no freedom for those whose evil madness led the rest astray. The leaders of the Achaean League will be executed. The city of Corinth was the root of the wickedness. All her citizens and their families will be sold into slavery.'

There was a collective gasp as the hopes of thousands were dashed.

'Those of you who have been pardoned can now prove your repentance by seizing the malefactors and handing them over to the troops.'

Scuffles broke out as those who had been spared rushed to prove their new-found loyalty to Rome.

That, Paullus thought, was one way of sorting the wheat from the chaff.

'O thrice and four times happy Greeks who perished then.' The child who shouted the line from the *Odyssey* was being held by a rough-looking man who gripped the boy's mother with his other hand.

Mummius smiled. 'We Romans are not barbarians. Homer was the divine poet. Let that child and his family go free.'

Such was the whim of a conqueror.

All the refugees had dispersed to the four corners of the Peloponnese. All the Corinthians and their families, with the exception of the boy that knew the *Odyssey* and his relatives, had been sold. Wherever there was an army, one that had not been defeated, there were slave traders, like fleas on a stray dog. So many men, women and children had been on the block that the prices had tumbled. You could have picked up an entire family for a few coins. A pretty boy or girl to take to bed had cost little more.

Corinth was deserted and defenceless. With much effort her walls had been torn down. Not all the walls had been slighted, but large stretches lay in rubble. Now it was the turn of the buildings and their contents. Those statues and pictures too heavy and bulky to have been taken in the frenzy of the sack were being crated up as plunder. The minor works of art were to be given to Rome's ally the King of Pergamum. The major ones were destined for the consul. But Mummius was a modest and virtuous man. None of the precious things would be displayed in his own home. Instead they would be dedicated in temples or sent to deserving communities in Italy and Greece. Modest and virtuous Mummius might be, but he was a man of great ambition. A flamboyant gesture of piety was good for the reputation of any politician. And gifts that created clients in towns across the empire were an asset to any patron. It might be that renouncing any personal claims to artistic masterpieces had caused the consul little pain. It was said that in the contracts with the shippers Mummius had insisted on clauses that any of the old masters damaged or lost in transit had to be replaced.

Paullus was unsure if the rumour about the consul was true. Using a block and pulley, they had just loaded the last of the statues from the Temple of Apollo onto a wagon. Paullus had helped his new tent-mates. He worked with them, but he was not a part of their tight brotherhood. All his own companions were gone. Naevius had assigned him to a tent that had suffered one casualty. The members of his new squad were respectful, but kept their distance. In part it was awe of a man who had won the civic crown. Yet any soldier who had lost all his previous companions might be considered the bearer of bad luck. And there was the disappearance of Alcimus and Tatius. Three men had gone to plunder, but only one had emerged from the burning streets. And Paullus had been carrying two laden sacks.

At least Paullus was well looked after. Onirus, the Bruttian camp servant, had taken it upon himself to care for him. When the other members of the tent suggested that Onirus should help the one servant they shared, the slender young Bruttian had refused point blank. If any of them were awarded the *corona civica*, he might consider cooking their food and mending their kit.

Despite their proximity, Paullus and Onirus had not become close. Paullus was considerate and had given the Bruttian a generous share of the plunder. Onirus was grateful and carried out his duties with diligence. Yet the unresolved fate of Alcimus and Tatius was always present and prevented any intimacy.

The war was over and the settlement of Greece underway. That was how it was styled by Mummius: the *settlement*. The Greeks might have called it something less anodyne. The territory of

Corinth had been handed to the nearby city of Sicyon. It was not a gift. The land was declared the property of Rome. The people of Sicyon would pay rent. Thebes and Chalcis, the two cities outside the Peloponnese that had supported the Achaeans, also had their walls demolished. To forestall any further act of rebellion, or attempts to cast off the benign oversight of Rome, every Greek city was disarmed. All leagues of the Greeks were to be dissolved. As well as the Achaeans, the ancestral confederations of the Phocians and Boeotians were abolished. The constitutions of many cities were changed. Rome had never trusted democracies. The poor were too easily worked up into a mob by demagogues. They were too volatile and they lacked foresight. Far better the cities were governed by oligarchies of the rich. Property owners were more likely to show prudence. Those with much to lose were likely to heed the will of Rome, especially if Rome had placed them in power. Such wealthy men of culture understood the realities of empire. If they did the bidding of Rome, then Rome would ensure their continued dominance over their fellow citizens.

The just cause of the war was not forgotten. Let no one think that Rome had fought for gain or her own advancement. The Achaeans were ordered to pay a fine of two hundred talents to Rome's ally Sparta. That it would take the Achaeans several lifetimes to raise such a staggering sum was of no consequence. Lest the Spartans grew too proud, or might be seduced by foolish dreams of past greatness, their petition to have the Temple of Diana, and its lands, restored to them from their neighbours in Messene was rejected. From now on Greece would be ruled by the Roman governor of Macedonia, and Sparta, and all other Greek cities, should accept their status as provincial backwaters.

Everything was done by the due legal processes of Rome. Mummius was advised by a commission of ten other senators. Of course,

it was quite fitting that one of the commission was Mummius'
own father.

'Right,' Naevius said, 'now for the statue in the house over there.'

They walked past the stoa that had contained the Achaean arsenal. All the racks of weapons and suits of armour had already
been removed. Nothing remained of the Achaean materials of
war except the great pyramids of artillery stones, which had been
judged too heavy and not worth taking.

This quarter of Corinth had escaped the fire. The house was
just as it had been the year before. The open archway without
gates, which gave a view into the atrium, was unchanged. Paullus
remembered the mob jostling through the opening, the embassy
with locked shields against the far wall, the old man whose throat
was cut at the feet of the statue, the child whose brains were dashed
out against the wall.

The statue was still on its plinth in the centre of the atrium. The
marble image of Philopoemen was undamaged. The old Achaean
general still advanced towards the gate in martial pose.

'Wait.' A young military tribune had followed them.

They had just got the ropes round the statue. It looked rather like
a lynching.

'The consul has ordered all statues of Philopoemen are to be left
standing.'

'Our orders are to remove them, sir,' Naevius said.

'Your orders have been changed.'

'Why?'

'That is not your concern.' After the brusque rejoinder, the good
manners of generations of senatorial breeding took over. 'Polybius,
the Achaean historian, has prevailed upon the consul. Philopoemen is known as the *last of the Greeks*, and Polybius is a confi-
dant of both Mummius and Scipio Aemilianus, the conqueror of
Carthage.'

'Which building next, sir?'

'Report to Lucius Aurelius Orestes back in the camp. The legate wants your maniple for a special mission.'

'Revenge is a duty,' Orestes said. 'Diaeus is alive. He fled from the isthmus and was not found among the dead or apprehended here in Corinth.'

'Much of the city went up in flames, sir,' Naevius said. 'There are many unaccounted for in collapsed buildings.'

'The last sighting was on the Acrocorinth. It was untouched by the fires. His home town is Megalopolis in Arcadia. Your maniple will act as my escort.'

'The countryside is still unsettled, sir.'

'A maniple should be enough to defend ourselves. To take more men implies we are anxious about our security.'

Orestes looked thoughtful, as if some further explanation was necessary. 'Diaeus was one of the instigators of the revolt. Enemies of Rome have to be hunted down. The Achaean general must be captured. It is necessary that he walks in chains through the streets of Rome behind the chariot of Mummius in the triumphal procession. Afterwards he will pay for his crimes.'

'When do we leave, sir?'

'In the morning.'

The march took five days. They went south from Corinth into pale, grey-brown hills. Ridge after ridge of blue crests showed in the distance. They passed through Nemea, and on the second day came down to the green plain of Argos. They camped by the sea at a place called Lerna. The next morning they ascended a river valley to the west, where the sides rose like walls. Further on the road zigzagged up to the heights, and opened views back to the sea and the mountains beyond the Gulf of Argos. They came to an upland plain and the city of Tegea. Picking up the headwaters of the Helisson in the next range of mountains, the road followed the river all the way down to Megalopolis.

Nemea, Argos, Tegea – all were known to Paullus from schooldays, from reading Herodotus and Thucydides. In reality they looked unprepossessing and run down, as if Corinth had sucked all the wealth out of the rest of the Peloponnese.

The stages were long and the route tough, but the legionaries had been toughened by the campaign. The locals were wary, but not overtly hostile. At the approach of the Romans, the peasants drove their flocks to hidden places in the hills. But peasants anywhere, if they had any sense, did the same when they saw soldiers coming down the road. In the towns the local notables, the heirs of the proud Argives and Tegeans of history, rushed to offer provisions and lodgings. They fell over themselves to execrate the leaders of the Achaean League. Never had they approved of the calamitous policies of Critolaus or Diaeus. Some admitted that they had seen Diaeus in headlong flight through their town. The silence of the others somewhat undermined their professions of delight at the new Roman order.

The Helisson river divided the city of Megalopolis into two. The civic buildings were on the north bank. The town councillors had come out of their offices and were waiting in the marketplace. They greeted Orestes effusively. The legate listened with good manners to the lengthy speeches, never betraying any doubts about the sincerity of their sentiments. The orations were couched in the Attic Greek of the past. It was the language of Demosthenes and Plato that the schoolmaster in Temesa had beaten into Paullus. It was the preserve of the educated. Paullus wondered how much was understood by the unwashed loitering in the marketplace. After a time, he stopped listening to the elaborate figures of rhetoric.

Eventually, Orestes replied. He too spoke in the antique dialect of philosophy. The Achaeans had been in the grip of a fever or madness. Their feet had been set on a calamitous path, as if by evil daemons. Only the guilty need fear. Where was Diaeus?

Orotundity was cast aside as they hurried to give up their fellow townsman. All gabbled at once. One or two, so overcome by their eagerness, even lapsed into the common tongue of the streets, used foul language and uncouth words. The traitor had returned. All Megalopolis had shunned Diaeus. No one would speak to the man who had brought tragedy down on the heads of all the Greeks. Diaeus had fled to his country estate. It was at no distance, to the south-west, on the road to Messene. You could not miss the house. It stood alone, next to the sanctuary of the Manes, and the tumulus of Orestes, the legate's unfortunate namesake. They gave every piece of information they could about the locality. Their offer to all act as guides was politely refused. One councillor could show the way.

The legionaries were just allowed time for a swallow of wine, and a hunk of bread and cheese, before setting off.

The house was indeed only about a mile from the city. It was square and solid, and presented a blank face to the outside world. There were only two doors and they were shut. The windows were high and they were barred. There was no sign of life. Orestes ordered the legionaries to surround the dwelling.

It was beneath the dignity of a legate of Rome to hammer on the door. The task was given to Naevius.

'Open in the name of Rome!' The centurion used the pommel of his sword to batter the boards.

There was no response.

It was hot standing in the afternoon sun in full armour. Swallows banked and turned in the sky. Cicadas called to each other in scrub by the roadside. From somewhere came the scent of wood smoke.

'Open the door or we will break it down!'

That would be easier said than done. The door was massive and banded with iron. There was no suitable timber nearby to fashion a battering ram.

Not far from the house, on the left side of the road, was the sanctuary of the Manes. The earth mound behind was surmounted by a finger of stone. The Manes was another name for the Furies, or the Kindly Ones. After the murder of his mother, they had hounded Orestes to this place. Here, in his madness, he had bitten off his own finger. The pain had done a little to bring him to his senses. The old women had no longer appeared to him clad in the black of the underworld, but the white raiment of the Olympian gods. A poor exchange for the pain and the loss of a finger.

'We will have to send a detachment for a ram, sir. Unless we take a beam from the sanctuary.'

'That might be unwise, centurion, especially given my cognomen.'

'Look, sir!'

Diaeus appeared on the flat roof. With him was a woman, who hugged herself so tightly it suggested that if she relaxed she might collapse. Diaeus himself was dressed as he had been when he confronted the Roman embassy the year before at Corinth, in the same immaculate Greek cloak and tunic. Again his posture was composed, his right arm across his chest, and the hand hidden in the folds of the material. But now he moved awkwardly, as if his joints did not altogether obey his commands.

'Surrender!' Orestes demanded.

Diaeus drew himself up. 'To be led in chains and jeered by the mob in Rome? To be strangled in the dark?'

'Give yourself up, Diaeus,' the guide shouted up. 'Think of your fellow citizens. Do not bring the wrath of Rome on Megalopolis.'

Diaeus made a gesture of contempt. 'Philopoemen was indeed the last of the Greeks. Even he could not unite us. Every Greek city

THE RETURN | 249

thinks only of itself, of its own temporary advantage or safety. That weakness had undone us. It led to Macedonian domination, and now to Roman enslavement.'

'The senate will decide your fate,' Orestes said.

'The same men who ordered the destruction of Corinth, of Carthage, of a hundred other places? Romulus was suckled by a wolf. Her milk runs in your blood. You are no better than voracious beasts. Your greed has driven you to rape the world. No people, no matter how poor, can escape your avarice. No isolated hamlet or remote mountain valley will ever be safe from your lust.'

'The gods know,' Orestes said, 'Rome only fights to defend herself and her allies. Victory is the proof of the justice of our wars.'

'The gods are far away and do not care for mankind,' Orestes said. 'You use their name to cloak your villainy. You care nothing for Sparta. You made a treaty with them to give you an excuse to crush Achaea. Our freedom was an affront to your pride, the riches of Corinth a spur to your desire. You yourself, Roman with an accursed name, demanded conditions you knew we could never meet. You forced us to war.'

'Sir,' Paullus spoke quietly. There were wisps of smoke issuing from the joints in the door. 'The house is alight.'

'Diaeus, this is madness,' Orestes said. 'Would you let your wife burn to death?'

'Better that than be outraged by your soldiers, then sold as a chattel.'

'You have my solemn vow, she will be unharmed.'

'Your word is worthless.'

Smoke was pouring out of the chimneys, coiling up from the roof itself.

'For the sake of the gods, let her go,' Orestes said.

Diaeus ignored him, addressed the others assembled there. 'You legionaries are fools. The plunder of every continent flows into Rome.

How many of you will see any of it? It all goes into the coffers of the senators and their high-born friends. You march and die to make the senators rich. While you are campaigning your farms are ruined, your families driven out, your land taken. Your own commanders steal your land. You are fighting to dispossess yourselves.'

There was a groan, and a roar, as something collapsed inside the house. The first flames could be seen above the parapet.

'It is not too late,' Orestes said.

'No, it is far too late. I took the hemlock when I saw you approach.'

Diaeus turned to his wife. She did not flinch, but stood as docile as a heifer at the altar. Diaeus took her in his arms, kissed her on the forehead. And then the knife was in his hand, and he drove it upwards into her body. She crumpled, clinging to him. Stiffly, they tottered towards the flames. And then she was gone.

Bloodied and defeated, Diaeus faced them one last time.

'*For I know this thing well in my heart, and my mind knows it:*
There will come a day when sacred Ilion shall perish.'

There was a dignity to the face with the heavy jowls, to the balding head, as he recited the words of Homer.

'I curse every last one of you, every son of Rome. May the earth lie lightly on you, so the dogs can dig you up.'

And he turned and walked into the flames, and was seen no more.

CHAPTER 25

Patria

609 Ab Urbe Condita (145 BC)

After the footsteps had gone, there was nothing to do but wait. The cave was tiny. Paullus was cramped and very cold. He shivered, hugged himself and bit his knuckles to stop his teeth chattering. Sometimes he could not help but cough. After every muffled bout, he was terrified. Were they still nearby? Had they heard? At any moment would he be dragged out, like a rat from its hole, and butchered? He listened, strained to hear every sound. There was nothing except the wind sighing through the olive trees, and further off the oxen bellowing their distress. Tied to the plough, the baskets on their muzzles, they would be thirsty and hungry.

Paullus imagined the knife brought close to his face, the agony as it punctured the soft globe of an eye. First one, then the other, the screaming darkness that would follow. His jaws wrenched open, rough fingers grasping his tongue, the serrated blade sawing. His own blood in his throat, choking him. Hands reaching for his manhood, the blade about its hideous task.

Would they mutilate him while he was still alive? He had seen what they had done to Hirtius and Junius. They took pleasure in what they did. But he was a veteran, trained to fight. Alive, he remained a threat, even unarmed and outnumbered, even if wounded and bound, and he would not let himself be bound. They would know he had killed before, and would have no qualms about doing so again. They would know about the bandits in the Sila, and a man did not win the civic crown without shedding blood. They would be cautious, not risk indulging their pleasure in torture. It would be a quick death.

There were two of them, and they took pleasure in what they did. From the start, Paullus had never believed the killings were the work of the Hero of Temesa. He knew what it was to be haunted. The Kindly Ones had seen to that. The murders were not the work of a daemon, but of men. At first, when he saw the desecrated remains of Junius, he had thought it was a brigand, a lone man driven mad by solitude and rejection, seeking a twisted vengeance on the world. But, in the wild, the bandits had a sort of community. Those taken at Blood Rock had known nothing about the mutilated corpses. And there were two of them. It had taken two men to force Hirtius into the boiling pitch. There had been two shadowy figures slipping away from the Temple of Polites, two men just now seeking his life. The odds were long against two individuals, both sharing a motiveless desire to inflict suffering and death, finding each other in a small town like Temesa. The insane did not work well in harness, like a team of biddable oxen. Madmen did not form compacts, then efficiently put them into execution.

Both the victims had been Roman. The Bruttians had more than enough reasons to want revenge on their conquerors. Their grandparents had been raped and killed, and enslaved in vast numbers. Their best land had been seized. Now they watched Romans living on their ancestral farms. They were outcasts in their own country. More than enough reasons. But they had come to kill the girl in the temple, and Minado was a Bruttian. Not the Bruttians, then. Yet Paullus was convinced the killings were not senseless. They were designed to spread fear. The causes must lie deep in the fractured community of Temesa, a claustrophobic small town where the poor hated the rich and the rich despised the poor, and petty animosities grew and blossomed into hatred. Paullus had his suspicions, but he had no proof.

At long last the light outside faded. Paullus had to leave, but it took a great effort of will to force himself to move. Suddenly the small cleft of rock seemed like a sanctuary. Like a timid animal, he was safe in his hole.

Be a man. He was unsure if he muttered the injunction aloud. The interminable hours of apprehension and discomfort had taken their toll.

Feet first, wincing at every noise, he wriggled out of his hiding place. Not pausing, he forced his way through the brambles and scrambled down the slope to the trees.

Back in cover, he leant against the bark of an olive. It was dark. There was a waning moon, but it was often obscured by the black clouds scudding in from the unseen sea. He listened intently. Small, nocturnal rustlings, as furtive animals sought to feed or to prey on each other. An owl hooted and was answered from far off. Occasionally, one of the oxen lowed miserably, and with little hope of succour. No sounds that did not belong to the peace of the night.

Paullus ached all over. Gingerly, he eased the stiffness out of his limbs, back and neck. Every movement hurt. He was light-headed with hunger and anxiety. Was there any fight left in him? There was nothing to be gained by staying here. He had to face whatever was in the darkness.

Slowly, he flitted from one tree to another. Stopping in the blackness under the boughs, every sense alert in the gloom of the night. What was it the brigand chief had said at Blood Rock? Every night must be like this for the slave-king of Nemi, always patrolling, always waiting for the next escaped slave who would steal up, intent on his death, and on taking his place. Every night must be a time of terror.

Paullus moved along through the plantation, then down along the drystone wall by the stream. His first thought was to get to his sword belt by the water trough. As he got near, he realised the danger. The slighter-built archer had shot from close by, and must have noticed the set-aside possessions. There was just enough light to take a shot. If Paullus had been setting an ambush, it would have been here. Like a hunter at a waterhole, you waited at the place to which you knew your quarry must be drawn.

When he was some thirty paces away, Paullus flattened himself to the ground. No matter how hard he tried, he could detect no lurking presence: no sound, sight or smell. It was hours since the attack. Perhaps they had left, abandoning, or at least postponing, the attempt. In a small town like Temesa, everyone knew each other's business. It was difficult to absent yourself from where others expected you to be for the best part of a day without drawing comment.

He thought about his own home. They would have expected him to return before dark. How long ago since nightfall? The oxen needed to be fed and watered, bedded down. Even now would Eutyches or Pastor be crossing the river and beginning the long climb into the hills? Might they too be walking innocently into danger?

The thought spurred him into action. He covered the distance at a run, grabbed the sword belt and dived into a small hollow some paces beyond. No arrows sped out of the night, no enemies rose up from the darkness.

One of the oxen called unhappily. It would be cruel to leave them. Yet they were exposed on the plough land, and he had not scouted the eastern extremities of the field. Paullus looked at the clouds, at the thick blanket of the night. It would take a good shot to bring him down. A strange fatalism stole over him. Naevius had told him it often came over soldiers who had been too many times in combat. They became careless of their own safety.

Fuck it, and Naevius too.

Paullus stood up, buckled on the belt and walked out across the furrows.

Despite his fatalism, Paullus had walked back with his head ducked and his torso between the solid shoulders of the beasts. There was accepting the will of the gods, and there was recklessly putting yourself in the way of harm.

A halo of light from a lantern had shown him Pastor trudging up the track from the Sabutus. As was his custom, the old shepherd travelled armed. That had been a relief. Paullus had offered no explanation until they were safe home in the farmstead, the oxen stalled and the whole *familia* gathered around the fireplace. For the rest of the night Pastor and Eutyches had taken turns to stand watch in the main room of the farmhouse. Probably it was an unnecessary precaution, but Paullus had slept soundly.

In the morning Paullus had gone down to Temesa and told the magistrates and council what had happened. Predictably there was consternation. Paullus had not expected the undertone of animosity. Although he was the victim of an unprovoked attack, there seemed to be an unspoken feeling that it was his fault, as if he had in some mysterious way been responsible for the return of an evil everyone had hoped was over.

Whatever stalked the hills, it was November and the ploughing had to be finished, the wheat sown. There were only nine and a half hours of daylight. And so, on the second morning, Paullus was back in the top field. This time Eutyches did the ploughing and Paullus sat with his back to the water trough, his sword – as well as a tall hunting bow and a quiver full of arrows – close to hand.

The trough was an old sarcophagus fed from the stream. It was ancient and had no inscription. The bones of whoever had lain there had long mouldered to dust and their name been forgotten. Temesa was built on the bones of the dead, so Kaido said. When asked to explain, the Bruttian witch merely repeated herself: built on the bones of the dead.

It was broad daylight, and any further attempt on his life improbable. But Paullus remained alert, and he heard the men coming before they emerged down through the trees. There were five of them: Solinus and the other two young kinsmen who had been at the boar hunt of Fidubius and Vibius, accompanied by two slaves. All of them were carrying weapons and their nerves were obviously on edge.

'There has been another murder.' Solinus gave the news without preamble. 'The magistrates want you there.'

'Where?'

'A farm up the Sabutus.' Solinus seemed surprised by the question. 'Marcellus is dead.'

'I would be happier if you left one of your servants to keep an eye on my ploughman.'

Solinus shrugged but agreed.

They went back over the ridge and took the path that ran along the northern bank of the river. Paullus walked with Solinus and the others followed. They did not talk, and Paullus had the impression that they were watching him. Since the civic crown, he was used to people staring. Sometimes it was appealing, especially when the self-important had to get to their feet at his entrance. Now it was vaguely irritating.

The farmhouse of Marcellus faced south at the top of the slope overlooking the Sabutus, well placed to catch any breeze in summer, yet sheltered by tall elms for the winter. It was an impressive structure: two wings jutting out from the main house to form an open courtyard. There was a walled compound down the incline containing the farm buildings and slave quarters. The homestead was set in an estate of many *iugera*, the land worked by half a dozen home-bred slaves. Yet the whole place had a shabby and neglected air. Plaster peeled from years of damp under uncleared gutters, and both wings of the house were boarded up and unused.

Although descended from an original colonist of Temesa who had equestrian status, and benefitting much from family inheritances, in other respects Marcellus' life had not been so fortunate. He had married late, and to a woman of shrewish character. Like many couples intent on handing down their holdings undivided to the next generation, they had had only one son. The gamble had failed; both son and wife had died of fever. Marcellus had never remarried. Never the most gregarious of men, he had withdrawn into his solitary grief. Paullus remembered that at school Lollius had compared the widower to Timon of Athens, a misanthrope who had shunned all company and come to loathe humanity. It was a fair comparison, if made with the cruelty of youth. Marcellus seldom ventured down to the town, never attended the festivals and had no friends or close family. Although rich in property, he was a miser, and, as Fidubius had described him at the hunt, a man of no account. Marcellus had never adopted an heir and, it was said, he had never remade the will that bequeathed everything to his long-dead son.

There was no one about and the courtyard was unpopulated, except for some chickens desultorily pecking the hard-packed surface. They squawked and scattered as the men crossed to the threshold of the farmhouse. The door was ajar. Paullus noticed that the lock was not splintered and the hinges were in place. Marcellus had known his killers and, however grudgingly, had let them into the house. Solinus led Paullus inside. The others followed at their back.

The main chamber on the ground floor was large, and everyone who mattered in the colony was there: the magistrates, the great landowners, Vibius and Fidubius, the latter shadowed by the intimidating figure of Croton, the priest Ursus, even the innkeeper Roscius and his little catamite Zeno. There was a solemnity about them, as if they were attending a religious ritual of which they did not totally approve, and whose outcome they considered dubious.

Those assembled greeted Paullus with stiff formality. Even Lollius did not embrace him, and the eyes of his friend were dull and expressionless, like the empty windows of a dark room.

The coldness was unsurprising, given what had brought them there.

What was left of Marcellus was arranged in front of the fireplace. The killers had not stinted themselves. They had taken their time. Two cups stood on the mantelpiece with an empty jug of wine and a plate with some leftover cheese and a crust of bread. This had been no frenzied attack. A table had been moved to give space to operate. A vase still stood on its surface. The table had not been shoved aside, but picked up with care. That would have taken both men. They must have overpowered Marcellus first, for there were no signs of struggle. Nothing in the room was broken, no furniture overturned, and nothing, except the table, was obviously out of place.

The domestic order of the room made the object on the flagstones yet more repellent.

All the dead man's extremities had been removed – penis, hands, feet, nose and ears – the tongue severed, and the eyes gouged out. The penis had been inserted in the mouth, but this time the other body parts had been fastened to a string which ran around the neck and were then packed under each armpit. It had taken skill to extract the eyeballs with enough of the optic nerve remaining to tie them to the string.

No effort had been spared to ensure that the shade of Marcellus would be unable to stalk his murderers: no eyes to see, ears to hear, nose to scent, feet to follow, hands to seize, tongue to denounce, and no penis to outrage in vengeance. The elaboration went beyond any folk memory. It reminded Paullus of the fate of Apsyrtos in the *Argonautica* of Apollonius of Rhodes. At least one of the killers was a man of some education. Perhaps, like Jason, he had knelt and three times licked then spat out the blood of his victim. It was impossible to tell. There was blood everywhere. Drowsy flies feasted on the dark pools on the floor.

And there was worse. Through the gore, rope marks could be seen on all the truncated limbs. Marcellus had been alive, at least to begin with, as they calmly and methodically tortured the defenceless old man. Paullus remembered his own terror in the cave the other night, and felt a terrible sympathy. Perhaps the pain had been inflicted to extract the location of hoarded wealth, but Paullus thought the motive was nothing but wanton cruelty. Paullus imagined them in the midst of their barbarity stopping to eat and drink.

No one had spoken since Paullus came into the room.

'Where were the slaves?' Paullus broke the silence.

'In the fields,' Ursus said. 'Everyone knows Marcellus only allowed them in the house to serve his meals.'

'When were you last here?' demanded Fidubius.

The question wrong-footed Paullus. 'Not for years. Marcellus did not encourage visitors. Probably before his son died, when I was a child.'

'You recognise this?' Vibius held out a small copper ornament in the shape of the Greek letter theta.

'Yes, it is mine.'

'Then how do you account for it being found in this room?'

Paullus felt something take a cold grip on his heart. 'It was placed here to implicate me.'

'Or you lost it in the struggle.' As always Vibius sounded well mannered, almost disinterested.

'There was no struggle.'

'And how do you know that?' Fidubius' interjection was triumphant.

'The room is undisturbed.'

'You are a veteran. An elderly man like Marcellus would not have put up much of a fight.'

'Why would I want to kill him?' Even to Paullus' own ears, his tone sounded pleading and desperate.

'The other victims were known to you,' Vibius said. 'Junius was your neighbour, and there was talk of you marrying Hirtius' daughter.'

'And it has been often observed that you are a changed man since you came back from Corinth.' There was a well of unspoken hatred behind Fidubius' words: *You returned from the wars, and Alcimus, my son, did not.*

'But there are two killers.'

'We only have your word for that,' Fidubius said.

No, Paullus almost blurted out, Minado saw them sneaking away from the temple. Even in extremis, discretion prevailed. He would not drag the girl into this. She was a despised Bruttian. They would never believe her.

'Or you had an accomplice.' Vibius was smooth as oil.

'Who?'

'Your slaves have been taken. Eutyches and Pastor will be questioned.' Fidubius seemed to relish the idea.

'They are innocent and elderly. You cannot torture them.'

'You know it is the law,' Ursus said.

'The only way to ensure the servile tell the truth,' Vibius added.

Paullus looked round at his fellow citizens. Most he had known all his life. Now all those pairs of eyes were devoid of compassion, vacant and black like the windows of an abandoned house.

Fidubius nudged one of the magistrates.

'Gaius Furius Paullus, I am arresting you for murder.'

CHAPTER 26

Patria et Militia

608–609 Ab Urbe Condita (146–5 BC)

THE ORIGINAL COLONISTS OF TEMESA were good Romans. They had tried to create a miniature Rome in remote Calabria. Even down to the gaol.

The Tullianum in Rome was at the foot of the Capitoline Hill, hidden away behind the senate house. It was a circular underground chamber, about seven paces across and twelve feet high. The cell was enclosed by strong walls and a stone vault. The only access was by a ladder let down from a hole in the roof. A spring of water drained through it, and the dampness added to the repugnant air of neglect, darkness and stench. It was not intended for long-term imprisonment, but simply a place of detention for those convicted of capital crimes or treason, or captured foreign enemies of Rome. All committed were awaiting execution, usually by strangulation. The only ones who were hauled out alive were destined to be thrown to their deaths from the high cliff of the Tarpeian Rock.

The colonists of Temesa had excavated a cavern of similar dimensions behind the basilica on the forum, where the town council met. There was a guardhouse above to shelter the public slaves who were detailed to prevent any attempt to escape. The prison was seldom used. Those detained by the authorities, for debt or more heinous crimes, usually were confined to house arrest in the home of a respectable member of the community. Often the householder was a relative, who stood surety for the accused. If many were arrested at once, or if there were debtors for whom no trusted citizen would vouch, they were held in a nearby slave barracks. It had shackles, stout doors and iron bars on the windows. The bandits taken at Blood Rock had been held there. But the man believed to have murdered and mutilated three citizens had to be confined to the deepest dungeon. That Paullus had not been tried, let alone convicted, was thought irrelevant.

Paullus climbed down the ladder. There was no point in struggling. There were far too many of them, and they would have just manhandled him to the edge and thrown him down. The fall would have broken bones, maybe been the end of him. The latter outcome would have been convenient for some.

There was no spring, but the chamber was very damp. The river was close, and it could not be much above the water level. It would not help his persistent cough. There was a filthy, mildewed mattress, a cup and jug of water, and a bucket in which to relieve himself. While there was still light, he sat down on the mattress. The ladder was pulled up, the trapdoor slammed shut, the bolts grated. The darkness was absolute.

Almost at once he heard the heavy, guttural breathing and smelt their stale sarcophagus odour. Although he could not see them, he knew the Kindly Ones sat close around him. They whispered to each other, as might the dead in the gloomy halls of Hades. Then one of them – Allecto, or another sister, Tisiphone or Megaera – spoke.

Remember Corinth. Remember the Last House.

*

The street was full of smoke. Soot, like black snow, eddied in the backdraught of the fires.

'One more house,' Tatius said.

'We have enough,' Alcimus coughed. It was getting hard to breathe.

'Alcimus is right,' Paullus said. 'The flames will cut us off.'

'No, one last house,' Tatius said. There was a strange, mad light in his eyes.

They gave in to the determination of Tatius.

The gate of the last house stood partly open. The courtyard was empty. Tatius led them into the house. There were signs of frenzied packing: bulging sacks, half-filled crates, treasured possessions dropped on the floor. It would take a small army to carry them.

They started rummaging through the baggage.

The roar of the fire could be heard clearly. It was getting close. A street away, perhaps nearer still? There was a breeze. It would carry burning embers. Fires could break out anywhere.

'We have to go,' Paullus said, 'while there is still time. Any moment now, we are going to be trapped. No wealth is worth dying for.'

'Nothing ventured, nothing gained,' Tatius said.

Alcimus gave a low whistle. From a packing case, he lifted a wine cooler. It was huge and heavy, beautifully engraved, and made of solid gold.

'Someone is coming!'

As Paullus spoke, dropping what they held, all three drew their weapons.

From deeper in the house, two Greeks burst into the room. They stopped, thunderstruck at the sight of the soldiers. They were unarmed, but for an instant Paullus thought outrage was going to impel them not to give up their belongings without a fight.

Then they turned and fled, and Alcimus set off in pursuit.

'Let them go!' Paullus seized Alcimus' belt, and pulled him back.

Tatius was turning the wine cooler in his hands.

'That is mine,' Alcimus said. 'I found the drinking set.'

'It is mine now.' Tatius was tracing the engraving with his fingers. He seemed entranced.

Alcimus went to grab the precious object. They tussled, like two children in the street. One hand still holding his sword, Alcimus was losing.

Paullus moved to separate them. He was too far away and never had the chance. Tatius' sword was back in his fist, then its point was buried deep in Alcimus.

Paullus stood as if turned to stone. In the heat and the smoke he was icy cold.

Tatius withdrew the sword and pushed Alcimus away with the wine cooler. Alcimus staggered back. His hands were pressed to his stomach, his blood pulsing through his fingers. The blade had punched through the rings of his mail. His round, innocent face was blank with incomprehension. Then he doubled up and collapsed. No one survived a gut wound.

'What have you done?' Paullus said.

Tatius turned and carefully placed his treasure on the table. 'I told him it was mine. I told you both.'

'You have killed him.'

'You should have listened to me.' Tatius' thin, delicate face was sad. 'How many times did I say that nothing and no one was going to stop me returning as a rich man?'

'But you killed him.'

'And now I am going to have to kill you.'

'What?'

Tatius pouted like a sulky girl. 'You know the punishment for killing a fellow soldier: tied to the fork, slowly whipped to death – the
ancient method of execution, the stern way of the ancestors. You
think I am going to let you run and tell your new little friend Centurion Naevius?'

Paullus stepped back, drew his sword.

Tatius followed.

Thick ropes of smoke were coiling through the doorway.

'If we don't leave now,' Paullus said, 'we are going to die in here.'

'One of us is.' Tatius advanced in a fighting crouch, half turned,
blade held up by his right ear.

From nearby came the crash of a roof falling.

Tatius was between Paullus and the door.

'It is your own fault really.' Tatius shook his head, but his eyes
never left Paullus. 'You both have farms to return to, and I don't.
Again and again I told you both that I needed enough to buy an
estate.'

Tatius jabbed to the face. Paullus flinched, but managed not
to raise his guard. As he suspected, it was a feint. Tatius thrust at
his stomach. Paullus turned the blow with the edge of his blade.
The momentum drove them together. Tatius' eyes were insane.
Paullus tried to stamp on his instep, but missed. Tatius shoved
him away.

Smoke was gathering in the ceiling. Paullus had to get out of
here. Soon there would be no air to breathe. He would suffocate
or burn to death. He aimed a backhanded cut, designed to drive
Tatius out of the way to the door. Naevius and the army could hunt
Tatius down, exact due retribution.

Tatius did not move to the side, but instead gave ground. He
was still blocking the path to safety. And now Tatius moved to
the attack. Long years with the eagles had taught him to fight.

He unleashed a combination of blows to the head and shoulders and torso, cutting and thrusting, varying the point of attack. The wound he had taken earlier to the shoulder did not seem to be any hindrance, and experience was on his side. Paullus was forced back, step by step, doggedly parrying, just trying to stay alive. One strike got through. Paullus staggered as the sword clanged and bounced off his mailed shoulder.

Paullus was standing in Alcimus' blood. A great pool of it was spreading across the floor. Alcimus was almost underfoot, not moving. Paullus did not know if his friend was dead yet.

Tatius was maddened, like a cornered beast, insensible to reason or pain. It would take a mighty injury to stop him. He had to be incapacitated. Paullus did not know if he had the strength. Tatius only wore a chest protector. But did Paullus have the skill to find an exposed extremity?

The back of Paullus' legs bumped against the table. There was nowhere to retreat. Tatius smiled, sensing his advantage.

'Time to join your friend,' Tatius said, unleashing a powerful right and left. Somehow Paullus got his weapon in their path. Steel rasped on steel, just in front of his face. Again he collided with the table, was forced halfway back over its surface. Something heavy shifted and fell on the wooden boards. Tatius' gaze flicked to the glitter of gold. It was enough. Paullus got his sword inside Tatius' guard and thrust its tip straight at his mouth. Tatius jumped back, but his boots slipped in the blood. Paullus thrust again. Tatius lost his footing and fell. Paullus was above him, plunging his blade down. Tatius rolled aside, knocking away Paullus' left leg.

The momentary advantage was gone. Paullus landed hard next to Tatius. The impact jarred and made him grunt with pain. They grappled, the left hand of each gripping the wrist of the other's sword hand. They wrestled in the gore, turning over, attempting to use brute strength to drive the sharp steel into the chest of the other.

Paullus felt Tatius' blade nudge into the rings of mail guarding his ribs. One snapped, then another. The steel was worming its way through the leather padding under the armour. Then it would be into the muscle and bone of the ribcage.

Making a last throw of the dice, Paullus slackened his own attack. Surprised, Tatius lost a fraction of his grip. Paullus altered the angle of his own weapon: not the chest, but the armpit. With a titanic effort he put his weight behind the thrust.

Tatius grunted with disbelief and pain.

'Poverty has undone me.' Tatius' tone was almost bitter. 'If only I had owned a coat of mail.'

Paullus twisted the blade deep into the wound.

Tatius dropped his sword; pointlessly his fingers clutched at the blade of Paullus' weapon.

Paullus drove the tip deeper still.

The heels of Tatius' boots drummed on the floor, and his eyes closed as his body convulsed.

Tatius was still. Paullus thought he was dead.

But Tatius opened his eyes. He looked through Paullus with an expression of horror, as if he had caught a glimpse of what awaited him beyond the great divide. Then his gaze focused on Paullus. His lips moved. Paullus had to bend close to catch the words.

'Hades, hear me – Furies hunt him across the face of the world.'

The final malediction, and Tatius was dead.

Paullus hauled himself to his feet.

The smoke was roiling down from the ceiling. There were only a few feet of clean air above the floor. More smoke was eddying in through the door.

Paullus went to Alcimus, knelt and touched his neck. There was no pulse. He looked at the two bodies. Soon the fire would consume both.

They had called themselves brothers. They had been inseparable. Naevius had called them the Three Graces. And now two of them were dead by the hands of their brothers. And Paullus knew that nothing in the world would ever be the same again.

CHAPTER 27

Patria

609 Ab Urbe Condita (145 BC)

THE ROUTINE OF THE PRISON did not change. Twice a day the trapdoor was opened. The ladder was not put down. No opportunity was offered for escape. Instead, one by one, a pail of food, a jug of water and a new slop bucket were lowered by rope. The prisoner had to tie the handles of the old ones to the rope to be hauled up. The trapdoor had opened three times. It was the evening of the second day.

The public slaves were in an invidious position. Doubtless they had been ordered not to talk to the prisoner. But, on the other hand, Paullus was both a local landowner and the holder of the civic crown. It was known he had high-ranking patrons in Rome itself. A turn of the stars, and his fortunes might change. If he were declared innocent and released, things would be very difficult.

The slaves volunteered next to nothing, but they answered his questions. Evidently there was no overseer of the two on duty at any time. If there had been, the guards would have remained silent. Their answers had mainly been negative. No, there had been no visitors. No one was to be admitted. Eutyches and Pastor were being held in the house of Ursus. No, they had not been put to the torture yet. The priest refused to give them up until there was a formal trial. No, there was no date set for the proceedings.

The grudging conversation over, they shut the trapdoor. Paullus was left to eat in the dark. The food was always bread and cheese.

Every Roman citizen accused of a capital crime was entitled to a public trial before a magistrate and jury in Rome. It was one of the foundation stones of the Republic. Without that right there would be no liberty, and it was *libertas* that made Rome the envy of the world. If the charges were treason or aiding the enemy, the prisoner would be kept in custody. Otherwise, even if he was to be tried for murder, it was accepted that he had the option to retire into exile.

Paullus knew that he would not be put on trial in Rome. There was no evidence against him, except the theta ornament, and it could not be proved that he had lost it in the house of Marcellus. Indeed, his own *familia* – his mother as well as his slaves – could testify that it had been mislaid or stolen some days before the murder. He had no motive and could not be argued to have gained from any of the killings. Eutyches was a witness that he had been in his own field the day Marcellus died. Of course, many slaves said what they thought their inquisitors wanted to hear under the lash, but, for all his surliness, Eutyches was loyal as well as tough. No conviction would be secured. Not if he were defended by senators of consular rank, his old commanders, Lucius Aurelius Orestes and Lucius Mummius, the conqueror of Corinth. Like most things in Rome, *libertas* was amenable to the influence of the powerful.

Paullus would not be put on trial in Rome. The real killers could not allow it to happen. Paullus would not leave this cell alive. They would have to ensure that.

Talking to the guards in the brief moments of light, Paullus had looked all around the subterranean chamber, searching for any-thing that could be used as a weapon. There was nothing – just bare, damp stone walls. If they came to kill him, he would not die quietly. He would fight with his fists and boots, his teeth and nails. If they came to kill him, they would also have to kill the guards. They might be suborned, but then they could not be left alive knowing the truth.

It would do no good explaining the danger of their predicament to the guards. Even if he convinced them, they would not dare turn him loose. If he escaped, the dereliction of duty would bring them torture and execution. For them the whirlpool of Charybdis was in plain sight, but the monster Scylla lurked out of sight in her cave.

Paullus had thought about poison. Yet he ate the gaol rations. It would be difficult to conceal toxins in plain bread and cheese and water. Poison was not always certain, and usually it left a trace, a black discolouration of the skin. The prefect of the Bruttians would arrive next month, and there would be an investigation.

There was an awful irony in this. The visit of the prefect was as regular as the seasons. November: thirty days; the sun in the sign of Scorpio; sowing of wheat and barley; the prefect holds court in the town of Consentia. December: thirty-one days; the sun in Sagittarius; olives gathered and beans sown; the prefect hears cases in Temesa. The prefect, of course, was Orestes, Paullus' old commander. With him, in charge of his bodyguard of soldiers, would be Naevius, the old centurion. It was November. They were in Consentia. So close, yet so far. They might as well have been on the other side of the Adriatic, back in Achaea. It was late in the month. Soon they would take the road to Temesa. Yet the imminent arrival of his patron, and his friend, promised Paullus no salvation. Rather, it hastened his end. The killers could not let Paullus talk to the prefect. They would have to ensure he was dead before Orestes reached Temesa.

Paullus sat alone in the dark, a foul old blanket draped around his shoulders. Had there been light to see, an observer might have taken him for a vagrant. At times he doubled up coughing. The damp was making it worse. Paullus' thoughts reached out beyond the stone walls to Minado: the way her hair curled over the nape of her neck, the perfect oval of her face and the way she lifted her chin without a hint of vanity. In her company he felt an ease, and a companionship he had known with no other girl. It was a cruel tragedy that he had found the woman he wished to marry, and now he would die in this dank cell. But he could not have married Minado. She was a Bruttian. She could have become his concubine. There was no shame in that. But their children would not have been Roman. Debarred from inheriting his land or wealth, they would have had a dismal life in the Roman colony of Temesa, forever trapped among the oppressed.

The bolts above rattled back. Paullus had not long finished the food. His heart quailed. So soon? He had not thought the killers would come so quickly, not the second night. He got to his feet, pressed his back against the wall.

Die like a man! There was nothing else to be done.

The hinges of the trapdoor squealed as it was raised. Paullus tried to shrink yet further back from the shaft of light. There would be questions. Orestes would see to that. But they would be too late. Paullus would be dead, his testimony gone and any evidence vanished.

The ladder was lowered. Paullus tensed himself. That would be his only chance. Take the first one while he was clambering down. Grab his legs, haul him to the ground, smash his head against the flagstones. It meant no escape. The others would kill him: shoot him down from above or stone him to death. There was nowhere to hide in the cell. But he might take one of them with him. Somehow he was sure he knew who they would send first down the ladder.

The feet of the ladder bumped on the floor. But no boots appeared on the rungs.

Paullus waited, almost keen to get it over with.

'Pssst.'

The sort of sound used to summon a hunting dog.

'Pssst.' It came again – low, but urgent.

Paullus kept quiet. If they thought to lure him out, they had mis-judged him.

'For fuck's sake, Paullus.' A big square head peered down from the aperture. 'We haven't got all night.'

Paullus was up the ladder as if wearing the winged boots of the god Hermes.

The slight figure of Onirus stood behind Dekis. The two guards were slumped in the corner.

'Have you killed them?'

'They are just sleeping,' the old huntsman said.

'With the help of one of Kaido's potions,' Onirus added.

'The guard changes in two hours,' Dekis said. 'We need to be long gone.'

Outside, the town was sleeping. A cold wind came up from the harbour. They crept along the back of the council house, then Dekis led them up the street that led away from the forum.

All went well for two blocks, then they heard the sound of the revellers. All the houses were shuttered for the night, but they were near the small temple of Hercules. Like the homes, it was locked, but the columns flanking its entrance at the top of the steps offered a modicum of cover.

A piper led the tipsy procession. Its tune got louder, almost drowned out by shouts and bursts of drunken laughter.

Crouching low, shielding the white of his face with his arm, Paullus peered around the base of a column.

A piper and a torch boy led four young men. The drinkers were well dressed, but the wreaths of rose petals were askew on their brows. Lollius was reasonably steady on his feet, but Solinus and the other two were staggering.

The guttering torch threw grotesque shadows down the street.

They had almost passed when Solinus stopped. He lurched towards the temple.

Paullus wondered how they did not hear the thudding of his heart. It seemed to be trying to burst through his ribs. *Six of them, three of us.* They were drunk and unarmed – the two Bruttians had swords – but the uproar would wake the whole street. The hue and cry would start at once. They would be chased down.

Solinus pulled up his tunic, fumbled with his undergarment. With a huge sigh, he pissed against the steps. The urine stank of wine. It splashed and started to run down the gutter.

All Solinus had to do was turn his head. No matter how inebriated, he could not fail to see them.

'Get a move on,' Lollius shouted. 'We need to knock up Roscius. I don't know about you, but I fancy having that Syrian of his, the one with the hot eyes and the big arse.'

'We can all have her,' Solinus slurred. 'Do her good.'

'Old Roscius could do with the company,' Lollius laughed. 'Gets lonely, now his catamite is out at Croton's place.'

Solinus shook his penis. A few drops stained his clothes.

Paullus felt the need to cough rising in his chest. He bit his own arm, held his breath.

It seemed to take Solinus forever to rearrange himself. Finally, he reeled off after the others.

The sounds receded. Paullus took a deep breath. The urge to cough had gone.

They remained in the shadows until they could not hear the revellers.

'Hercules' hairy arse, that was too close,' Dekis muttered.

'A metaphor for life,' Onirus said. 'Romans pissing on us.' He turned to Paullus. 'No offence.'

'None taken.'

'We have got you a horse,' Dekis whispered, 'a good one. It is tethered in the grove outside the east wall. Fidubius owns so many, he will hardly miss one.'

'The gates will be locked,' Paullus said.

'There is a hidden door, used by Bruttian smugglers.' Onirus grinned. 'You Romans have no idea what happens in this town.'

'Why are you helping me?'

'Fuck knows,' Dekis said. 'My daughter is very persuasive.'

'You looked after me in the camp, and saw me right with the plunder after Corinth,' Onirus said. 'Besides, some of them wanted to blame the murders on the Bruttians, and you are no more guilty than us.'

'We should get moving,' Dekis said.

'I need you both to do something for me,' Paullus said. 'I am going to the deserted village near Blood Rock. Dekis, tomorrow at noon, not before, go to Lollius. Tell him I left you a message saying where I am hiding.'

'Are you sure? Lollius . . .'

'Quite sure.' Paullus turned to Onirus. 'I want you to do something else. You will need the horse. I can take my own mules, and get everything else I want from my farm. Although I could do with some food, especially raw meat.'

'You are hungry,' Onirus said, 'and at a time like this?'

'Not exactly. Is there any of Kaido's potion left?'

'Yes,' Dekis said. 'What are you planning?'

And Paullus told them.

CHAPTER 28

Patria

609 Ab Urbe Condita (145 BC)

THE CRESCENT NEW MOON hung in a soft blue sky. Its light speckled the ground through the bare branches of the beeches and oaks. Leaving the road, Paullus had given a low whistle. Now he whistled again so the hound could find him.

Niger came bounding through the trees, bursting with pleasure and excitement. He wound through his master's legs, hackles raised, baring his teeth in welcome. Paullus made much of him, fussing his ears, talking gentle nonsense.

There was little time to spare. When the alarm was raised at the gaol, his own farm was the obvious place to look. Signalling Niger to follow silently, Paullus went through the belt of trees and into the farmyard.

Always secure a line of retreat. The army had taught him that. The Achaeans had paid a high price at the isthmus for ignoring the lesson. Paullus went straight to the stables. It was dark inside, but Paullus could have moved around them blindfold. He took down two riding saddles. The mules were sleepy and docile, although, true to their reputation, one took a deep breath as he fastened its girth. Paullus kicked it in the stomach, not hard, but enough to make it exhale. He cinched the straps tight, then hung some lengths of rope, along with the provisions Onirus had provided, from the saddles. He made sure the bag containing the potion concocted by Kaido was not touching those that held the food. When meddling in such things, you could not take too much care.

Leaving the saddled mules standing in their stalls, he went across to the hay barn. With a pitchfork he shifted aside the hay, then got a spade and started digging. It took no great time to unearth the two swords. He had wrapped them in oilcloth, and they did not look too spotted with rust. He scooped up a handful of the hidden coins. It seemed profligate not to rebury the others, but there was no time. Anyway, if his plan failed, he would only need a single coin: wedged between his teeth to pay the ferryman across the Styx.

Paullus collected his old army entrenching tool from the store shed, then led the mules out as quietly as he could. If the noise carried to his mother and her maid in the house, the silence of Niger might reassure them. He stood for a moment, debating which way to go. The road was more exposed, but the track at the rear of the farm slower. He swung up onto the lead mule, turning its head towards the treeline and the road beyond.

Paullus told Niger to stay. Looking back, he saw the black dog watching him go.

Fidubius himself now lived in his town house in Temesa. It was close to the council house and the baths, the other amenities of civilized life, altogether comfortable for an affluent old age. His rural estates stretched along the valley of the Sabutus, with outlying holdings north towards Clampetia and south in the direction of Terina, as well as sheepfolds and pastures far to the east in the high Sila. But the main villa was several miles up river near the bridge at Ad Fluvium Sabutum. It had been Alcimus' childhood home, and Paullus knew it intimately.

The villa consisted of a central building with wings added. Its layout was like the house of the murdered Marcellus, except on a grander scale. Domestic servants, all home-bred slaves, lived in the main house to keep it in constant readiness on the off chance that Fidubius should decide on an unannounced visit. The domicile of the owner was separated from the farm buildings and the quarters of the agricultural slaves by a low wall, and the whole complex was surrounded by a somewhat taller perimeter wall. The house of the bailiff stood between the working farm and the villa, from where both could be overseen. It was set in the corner between the outer and internal walls, and two further walls created a separate small interior compound.

Paullus approached from the west, through the olive groves that grew almost up to the boundary. They were behind with their autumn work. New trenches had not yet been dug around all the trees. About a hundred paces out, after taking what he needed from the saddle packs, he tethered the mules, leaving them enough rope to graze.

At the edge of the trees, he stopped and listened. There was nothing to hear. Looking at the new moon, he estimated it was just gone midnight. Everyone should be asleep. He secured the coils of rope across his shoulders, and one of the swords, the entrenching tool and the bag of meat all in his belt.

Stepping out of the shade into the blue moonlight, he felt very exposed, although, at this hour, he was reasonably sure there would be no one to see him. There was a wicket gate, but it would be bolted from the inside.

At the foot of the outer wall, he halted again and strained his ears to catch any suspicious sound. Again, there was nothing. The wall was about eight feet high, designed to keep out wolves from the forest, not a determined man. The top was smooth, not set with broken shards of glass. It would be a foolhardy thief that broke into the *villa rustica* of Fidubius. Paullus took a firm grip on the coping stones and hauled himself up.

Lying along the top, he studied the bailiff's house and its court-yard. Nothing moved in the cold light. The sentinels were out of sight. Paullus gave a low bark, like that of a rutting deer. It was the wrong season, but the bailiff should be sleeping, and anyway was not bred in the countryside.

The hounds appeared from around the house. The two huge black mastiffs wore collars spiked with nails. There was no need to make another noise. They had scented his presence. They padded towards where Paullus lay. Hackles raised, fangs and eyes very white in the half-light, they silently stalked this unexpected prey that sounded like a deer, but smelt like a man. If he descended into their terri-tory, they would pounce and tear him to bits, baying for blood. They would wake the entire farm.

Paullus threw the first two chunks of meat at their feet. Beasts like these were always kept hungry to increase their natural savagery. Neither hesitated, but gobbled down the food in one or two gulps. Paullus tossed down the rest of the meat, and they fell on it.

The mastiffs settled on their haunches, but remained alert. No gift of food would win them over. They were still intent on ripping this intruder limb from limb. Just let him set foot in their domain.

A man can outwait a dog. Suppressing the desire to cough, Paullus stayed very still, and looked over at the house. It was right a bailiff should have something of his own. It made him more loyal. Paullus remembered from his childhood Fidubius, up at the villa, holding forth on the duties of a bailiff. He must be the first out of bed and the last to go to bed, must see the farmstead is closed, that each one is asleep in his proper place, that the stock are bedded down and have fodder. He must be sober and honest and hard-working. He must withhold his hands from the goods of others, and turn his face from wrongdoing. The bailiff should be given a female slave as a mate to make him steadier and more attached to the farm. The litany of desiderata had gone on and on. Presumably it had been intended for the education of Alcimus, but Fidubius had not adhered to his own injunctions.

One of the mastiffs gave a low, unhappy whimper. It got up, turned round, then curled up in distress. The other looked over, ears pricked. Either in sympathy or sensing weakness, it too got up and began to sniff its kennel mate. Then it became unsteady on its legs and fell to the ground, as if felled by a slingshot. Both hounds were still.

Paullus dropped off the wall. Drawing his sword, he moved to the stricken animals. They did not move. Cautiously, he prodded them with the flat of the blade. Their flanks were moving, but they did not react. Not knowing what was in Kaido's potion, he had no idea of the strength of the drugs he had put in the meat. It might be enough to kill them, but they might come round before he was gone. They were guard dogs doing their duty, but there was no room for pity or sentimentality. Legionaries also died doing their duty. Such was life. Paullus cut both their throats.

Both front and rear doors of the house would be locked and bolted. The kitchen window was the place. It had shutters, but no bars or glass. Paullus slid the sword back through his belt and took out the entrenching tool.

Inserting the tip in the join of the wooden boards, he paused and let his memory trace his projected journey through the house: through the kitchen, across the main room, up the stairs, where the door of the bed chamber was to the right on the landing. When he was young, he and Alcimus had played in the house with the children of the then bailiff. The layout would not have changed. From breaking open the shutters to reaching the bedroom would be the work of a few moments. With luck, too few for a sleeping man to wake and gather his senses.

No point in waiting. Paullus put all his weight behind the tool. The shutters cracked – all too loud in the quiet night – and sprung open. Entrenching tool in hand, Paullus vaulted the sill. He stumbled over an unseen stool, kicked it away, and set off.

Racing up the stairs, he heard something. Reaching the landing, he wrenched open the bedroom door. The chamber was lit by a tiny lamp, and smelt of sex and perfume: spikenard and cinnamon. Croton was out of bed, barefoot, tugging on a tunic. Hades, there was another figure in the bed.

For a burly man, Croton was quick. The bailiff snatched up a sword – a guilty conscience sleeps with a weapon – and lunged. Paullus parried with the entrenching tool. The bigger man used his weight to smash Paullus back against the wall. No chance to draw his own blade. Croton's left hand had him by the throat. Paullus managed to seize the slave's sword hand.

Croton's hand was like a vice. The fingers closed, crushing Paullus' windpipe. He could not breathe. He tried to bring his knee up into Croton's crotch. The big man half turned.

'You are a hard little bastard to kill.' Croton's breath was hot and stank of stale wine.

The fingers tightened. Panic rose in Paullus, like a tide of bile.

'But you are finished now.'

Sparks of light were flaring in Paullus' darkening vision. He could feel his own grip on his opponent's sword arm weakening. Slipping towards unconsciousness, he made one last effort.

Paullus stamped down with a boot. The heel landed on Croton's unprotected toes. The slave roared with pain. The grip on Paullus' throat slackened, he twisted free and retreated towards the far corner.

Croton went to follow, but stopped, limping badly. 'Zeno, stab him in the back.'

So that was who was in the bed. Paullus should have known.

'Move and I will kill you too!' Paullus' shout came out as a croak. His eyes did not leave Croton as he shifted the entrenching tool to his left hand and drew his sword with his right.

'Him *too*,' Croton mocked. 'You are finished, civic crown and all, soldier boy.'

It was all bravado. Paullus was a trained swordsman, Croton was not. But Paullus wanted him alive.

Before Paullus could decide what to do, Croton lunged. Paullus blocked the blow with his blade. The heavier man dropped his shoulder, intending to hammer Paullus against a wall again. This time Paullus was ready. He sidestepped. The force of the attack drove Croton past, put him off balance. Paullus left a leg trailing and tripped his assailant. It was an old wrestling move from his youth. As Croton went down, Paullus hit him on the head with the entrenching tool. Not a clean blow. Croton was on his hands and knees, but still moving, pushing himself up. Paullus brought the solid implement down hard on the back of the slave's head with a sickening thump. This time Croton did not move.

Paullus swung round on Zeno. The youth was cowering among the sheets, clutching them, as if they offered protection.

'Turn over, face down, arms and legs spread,' Paullus said.

The youth did as he was told. His naked buttocks were white and smooth and rounded, like those of a girl, or a statue of a hermaphrodite.

'Please, don't hurt me.'

'Just don't move.'

Paullus took the lamp, and crouched by Croton. Blood was oozing, matting his hair. A lump was already swelling on the back of his head. Paullus felt behind his ear. There was a pulse. A big brute like Croton probably had a thick skull.

Putting sword and entrenching tool back in his belt, Paullus took the rope from around his shoulders. He went to turn Croton over.

The man weighed a ton. When Croton was on his back, Paullus bound his hands.

Paullus wanted Croton alive, but now he was unconscious.

'Zeno, come here and help me lift him.'

'Can I get dressed?'

'I am not concerned about your modesty.'

Taking one armpit each, together they dragged Croton down the stairs. It was hard work. There was no possibility they could manhandle his dead weight through the kitchen window.

'Where does he keep the keys?'

'By the bed.'

This was all taking time. Paullus marched Zeno back upstairs, collected the key, and went down again. The back door of the house unlocked, they hauled Croton to the wicket gate in the outer wall. Its bolts screeched noisily. Thank the gods, the house of the bailiff stood alone. Even so, Paullus made Zeno hurry to get his captive to the olive grove where the mules waited.

Slinging Croton face down over the second mule was the most difficult manoeuvre of all. Eventually it was achieved, and Paullus tied the bailiff's dangling hands and feet together under the animal's belly.

Despite the exertion, Zeno was shivering. It was not a cold night for November, but cold enough.

What to do with the youth? If he raised the alarm, Paullus would be hunted down within the hour. Zeno was innocent of everything, except the weakness that made him a victim of men like Roscius, and now Croton. Paullus did not want to have to kill him. Taken along, he would be an encumbrance. There were only two mules. He would slow them down. Some of Kaido's potion was left. Yet given too little Zeno might come round almost at once, and too much might kill him anyway. Paullus did not want to have to kill him.

CHAPTER 29

Patria

609 Ab Urbe Condita (145 BC)

'THEY WILL FIND YOU, and they will kill you.'

Croton was tied to a broken pillar in the middle of the ruined marketplace. He was seated, arms drawn back, wrists secured behind the pillar. The big slave was unshaven and dirty. He sat in his own filth. There was a swelling the size of a goose egg on his head, and his hair was stiff with dried blood. But he was alive. Croton obviously had a thick skull.

'They are not fools. They will not come today, but they will hunt you down. You will never be safe.'

Paullus did not answer, but checked the bindings and looked round what had once been the market of the remote and long abandoned Bruttian village. The buildings had collapsed many years ago. On all four sides of the square were cliffs of jumbled masonry. In the bright winter sun, where weeds had not caught hold, the jagged slabs and crumbling inclines shone dazzling white. Here and there the tumbled material had made cavities, like black and precarious caves, where a man might conceal himself. There was a gap where the road had once run. It was the only way in, and the only way out. That was why Paullus had chosen this place.

Perhaps Croton was right and they would not come today. But Paullus thought they would. Croton knew something they did not.

From out of sight a horse called, and close at hand one of his mules answered.

'They will kill your family, and your Bruttian whore.'

'You talk too much.' Paullus sat down. He was tired. It had been a long night and day.

Paullus had left Zeno roped to a tree. It had been cold, and the youth was naked. He would have suffered, but he would not have died. The labourers would have found him not long after first light, when they had come to continue digging the trenches around the olives. Unless, of course, before going out to the fields, the farm workers had discovered that Croton was gone and seen the evidence of a struggle in the house. But then there would have been a search, and they would soon have stumbled across Zeno. Either way, the youth would have been released.

After leaving Zeno, Paullus had crossed the river at Ad Fluvium Sabutum and followed the road north in the direction of Consentia. In the dead of night, there had been no one at the bridge and no travellers on the road. Paullus had pushed the mules hard, riding the foremost and controlling the other with a lead rein. Unconscious, Croton had hung over the back of the latter like a sack of grain, head and feet dangling. As the crow flies, probably it was no more than five miles from the bridge to the turning to Blood Rock and the Pass of Laboula. As the road twisted, it was nearer ten.

Reaching the turning without incident, Paullus had set off east. The high Sila had closed around him – the dark slopes of ash and oak, higher up pine and fir. The clop of hooves was lost in the solitude of the forest. They startled a herd of roe deer that bounded effortlessly away, their white tails showing through the trees. Once the mules shied to the side of the track, rolling their eyes and shuddering with fear. In the moonlight, Paullus had seen the white face, the lolling tongue, the pale tawny shoulders. A big old wolf, perhaps hungry, but it had watched them pass.

It was November. The last of the sheep would have been driven to lower pastures the previous month. The Sila was deserted in the winter. But Paullus had had to get off the road before dawn. There was always the danger of encountering charcoal burners or gangs of pitch-tappers whose desire for profit had made them tardy in their descent.

After a few miles, Croton had begun to come round and started groaning. Paullus had dismounted, considerately given him a drink, and told him that if he made another sound he would cut his cock off and shove it down his throat.

They had reached the ancient settlement as the sky began to lighten. Paullus had tethered Croton to the pillar, hobbled the mules and built a fire of juniper and pine. The mules he had unsaddled and fed and watered. Croton he had left. A man could live for three days without a drink, much longer without food. Croton had a strong constitution. It would do no harm if he were weakened.

Most of the morning Paullus had sat in the bitter, fragrant smoke by the fire. Occasionally he chewed some of the rations Onirus had provided, and from time to time went out and checked the approaches to the village.

'It is not too late.' Croton tried a different approach. 'You could just slip away. Get to the Adriatic, take a ship to Syria or Egypt. The kings there always need mercenaries. You won the civic crown.'

Paullus regarded the dishevelled figure. 'Let us not talk like fools. It is far too late for either of us, especially you.'

'It does not have to end like this.'

'Yes, it does,' Paullus said. 'But in silence.'

Paullus cut a short length of rope and went to gag Croton. The slave struggled, clenching his jaws, throwing his head from side to side. Paullus drew his sword and used the pommel to hit Croton on the lump on his head – not at all hard, but probably enough to cause agonising pain. Paullus forced the rope between Croton's teeth and lashed it tight.

It was past mid-afternoon. Again Paullus ran through his estimates of distance and time for men riding flat out: from Temesa to Consentia, from there to Blood Rock, and from Temesa to Blood Rock. His first calculations had proved correct; if the latter did likewise, they would come when the shadows were lengthening.

Paullus eased his back against a slab of masonry. Croton was glaring at him above the gag. In the quiet of the afternoon, Paullus knew he was being watched, and by more than mortal eyes. *Remember Corinth*, they whispered in his mind. *Remember the Last House.* But he would not do so; not now, not yet. If things fell out as he hoped, he might get a chance to tell the person who most needed to know.

Paullus' thoughts drifted to Minado. To Hades with Rome. If she would have him, he would live with her as if she were his wife. If he survived. As for children, who could tell what the future held? *Carpe diem.* Yes, he would seize the day. If he survived.

An owl hooted in broad daylight.

They were here.

Paullus got to his feet. They were earlier than he had thought. Their mounts would be near broken. Paullus stretched, looked about, checked everything was as it should be.

Lollius strode into the remains of the marketplace. He was dressed for hunting: a broad-brimmed hat, thick leather tunic, stout boots, and a sword on his hip.

'You came,' Paullus said.

'Of course I came, old friend, when I got your message.'

Lollius came over and embraced Paullus. If he showed a little reluctance, that might be because he was embracing a man accused of several murders.

Lollius let go and stepped back. 'So, Croton was the killer?'

Paullus said nothing.

'What gave him away?'

'His smell – that perfume of spikenard and cinnamon is expensive and distinctive.'

'Stupid of him.' Lollius walked a few steps away. He kicked some loose pebbles. 'That is all the evidence?'

'He will confess under torture.'

'Slaves spout all sorts of lies under the lash. So old Ursus says, and who are we to doubt a venerable priest who knows the ways of the gods?'

Paullus remained silent.

Lollius tipped his head on one side, thoughtfully. 'But a jury might believe his evidence extracted under duress, and that would get you off the hook.' Lollius put two fingers in his mouth and whistled. 'Best be on the safe side.'

The others entered the market. Fidubius and Vibius were preceded by Solinus and the other two young relatives from the boar hunt. Like Lollius, they were all accoutred for the chase. The three younger men also carried boar spears.

The newcomers fanned out.

'That is far enough.' Paullus drew his sword, put the blade to Croton's throat.

They halted in a rough semicircle, facing Paullus. Ten, twelve paces away. Odds of six to one.

'The Fates play unexpected tricks,' Lollius said.

'Often, but not this time,' Paullus said. 'I already knew you were the other killer.'

'How?'

'The way you walk. That overconfident swagger of a man who has no confidence or courage.'

'Really?'

'And the theft of the theta ornament from the house. Niger never barks at those he considers a friend. He never barks at you. Foolish old dog.'

Lollius smirked. 'A flimsy argument to put before a court. Not that you will get the chance.'

'And the mutilation. We read Apollonius of Rhodes together at school. You were excited when Jason dismembered Apsyrteis. There has always been a cruelty in you. Remember the merchant you beat half to death just for pleasure, the other side of Mount Ixias, down near Terina?'

'Yes, that was a lot of fun.'

Vibius spoke. 'It did not have to come to this.' His suave tones were alien to this bleak place and murderous occasion. 'You could have joined us. We made the offer after the hunt.'

'That was a bad mistake,' Paullus said. 'Until then you had done well spreading fear and doubt. From the start many believed that the Hero had returned. Ironically, I played into your hands by blaming the brigands. When it was shown not to be them, few doubted the killings were the work of the daemon. Then, after the temple, when the sword and arrow were proof the killers were human, things were almost worse. The killers had to be local, and it could have been any- one. Superstitious old Roscius pointed the finger at some cult, you at the Bruttians, and Lollius the poor. Perhaps it was just a madman. No one could be trusted. I had my suspicions, but until the hunt I could see no motive. It was slow of me. The motive was in plain sight. You created terror so men would give up their land to you for next to nothing. The pettiest of motives, nothing more than greed.'

'The same motive that has given Rome an empire,' Vibius said.

'Even Rome seeks a just cause for her wars,' Paullus said.

'A threadbare pretext. No one should know that better than you after Corinth.'

'Rome kills when it is necessary, according to the laws of war.'

'We also killed out of necessity.' Vibius smiled unctuously. 'We followed the laws of nature: the strong kill the weak.'

Lollius broke in. 'One thing that always bored me at school was a long-winded philosophical dialogue: Socrates said this, his inter-locutor that.' Lollius waved Solinus and the other two with spears to move forward. 'Farewell, Paullus, my old friend.'

'One more step,' Paullus said, 'and Croton dies.'

They stopped and looked back to the older men.

Vibius shrugged elegantly. 'Probably save us the task. Fidubius is fond of him, but he knows too much.'

'See!' Paullus looked at Solinus and the spearmen. 'None of you were party to the murders, but now you also know everything. Think they will have any more qualms with you?'

Vibius actually laughed. 'A clever effort, my dear Paullus. But Croton is an expendable slave. They are our flesh and blood.' He gestured them to move.

'Wait!' The voice of Fidubius was peremptory, used to having its way.

The sun lit the motionless tableau.

Fidubius hesitated, for once unsure of his words. 'If you grant one request, you will have a quick death, no mutilation, a coin for the ferryman, a proper grave. I give you my oath, as I loved my son. Tell me the truth. How did Alcimus die?'

And, before man and gods, Paullus told everything that had happened in the last house in Corinth, stated the facts without omission or embellishment. As he voiced the story for the first time, Paullus sensed the Kindly Ones take their leave, and he knew he was purified of the blood-guilt. Whatever happened in the next few moments, the pollution was cleansed, and he would not be haunted, either in this world or the next.

'You swear that is the truth?' Fidubius asked.

'I swear.'

'Then, thank you. You were not to blame.' Tears of pity and grief ran down the large, flinty face of Fidubius. 'I am sorry you have to die.'

Paullus did not wait, but turned and ran. He swerved around the mules. Behind him, taken by surprise, the spearmen were slow setting off in pursuit. The alarmed mules stamped, and got in their way. There was nowhere to run, nowhere but the teetering precipice of rubble. Paullus pulled up in front of the incline.

A dusty figure emerged from the shelter of a pile of toppled stones.

Paullus heard exclamations of shock. In the face of this apparition, his pursuers skidded to a stop. Who had summoned this warrior sprung from the earth? Was he even mortal? Strange things happened in the Sila. Was he some daemonic guardian of the place roused from eternal slumber?

Naevius tossed a light shield over. Paullus caught the buckler one-handed, and together they turned to face the enemy.

Vibius recovered fastest. 'There are only two of them. Kill them both!'

Solinus and the other two spearmen glanced at their companions, drawing strength from each other, steeling themselves to attack. In the hiatus, Naevius produced a hunting horn, put it to his lips and sounded one long note.

'Ignore him,' Vibius shouted. 'It's a bluff. They are alone. Get in there! Finish them! Lollius, you too!'

The four attackers shook out into formation. Each pair facing a lone man.

Solinus and another man edged towards Paullus. Their bodies half turned, feet close together, left boot leading, left hand guiding the spear; they approached as tense as a huntsman creeping upon a thicket containing the lair of a boar.

The reach of the spears was greater than that of Paullus' sword. They jabbed and probed, seeking an opening. Paullus kept shifting his stance, covering the spear points with shield and sword. Then Solinus thrust in earnest. Paullus pivoted clear, chopping down at the shaft as it sliced by his legs, trying to sever the tip. His blade clanged harmlessly off the long metal collar of the boar spear. Solinus recovered, and the cautious dance resumed.

It was like facing the Achaean phalanx. Get inside the reach of the spears and they were helpless. With a sweep of the sword, Paullus forced Solinus' weapon off to his right. It fouled the other spear. Shoulder tucked into shield, Paullus drove forward. Legs pumping, he crashed into Solinus. The shield thumped into Solinus' chest. Solinus toppled back, measured his length on the ground, his head cracking on a paving slab.

Paullus whirled round. He was close to the other assailant. The man was attempting to bring his weapon to bear. It was too long, too cumbersome. Paullus thrust down overhand at his face. The man went to jerk aside, but failed. The steel punched into his throat. Hot blood splattered Paullus' forearm. Mortally injured, the man went down.

And then Paullus yelled with pain and his right leg gave under him. Dropping shield and sword, he fell, hands clutching at the rear of his thigh. Paullus writhed, defenceless, on the stones. Lollius, blade in hand, stood over his childhood friend.

'You always were tiresomely virtuous.' Lollius hunched his shoulders to put all his weight behind the downward thrust that would skewer Paullus. Lollius grinned with expectation.

A disturbance in the air. A dark movement in the bright sunshine. A flash of steel. Lollius quivered, like a sapling struck with an axe. Another fast blur of motion and Lollius was gone, felled like a tree, and Naevius stood in his place.

'Well, that evens things up between us,' Naevius said. His other opponent lay in the dust behind the centurion.

Now there were soldiers in the marketplace, a dozen or more. They had surrounded Vibius and Fidubius, and were herding them towards where Croton remained impotently tied to the shattered pillar. Through the agony, Paullus felt a fierce exultation. It had worked. His calculations had been good. Onirus had played his part, ridden through the night to Orestes at Consentia, brought help in the morning. The killers had not detected the prefect's bodyguard lying in wait in the outskirts of the abandoned village. The stratagem had succeeded.

Naevius crouched and inspected Paullus' leg. 'Stop making such a fuss. It is nasty, but you will live.'

Naevius leapt to his feet, snapped to attention.

The prefect of the Bruttians had entered the ruins. More soldiers guarded him.

'Did they confess?' Orestes asked Naevius.

'Yes, sir. I heard every word.'

Orestes looked at Paullus. 'Are you badly hurt?'

'It is nothing, sir.' Naevius answered for him.

'Centurion, take the survivors into custody. They will be charged with murder. The law will take its course, but there can be no doubt about the verdict.'

'Yes, sir.'

'Then it is over,' Orestes said. 'The killings are at an end. No evil stalks the hills. The Hero of Temesa has returned to the depths of the sea.'

Epilogue

Patria

Three Years Later

612 Ab Urbe Condita (142 BC)

UBI TU GAIUS, ego Gaia: the wedding vow was so ancient no one really knew what it meant. Paullus slipped a ring on her finger, a band of iron set in gold. Some doctors claimed a fine nerve connected the ring finger to the heart.

Minado was veiled. She looked different. Her hair was teased into an elaborate coiffure with six braids of artificial hair. Then she lifted her chin, and she looked the same, and Paullus was happy.

'*Ubi tu Gaius, ego Gaia.*' She said the words, and they were man and wife.

'*Feliciter!*' The guests wished them good fortune as Paullus led her to the couch.

There had never been a wedding like it in Temesa, not one graced by the presence of two senators of consular standing. The place of honour was taken by Lucius Mummius, the conqueror of Corinth. This year he was serving as one of the two censors. Elected every five years, in the eighteen months they held office the censors were empowered to revise the rolls of Roman citizens, and to both admit and remove men from the equestrian order and the senate. A position of immense power and prestige, it was the pinnacle of a political career in Rome. Seated by his side, Lucius

Aurelius Orestes might have considered himself overshadowed. *Dignitas* was everything to a senator. Yet they were close friends. Orestes had served as legate to Mummius in the east, and they were bound by ties of *amicitia*. And both were patrons of the groom.

'Thank you,' Paullus said to Mummius. 'Without you—'

The great man made a small gesture of demurral. 'Her father showed the loyalty and courage of a citizen of Rome. It was only right the formal status was conferred on him and his family. The same held true of Onirus.'

Orestes smiled. 'It was lucky Onirus had been a camp servant with the army. Even so, the guards were in two minds about admitting him when he came to me in Consentia. If they had not, things would have turned out very differently.'

Paullus acknowledged the truth of this, and Mummius proposed a toast to Good Fortune.

When they had drunk, Mummius asked Paullus if he was sure he had not bid too much for the right to fell timber and tap pitch in the mountains around Drys, Laboula and Section. Wedding or not, public business was never far from his mind, and auctioning such contracts were part of the duties of the censors.

'I do not think so, if the gods are kind. The Sila is a wild and dangerous place. It needs a man who knows its vastness. But there are profits to be made, and without any fraud or loss of honour.'

Mummius nodded weightily. 'As I have said, now you wear the gold ring of an equestrian, a political career in Rome is open to a man who won the civic crown. Military glory brings many votes. There are those of us who would be honoured to support you.'

'Thank you again, but no, I am content to remain in my home town, to raise a family.'

'You may be called to the standards again.'

'If so, I shall do my duty.'

Servants brought in the first course: snails and anchovies with salad, washed down with wine from Tarentum. It was good quality, but nothing ostentatious. There would be lamb to follow, before the apples and nuts.

Paullus looked round the room. It was decked with luxuriant greenery and spread with rugs. Three years before, it had been the town house of Fidubius. Now it was the residence of Dekis, the sometime Bruttian huntsman.

The trial had brought a seismic shift in the colony of Temesa. Lollius, of course, was dead, along with two of his cousins. The verdict on his father and Vibius' accomplice had been a foregone conclusion. The evidence had been overwhelming. Some had been provided by Solinus, on promise of immunity. More had been wrung out of Croton under torture. The latter subsequently had been crucified outside the main gate. Vibius and Fidubius had fled into exile.

'Fidubius is still in Massilia?' The exiles were the only thing that still troubled Paullus.

'An old man sunk in lethargy and bitterness,' Orestes said, 'only rousing himself to drink and gorge on seafood. Haunted by his crimes, he will never leave.'

'And Vibius?'

'As far as anyone knows, still in the east. There is no cause to worry. Denied fire and water, if he sets foot in Italy, his life is forfeit.'

Both had been condemned to death in their absence. Their estates had been confiscated. By due process of law, one quarter of the whole had been awarded to Paullus. From the bounty, Paullus had gifted this house and land to Dekis, a more modest property to Onirus, and provided a smallholding on his own enlarged domain to old Kaido.

The lamb came in, tender and succulent, filling the room with its aroma.

'Do you ever think of Corinth?' Orestes asked.

'Sometimes, hardly ever,' Paullus said. 'I try not to dwell on what was done.'

'We did our duty,' Mummius said. 'We had our orders. It was a terrible thing, but perhaps for the best. Polybius the Achaean argues that it spared Greece the agony of a long-drawn-out conquest.'

They had not been long at dessert when Ursus, the officiating priest, rose to his feet and announced it was time.

Flute players led them out into the street. Five torchbearers were waiting, even though it was still broad daylight. Bystanders called out blessings on the procession as it wound down to Paullus' new house overlooking the water. There were ribald jokes and snatches of song. Naevius led the way in this traditional licentiousness. For once, half gone in his cups, the centurion looked not angry, but beatific. As they got near, children threw handfuls of nuts. They rattled on the pavement, supposedly a symbol of fertility and happiness.

Minado had been silent and demure throughout the meal, and separated from Paullus in the procession. She was preceded by a boy carrying a torch of tightly twisted hawthorn twigs. Her hands were held by two other boys. Her bridesmaids followed, carrying her spindle and distaff.

There had been no chance to talk.

Finally, at the door, her entourage stood back.

She lifted her veil, and Paullus kissed her. She smelt of verbena and sweet marjoram. Paullus lifted her into his arms and carried her across the threshold, and they were gone.

Afterword

Calabria

THE ORIGINS OF THIS NOVEL go back to a story I read many years ago in Cicero's *Brutus* (85–8). Several persons of note were murdered in the Sila forest. Some slaves of the *publicani* involved in the production of pitch, as well as some free members of the corporation, were prosecuted for the killings. After a drawn-out trial, featuring some of the best orators of the time, the defendants were acquitted. Cicero does not say if they were innocent.

Calabria was a remote and wild place in antiquity. The Romans knew it as Bruttium. The modern name migrated from the Sallentine Peninsula in south-east Italy sometime after the Lombard invasion in AD 700. To avoid confusion, the modern usage is followed in this novel.

Calabria is a backwater of modern scholarship. The most useful study I have found is the doctoral thesis of I. Matkovic, *Roman Settlement of Northern Bruttium*: 200 BC–AD 300 (McMaster University, 2001); a PDF is available online (Google: Matkovic Bruttium).

The Roman colony of Temesa (or Tempsa) was a port somewhere on the lower Sabutus (modern Savuto) river. Its precise location is uncertain (Matkovic, op.cit., p.39, n.1).

Versions of the ghost story of the Hero of Temesa are found in Pausanias (6.6.7–11), Strabo (6.1.5), and Aelian (*VH* 8.18).

Roman Farming

The texts translated by K.D. White in *Country Life in Classical Times* (London, 1977) offer an enjoyable way into the subject. Much in this novel has been drawn from Cato, *On Agriculture*, an invaluable contemporary source. My eyes were opened to rural life and peasant farming in classical antiquity by R. MacMullen, *Roman Social Relations 50 BC to AD 284* (New Haven and London, 1974), 1–27, and L. Foxhall, 'Farming and Fighting in Ancient Greece' in J. Rich and G. Shipley (eds.), *War and Society in the Greek World* (London and New York, 1993), 134–45.

The Agrarian Crisis

Modern scholars often argue that in the last two centuries BC the Roman peasants recruited into the legions were in effect fighting to dispossess themselves, as, while they were serving overseas, their farms were ruined and taken over by the rich. The classic statement of the case is K. Hopkins, *Conquerors and Slaves* (Cambridge,1978), 1–98. Recently the view has been repeatedly challenged. An overview of the arguments, inclining to the traditional view, can be found in H. Sidebottom, *Ancient Warfare: A Very Short Introduction* (Oxford, 2004), 43–9.

Roman Imperialism

In the nineteenth century Rome was seen as a 'defensive imperialist', reluctantly drawn into expansion by the needs of her own safety and those of her allies. Now analysis tends to focus on the 'expansion-bearing structures' in her culture and society, above all the senators' needs for military glory, as well as the profits from successful war-making. Two summaries of the modern historiography are T. Cornell, 'The End of Roman Imperial Expansion', in J. Rich and G. Shipley (eds.), *War and Society in the Roman World* (London and New York, 1993), and H. Sidebottom, 'Roman Imperialism: The Changed Outward Trajectory of the Roman Empire', *Historia* 54.3 (2005), 315–30.

The Campaign Against Corinth

The ancient references for the Achaean War, which culminated in the sack of Corinth, are scattered and poor, and often contradictory: Polybius 38.9–18; Pausanias 7.14.1–16.6; Livy, *Per.* 51–2; Justin 34.1–2; (Aurelius Victor) *Vir. Ill.* 60.1–3; Orosius 5.3.1–7; Zonaras 9.31.

Modern scholarship tends to concentrate on either the origins or the effects of the war. Among those who discuss the events, even if only in passing, are A. Fuks, 'The Bellum Achaicum and its Social Aspect', *JHS* 90 (1970), 78–89; W.V. Harris, *War and Imperialism in Republican Rome 327–70 BC* (Oxford, 1979), 240–4; E.S. Gruen, *The Hellenistic World and the Coming of Rome* (Berkeley, Los Angeles, and London, 1984), 514–23; G. Shipley, *The Greek World After Alexander 323–30 BC* (2000), 383–6; and P. Erdkamp, 'The Andriscus Uprising and the Achaean War, 149–146 BC', in M. Whitby and H. Sidebottom (eds.), *The Encyclopedia of Ancient Battles*, volume II (Chichester, 2017), 842–4.

The Roman Army

An excellent introduction to the mid-Republican legions is L. Keppie, *The Making of the Roman Army from Republic to Empire* (London, 1984), 14–56. There is a more comprehensive discussion in M. Dobson, *The Army of the Roman Republic: The Second Century BC, Polybius and the Camps at Numantia, Spain* (Oxford, 2008), esp. 47–66.

Combat Stress in the Ancient World

There is a keen debate among modern scholars as to whether combat stress existed in the classical world. Broadly, there are two camps. The 'universalist' approach argues that as it exists now, so it must have existed then. The 'specificist' view points to the lack of unambiguous ancient evidence, and the very different conditions (physical and cultural) prevalent at the time. A sketch of both sides can be found in *Ancient Warfare* magazine IX.4 (2013), 70–4. A convincing example of culturally specific scholarship is J. Crowley, *The Psychology of the Athenian Hoplite* (Cambridge, 2012).

Quotes

The song the legionaries sing in Chapter 21 is taken from Plautus, *Miles Gloriosus*, translated by E.F. Watling (Harmondsworth, 1965), pp.160–1.

The various lines from Homer are from the translations of the *Iliad* by Richard Lattimore (Chicago, 1951), and the *Odyssey* by Robert Fagles (London, 1996).

Other Novels

All my novels include a couple of homages to other writers. Here I have reworked images from *Christ Stopped at Eboli* by Carlo Levi (Eng. tr., Harmondsworth, 1982), and *Across the River and Into the Trees* by Ernest Hemingway (London, 1950).

Acknowledgements

In every novel the usual suspects are thanked, but sincerity is not undermined by repetition.

First my family: my wife Lisa, my mother Frances, my aunt Terry and my sons Tom and Jack.

Next the professionals: James Gill at United Agents; Kate Parkin, Clare Kelly, Francesca Russell, Stephen Dumughn, and (sad to see him leaving) James Horobin at Bonnier Zaffre; Maria Stamatopoulou and Bert Smith at Lincoln College, Oxford.

Finally other friends: Peter and Rachel Cosgrove, Jeremy Tinton, Peter Hill, Sara Fox, Fiona Dunne, Mary and David Palmer, Sanda Haines and Jack Ringer. This novel is dedicated to the latter.

Dear Reader,

I hope you have enjoyed reading *The Return*. The inspiration for this novel was an anecdote in Cicero's treatise *Brutus* about the murder of several men in the forest of Sila, and the trial which eventually ended in the acquittal of the defendants. Cicero discusses the tactics of the orators speaking for the defence, but he does not say if the accused were innocent.

Calabria was a wild and dangerous region in antiquity. Roman law frequently did not reach into the depths of the Sila. Calabria was a strange place, where anything could happen. It was also the setting for one of the most chilling ghost stories in classical literature: the Hero of Temesa, told by Pausanias. That was another reason for my choice of this wonderfully atmospheric location.

Readers of my previous novels will know that I like to explore important themes of Roman history in my fiction. These themes were important then, and they remain so today. The Romans are always 'good to think with' about both the past and the present. *The Return* investigates Roman imperialism; its causes and effects, as well as its ancient justifications and critiques. It may be a surprise that at times the Romans could voice severe criticisms of their own rise to empire and deplore the effects on themselves.

The Return marks something of a departure for my novels. Although I have flirted with the genre before (in *The Wolves of the North*), this is my first murder mystery. I aim to bring the dark, brooding menace of the best Scandi and Italian Noir to the past, while not stinting on the military action of the historical novel. The reader is posed several interlocking questions. Who or what is behind the killings? What terrible event in the war changed Paullus? What happened in 'the last house in Corinth'?

I have never had more fun researching and writing a novel than with *The Return*, and I very much hope that you enjoyed the story. Please tell your friends about the novel and discuss it on social media. Finally, do find me on Facebook or my website www.harrysidebottom.co.uk. I would love to know what you think of *The Return*.

Best wishes

Harry Sidebottom